DESERT BURIAL

BRIAN LITTLEFAIR

HENRY HOLT AND COMPANY NEW YORK

Henry Holt and Company, LLC
Publishers since 1866
115 West 18th Street
New York, New York 10011

Henry Holt® is a registered trademark of
Henry Holt and Company, LLC.

Distributed in Canada by H. B. Fenn and Company Ltd.

Library of Congress Cataloging-in-Publication Data

Littlefair, Brian
Desert Burial : a novel / Brian Littlefair.
p. cm.
ISBN 0-8050-6723-X
1. Americans—Mali—Fiction. 2. International business enterprises—Fiction. 3. Radioactive waste disposal—Fiction. 4. Refugee camps—Fiction. 5. Geologists—Fiction. 6. Mali—Fiction. I. Title.

PS3612.I88 D47 2002
813'.6—dc21 2001024379

Henry Holt books are available for special promotions and premiums. For details contact: Director, Special Markets.
First Edition 2002

Designed by Paula Russell Szafranski

Map illustration by Jackie Aher

Printed in the United States of America

10 9 8 7 6 5 4 3 2 1

To my parents

There then he passed his life, and endured such great wrestlings, "Not against flesh and blood," as it is written, but against opposing demons, as we learned from those who visited him. For there they heard tumults, many voices, and, as it were, the clash of arms. At night they saw the mountain become full of wild beasts, and him also fighting as though against visible beings . . .

—Athanasius, *Life of Antony*

Author's Note

This is a work of fiction. Names, characters, places, and incidents either are the product of the author's imagination or are used fictitiously. Any resemblance to actual persons, living or dead, to events, or to locales is entirely coincidental. The near-future setting projects historical forces and trends to fictionalize Mali, a country that at this writing is one of Africa's more vigorous democracies.

DESERT BURIAL

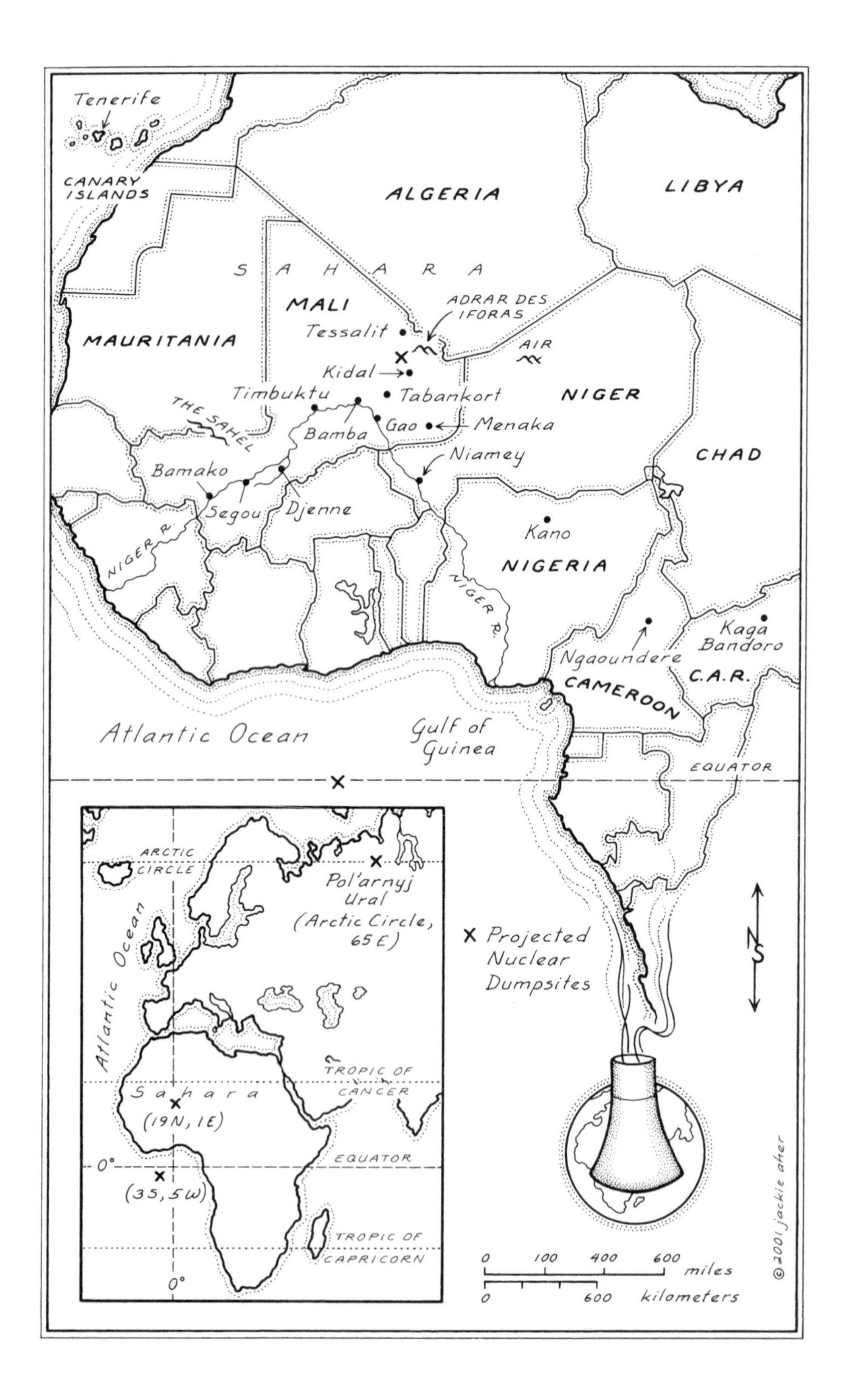
Tenerife
CANARY ISLANDS
ALGERIA
LIBYA
S A H A R A
MALI
ADRAR DES IFORAS
MAURITANIA
Tessalit
AIR
Kidal
Timbuktu
Tabankort
NIGER
THE SAHEL
Bamba
Gao
Menaka
CHAD
Niamey
Bamako
Segou
Djenne
Kano
NIGER R.
NIGERIA
NIGER R.
Kaga Bandoro
Ngaoundere
C.A.R.
CAMEROON
Atlantic Ocean
Gulf of Guinea
EQUATOR
ARCTIC CIRCLE
Pol'arnyj Ural (Arctic Circle, 65 E)
Atlantic Ocean
Projected Nuclear Dumpsites
N
S
TROPIC OF CANCER
Sahara (19N, 1E)
EQUATOR
0°
(3S, 5W)
TROPIC OF CAPRICORN
0°
0 100 400 600 miles
0 600 kilometers

The stillness here is so profound that its subtlest lapse can unsettle me. What alerts me now is not movement, or sound, but evidence of a brief insensible change in the air. The air has changed back, and the variation was too slight to be termed weather or wind or even haze. But it compels attention as storm clouds do elsewhere.

When I reach past the ladder to touch the roof, runny yellow mud adheres to my fingers. To collect drizzle and dew I stretch a plastic tarpaulin over my shelter. Last night, however, some disturbance raised dust with the texture and adsorbent properties of talc. The finest motes of it settled on the tarp's silver plastic, blotting the dew before it could trickle into my cistern.

With one night's dew harvest lost, I will have to draw water again soon. My roof drains yield just a few gallons a day. They cannot replace my well. But sometimes the dew from my roof lets me put off a trip to the pump. On indolent days I am grateful for this. The well lies a quarter mile away. My jeep cannot come within fifty yards of it, and to draw water takes a steep climb and a grunting descent, repeated for each of the six plastic bottles I fill.

The work of drawing water is no hardship. I have little else to do. Still, the dust pall weighs on my mind. Even here in the desert, air this calm seldom carries so much dust. This may be a sign of a great distant storm, but it has an unnerving feel. It feels like the sticky dust communities raise as fat sizzles and feet shuffle and life closes in.

In a shrinking world that daily grows better known and tighter knit it is no small thing to escape notice. But I do. I have so successfully perfected my solitude that no one thinks to label me a desert hermit.

My home is a shuttered shipping container, purpose-built to house those in flight: refugees, exiles, dazed victims of disaster. Inconspicuous, portable, disposable, it suits those in hiding as well.

The elements guard my solitude. Flat desert surrounds this knob of rock like a moat of molten lead. I survive because everything here helps temper the heat. My home sits in a gulch between two conjoined hills, sheltering in their shadow several hours each day. Perched on foot-high stilts to expose and discourage the scorpions and snakes, it traps cold night air underneath. Some mornings I rub lacy frost off the steel walls.

I coax some food from the dying soil, watering terraced dust with an underground hose that seeps moist sewage. I grow beans and tubers and, for tradition's sake, a potted oasis: a single date palm that will not bear fruit. I keep fierce hardy bees with safe modern methods. Officially, my enterprises set an example for my neighbors. In truth, self-sufficiency helps me cut more ties with a distant and oblivious world.

I keep my handheld radio. That is the one unbreakable link. It connects my obsolete computer to a swarm of satellites circling overhead. I could speak over my radio, but I prefer to interpose a keyboard and type stock phrases.

The United States government supports me in my hermitage. They pay me to search for water trapped deep in rock. I dowse for this lost water as I search for peace, wistfully, learning all about things that will always be out of reach.

Living things recover in characteristic positions and in characteristic places. Injured men lie prone, head pillowed on an arm. Wounded creatures drag themselves away to hide alone.

My life affords the inert solitude needed for recovery, or for hopeless endurance. Now I have come to rest again, on black canvas stretched on a skeletal plastic pipe chair. In this, my only chair,

I slacken my body until my eyes stream and wait long sated intervals without taking a breath.

A toy sink sends dishwater back to my cistern. My gravity toilet uses the dishwater to sprinkle its pedal-operated trap door. I squeeze this fouled water through a membrane and back to the sink. A clever mirrored box focuses the sun's rays to boil my food in the filtered water. My thoughts circulate as my water does, more tainted and stale each day.

I wear a thin cotton shirt, in which I have slept, and nothing else. The shirt was blue, but it is white now, thin as tissue across my back and shy two adjacent buttons. It is almost cold enough to put on a hat. Here I can ignore the societally ordained conventions for covering myself. When I am cool I cover my ribs. When I continue to be cool I cover my head and perhaps my feet and legs. I sleep as I dress and eat and drink, for reasons logical, not conventional. I may sleep through the heat and wake to dowse at night. I may stay on the move for days on end. I have no routines and no discipline—those things reassure others, not me. I behave as I choose here. I may have more privacy than anyone in the world. This kind of privacy does not need to be guarded. To the agency that employs me I am records in a system, budgets and disbursements trickling into indifferent computers without human intervention. My work amounts to bits in a digital map no one sees. Computers remember me so people can forget.

The close-pressing walls of my container are a hazy streaked blue, as the dawn sky outside might look if I could see it. I have shuttered the windows. I do not fear prying eyes. I simply have no need to see out. I know what is outside now and what has always been outside and what will be outside forever. Sometimes there is weather, but not now.

Having sat inert for uncounted dark hours, I move. When I rise I must move gently; the floor is a warren of passageways threading past cases and cabinets. By habit I hunch in my home. The ceiling is low.

The yellow earth outside my door careens out, down and sidelong like a bobsled run to settle in an old ravine full of faceted stones. Nomads have not grazed here for years. I have seen no rain for months. The footprints that weave among the gullies toward my home are mine alone. Africa's upheavals intensify the stillness of this place.

Mali, for all its terror and misery, is stable now, even peaceful, by the standards of Africa. Mali's turn-of-the-century democratic golden age is gone, of course. The African War put paid to that when it ended the innocent age of little wars. Here in Mali the Flame of Peace has sputtered out; the monument's oxidized gas pipes have long since been looted for scrap. This is the new millennium, and the people of Mali are not among the chosen.

Mali is a faint butterfly shape traced in desert sand. The government controls a bit of the south: Bamako, the capital, and the Niger River valley. Two warlords crouch like spiders on the wings.

The self-styled emperor Mansa Muru reigns in the southeast. He leads a tribal movement of black settlers called the Creepers of Niani. In the songs of the *griots,* the ancient bards, the creeper symbolized indomitable persistence: *The vine will entangle the tallest of trees.* Now the creeper evokes Mansa Muru's stealthy raids and silent abductions. With night-vision gear and special-forces tactics, the Creepers of Niani can depopulate half a town, or half a hut, and leave the other half asleep. *The Creepers will wait till you doze* is the new refrain.

Ibn Inhad owns the north and its ancient salt mines. He leads the Holy Garrison, an Islamic movement that preserves Tuareg identity and nomad culture. In Inhad's gabbling mind this means a rigid caste system built on black slavery. Inhad supplies the "guests" and "students" who attend you in the homes of Libyan oil men and Algerian gas magnates. Inhad draws his warriors from the caste of metalsmiths, but they are ranchers now, trading human livestock. The rich world hunts them, but Inhad's Holy Garrison leaves no spoor on satellite photographs. Black captives move invisibly among an elusive stipple of camps and auction pits.

The democratic dream persists only along the Niger River. Mali's president, Aras Bozo, governs an upriver enclave there. The papers in America play games with his name, but Bozo bears the name of Mali's fisherpeople. He almost saved Mali; for that he is revered.

But the fault lines opened once more, as Bozo knew they would. Muslims versus Christians versus traditionals. Light-skinned people versus dark. Farmers versus herders versus fishers versus government drones. Mali dropped piece by piece into the crosscutting chasms.

Muslims enforced their laws on migrant Christians. Christians mobbed magicians. Magicians led witch-hunts. Dark-skinned farmers penned light-skinned herders into maximum-security refugee camps. When the herds died the herders escaped to raid and sack. City dwellers pushed the fisherfolk downriver and across the border, and Mali's neighbors drove them back more desperate than before. Through it all free food poured in, ruining farmers and herders and fishers alike, enriching the parasites. Guns flowed in, not free, but affordable with the money to be made hoarding and selling free food.

Now Mali is triune. It is the country of Inhad, of Muru, and of Bozo—two hells and a fouled river hopeless as the Styx. This is not chaos, or collapse. Mali's new order may endure for generations. The warlords get ample supplies of arms, precisely apportioned to ensure stalemate. They have learned what the rich world's special forces know: they can strike deep and evaporate like mist until peacekeepers' corpses are heaped like dates in the market, and priced like dates, too high. The rest of the world will not intervene.

The two warlords shun confrontation. They prey on the government's towns. Inhad and Muru have carved out an empty buffer zone to demarcate their wasteland empires, moving people, demolishing homes, and poisoning wells.

Here where Mali has been divided, the earth is rent. The Adrar des Iforas is a billion-year-old wound. It stopped suppurating lava long ago, leaving lacerated rock.

When the helicopter set my home down, the swath of destruction still smelled faintly of hasty interment and fire. But now I am safe, here in no-man's-land. The frontier is set, once and for all. In the oases, not even mosquitoes survive. I am the only infestation.

I radio for supplies twice a month, and some intrepid trader leaves a crate at the bottom of the hill. Once each month, to keep the money trickling in, I boast about the water I have found.

Water is easy to find in the Sahara. Beneath my feet, entombed in rock, is a great sea: fossilized water. Some of it tastes of the earth before life. Once I hired a work crew to drill into one of the oldest vessels. I drew some of its water at great expense. I have all the water I need. But water that has never been swallowed and sweated away or pissed back to earth: that is a drink to be savored alone.

I had a wife. I counted many friends. Greetings buoyed me, as they should do. I would swarm at the appointed times: Christmas, summer Fridays, nine A.M. But now it is inconceivable that I should have to face society or companionship. The thought of it roils my mind. Perfect solitude is the closest I come to peace. Concern repels me. Empathy and pity endanger me, like a tear in the headgear that protects me when I tend my bees. For a long time pity dogged me here: plaintive messages on my computer screen, pleading voices of bereaved friends. *Where is the man I knew? You have to get on with your life. You can't just disappear, we need you too.* I absorbed it in silence until it stopped.

I must be careful. I am weak. An American thrill seeker once stumbled on my home. I found myself clinging to him. I told him my life story and my secret thoughts. I scratched for common ground with talk of grants and contracts and names he might know at the Agency for International Development. I called it by its friendly nickname, "AID." I had always valued AID as an impersonal source of funds, the guarantor of my solitude. Now it became my claim on the world and on him. My net of mutual acquaintances came up empty but I offered him my best food, my smuggled liquor, even a glass of fossilized water from my diminishing store. I saw him fidgeting, then rising and shuffling. I detained him with contrived questions. To escape he had to sidle out shouting and laughing, boisterously drowning out the needy keen in my voice. By then I had disclosed almost everything. I did not speak of my wife. Just the thought of her, showing in my eyes, was enough to drive him off.

The memory of that visit still catches me up at times, and I find myself acting out our conversation, polishing and refining it. But the memory is enough. I am through with hospitality. The world is a snare with each soul knotted to all the others. Touch one and you are caught in their net.

I like it in the desert. I do not like green.

Green reminds me of my path through the jungle on my wife's last day. Plants visibly growing if you stop to watch. A clatter of insects that drowns out your voice. Vertical brightness plummeting down and slicing sharp-edged shade. Air that holds more water than the ground, wet air, still cool in the morning and almost drinkable. My wife half a step ahead, reaching back, green eyes drawing me after her. Wherever our lives took us, she got there first and waited patiently for me. I am left behind again now.

I spend hours on end replaying that day in my mind. My intent is not to harden myself to it. I want to know what happened next, behind her eyes. If she has gone to extinction, extinction will satisfy me too. This is the only secret she has kept from me. It must be good news, because she always kept good news to herself for a time. She would wait until she could announce it poker-faced, hesitate two beats, and erupt in pent-up joy.

The people of the village carved swirling patterns on her coffin. She never wanted to take up space, she wanted to be windblown ash; but the children needed to see her interred. She is dead, I thought. She won't know. Shut her up in a box underground.

Dusk makes the plateau cinder gray, cinder cool, and cinder dead. When hell burns out it will look like this, defiantly inert. In an older and darker world underground, cool waters tantalize. Somewhere below, a streambed runs south in a channel on top of bedrock. This river of porous aggregate carries more water than the Nile.

I am tracing its course. Having laid out scores of sensors in a perfect grid, I bury a blasting cap deep in the sand. My computer chugs and whines and draws pretty rainbow pictures of shock waves hammering the earth. I can see the sound and touch it now. Raw seismic data looks like close-up photos of a harp, or a lyre: a thousand bright vertical strings, writhing and pulsing in waves.

I can choose the waves I trust to paint a picture of the stream: short waves or long waves, fast waves or slow. Short waves are best. They push straight ahead until they give up and ricochet back. The long waves slip around my underground river and die out deep in the Earth.

I pick neat bright streaks out of multicolored blurs of shock and noise. I choose fifty-foot waves, tiny and jackhammer-quick. Some are fast, some are slow. The best creep along at a mile a second. They will give me beautiful clear echoes. But they are quiet, almost lost in the split-second crash.

Some of the sensors have gone wild. Some seem dead. These I kill. I gag the rock to silence its stricken crackle. I strip out some waves that shattered bouncing off a salt dome. I clip the sound of the blast and make the resonant bang into a pop.

Then I torture the echo I've culled to make it give up its secrets. I mow down the spikes of noise and beat back the overtones. I bind the waves that remain with a tangle of sinuous curves. The ordeal is pure mathematics, silent inside my computer.

At the end of it I have a hint of a picture, sonogram-shadowy, all judgment and guesswork and art. With enough imagination you can find almost anything down there. A whole consoling underworld, perhaps. Somewhere out of view beyond the stream is the place where lost brides go.

I have come to the well to replace the dew I lost that dusty night. It's just as well I came again so soon: the pump is in distress.

I am squatting in front of the tortured pump. Black heat and painful noise come from the cabinet that contains it. Fresh blood prickles in my haunches as I stand up to search my shirt for a dry patch. It has been thirty seconds since I last blotted the sweat pooling in my sunglasses. The glare scrapes at my bare eyes until I cover them again. Peering through the salty smears I can just see a caterpillar of dust writhing on the plain below. I can't hear whatever is raising the dust; the north wind has picked up, and it carries the sound away. Traders, probably. They will slink by without sensing me.

I prostrate myself in front of the generator to tune it, but it's no use. I can't put off changing the oil anymore. It's already been a month. The dipstick collects specks of grit as I withdraw it. The sand crunches in my head when I set my teeth. It's grinding remorselessly at the motor's works.

By the time I finish, the sun has moved to confront me. My head is pounding but the oil is fresh again. I suck from my canteen. The pump flutters with a mothy sound right at the pain threshold. I cut the engine. Before my ears stop ringing I hear a smiling voice, shockingly close, rushing through the channels of my mind that hear English. "What's the good word?"

I don't look up. I wait patiently for my ears to settle down. Then I turn to make sure I imagined it.

The sight registers in stages. A slight figure. A woman. Wearing boots and cuffed shorts and a coarse short-sleeved shirt. A woman with short blond hair, wavy but oily at the crown, and orange-brown eyes creased from squinting. Soft features, fair and ruddy in an old-fashioned sunbaked way. Two front teeth slightly lapped.

How did she get here? There's no food, no water, no shade, no traction for a hundred miles. The question comes out in twitches and blinks, not words.

"Nice well you got there."

My mind stumbles along in pursuit of the words, more words than I've heard in months. If I can trust my eyes, she frisks on flat feet, jaunty and impersonally engaging like a panhandler. Her eyes probe mine, flirting pugnaciously. "Well?" She's not repeating the noun but telegraphing her impatience for an answer.

Any soul appearing here would shock me. The sight of an American feels like a hallucination. I try to grind it down with steady attention, but the figure remains. It's been a while since I used my throat to speak. "Who are you?"

She reads my lips. "I'm Lila. I'm with Ecumenical Alms," and more words, "they're bankrupt. I didn't think a charity could go bankrupt, sounds weird, doesn't it?" Words in torrents. "Embezzlement or something, I guess. The receivers called and told us to come home but I said, Screw you, come and get me." A *tidal wave* of words. "They're scared to cut us off so they keep sending supplies. It works out fine. We don't get enough, but then we never did. So what's your name?"

I'm working to separate coherent thought from shock and noise. She doesn't understand that it's slow, painstaking work, like reading the seismic sensors after a shot. Finally: "I'm Ty Campbell. I'm a contractor. To USAID."

"What are you doing here?"

"Hydrology."

Her eyelids arch despite the sun, and she leans in. "So you could wave your divining rod over our camp and find us a well, maybe? Come and see the camp."

Camp? My life depends on a million-dollar clockwork of contracts and wayleaves and bribes. She thinks she can just camp out here? It comes out, "Camp?"

"We're new in town," she says. "We're between the ridge and the wadi where the trail stops. Any groundwater there?"

"A lot. But it's underneath two hundred meters of chert. You could get to it if you had an oil rig and six weeks to kill."

She dusts off slack palms. "Well, that's that. We came here with one leaky pillow tank that will last us maybe two more days. We're in your hands, ol' pal."

"Not so fast," I say. "Nobody's in my hands."

"If you don't find us water, we're going to die. Don't get me wrong, I'm not trying to manipulate you, but there it is. I've been in this situation a dozen times before, and no one has ever turned us away. Not Tuaregs, not blacks. Not settlers, not nomads. Not slaves, not bandits." She brightens. "So how many gallons a minute you get?"

Numbly I say ten.

"Wow, that's a lot," she says.

"How many in your camp?"

“Four hundred.”

My voice breaks. “Four *hundred*? Supporting four hundred people, the well won’t last six months.”

Her gaze softens and meanders toward some middle distance. “Six months sounds like a long time to me.”

2

It took a week of subtle signs to convince me, but I have come to believe in four hundred lost souls delivered here alive by some godly drudgery of miracles. The idea routs my thoughts. I prepare continually for further intrusions, planning evasion, rehearsing repulse. I am on guard for a caller at the door, an eye at the chink between the shutters, a shout outside. I can no longer sink into helpless repose. I cannot move freely. Holing up in my stifling box by day, I venture out only at night. I give the camp a wide berth. If I show myself too often they will soon know me by my comings and goings. Even that degree of intimacy is too much.

So I go about my business without ever seeing them. Despite that, they make their presence known beneath the well's white steel tripod. They leave such gifts as the destitute can leave: a small goat-hair blanket, undyed and dusty but lovingly folded; a child's drawing on coarse pink paper weighted with a stone.

The drawing is captioned in Bambara: *Nye bifé.* I love you. It shows a flower that the child could not have seen except in books, an indigenous lily the desert pushed far to the south. I can see Lila coaxing a dull-eyed girl to imagine something unknown and unthreatening and beautiful.

I take the picture home, not wanting to discard it where the artist might find it and be hurt. I toss it in the trash, but soon after,

I freeze in the act of scraping damp couscous off my plate. The picture lies on top of the trash. I cannot soil it.

The stem is rendered in blue, the petals in black. The stem is thick and crooked like a twig as though she can't imagine the frail beauty of gentler places. I tape the drawing to my wall and wait for its hold on me to weaken.

In time I turn to it more and more and begin to think, abstractly at first, then with diffuse sentiment, but never with intention: *Who drew this picture?* Early one morning I wake to a wordless disquiet that means *I have to see that child before it dies.* I set out for the camp before dawn.

I first see the camp from above, as I slip across a hillside. I expected platoons of calm Nordic staff, humming inflatable warehouses, neat khaki tents, and plump pillow tanks. But *camp* is a grandiose term for this huddle of prone and squatting stick figures, this ragged motionless queue. They straggle from a single ten-ton truck. Sand drifts up against its wheels. Some have shelters: crude windbreaks of driftwood-gray tree limbs and rags. The fortunate squat in dome-shaped wrecks of tents. Most sit outside with cookpots and bundles of sticks. They sit heaped in families with knees drawn up, or lie scattered like matchsticks. They wear cast-off Western sportswear, colorful under the dust, not bright but livid and unhealthy like wet gangrene.

I wallow downhill into the sand sea and nose up to the destitution's verge. Heads turn, but no one gathers. I can see the nearest of them blinking patiently in the dust I have raised. They are wraiths, existing dimly. The haze grays all but the nearest forms. In the distance haze swallows them up. Depth is not perspective but submergence in turbid air.

Out-of-place energy draws my eye—Lila at the center of a group of refugees. I pick my way toward her. She is swinging a shovel with incongruous vitality, slick with sweat in a halter top and shorts, tiny dugs twisting in and out of view as she tosses dirt. She's got a lot of ribs. Her earthwork sags in sandy apathy around her.

I had planned to acknowledge their gifts, but my dismay spills out first: "This is it?"

"Home sweet home," she says. "Like it?"

"It's—"

"Appalling?" she says. Crooked grin, glazed eyes, as though it's funny.

"What are you digging for?"

"This is the heart of our new playground complex. We are constructing a sandbox. The irony of putting a sandbox here is not lost on me, but the rules say food for work, after all. A sandbox is about all we can make with indigenous materials. Someday if we have a spare tent maybe we'll break it down and make monkey bars."

Relentless need. Lila sees my dismay at them, helpless and inescapable. Mistaking it for compassion, she says gently, "We'll make it." She's hanging lightly on my arm. Little tugs make me settle in the sand. "Feel like mixing up some mush?"

And I am caught.

In the city, as a white, I would be mobbed by beggars and helpers and new friends of all kinds. Here I hardly draw a glance. Lila is at my side, churning powdered milk in a blue polyethylene drum, choking on the flying powder, giddy to be burbling idiomatic English. I am silent.

"Please be careful, you are splashing, let me show you." This from a regal girl behind me.

"Ty, meet Fatimatou," Lila says. Fatimatou has a shaved head, as many do, to help keep on top of the lice. She keeps a brilliant smile mostly under wraps. Instead she flashes deep-set, slightly bloodshot eyes. She's a perfect little Fulani milkmaid with delicate bird bones and sable skin.

Her hands move me without pushing. "We can't slop food around like that, you clumsy man." She speaks briskly, with a teasing intonation that heightens the lilt of her accent.

"Lila, why don't you show Mister Ty around?" She is comfortable in command. Comparing Fatimatou's face and Lila's, I cannot tell who is in charge. Lila is not subordinate. Her eyes radiate some regard that threatens to burst her: pride, or admiration, or a friendship that surpasses my understanding. Fatimatou takes up the ladle like a scepter and Lila steers me around the camp.

Lila leads me down a slope between tents shaped like soap bubbles. Sand scoured and torn, faded and patched, they seem ephemeral as soap bubbles, ready to pop and disappear in a mist one by one. Some of the tents are skeletal, geodesic tubing woven with dead branches.

The heat is building, and the refugees have yielded to it. Lila's voice is the only sign of life. "Peulhs and Bambara, sworn enemies, right? Don't believe it. They were melting together until the warlords came. The Bambara were keeping livestock like the Peulhs, and the Peulhs were settling down, tending gardens. Listen to them—not a hint of hostility. I haven't met anyone yet who's fighting. All I ever see is victims. Farmer or herder or fisher or smith, everyone's a victim."

Despite the dry air, a miasma fills the camp. The air brings faint alarming smells in unhurried succession, some recognizable, some not. Feces, rotten fruity sweetness, sour retched-up smells, old sharp sweat or urine. Each one leaves a trace on the back of my tongue. I feel contagion probing me for weak points.

Lila has an odor too, a healthy unremarkable goaty odor. It is a comfort to huddle inside it.

From a sagging canvas lean-to comes a sound like puppies. Starving children don't cry; they cough. "That's where we do therapeutic feeding," Lila tells me.

I twitch in clouds of flies, a dozen tickling phantoms for each real one. The flies here, they're not like the flies back home. If there's water to be had in noses or eyes or sores, whatever kind of ooze it's in, they come and wallow. You can't simply wave them away. They have to be picked off, pulled out like little dogs straining at a leash. The starving have no patience for that. For them there's a kind of peace in letting the flies have their way.

Here it's as though we exist for the sake of disease.

Lila takes one dull-eyed boy by the shoulders. He is Lila's height and weight, but bonier still on a bigger frame. He has a stylized red camel on his shirt. Lila converses with him, speaking in three-word bursts of Bambara. He speaks in a language all his own: *unh, unh unh.*

"There's a lot of retardation from chronic malnutrition," she says. "It doesn't matter so much, life is simpler here: you're surviving or else you're dying. Doesn't matter how smart you are."

Lila points out what has been done here, what is needed. The latrine clearly needs to be limed. The shriveled pillow tank should be drained and patched. They need a source of smuggled diesel fuel, and I stop dead, dragging Lila to a halt.

I gag on it begging there in the dust, asking to be looked at. Its head lacks hair or ears or lips or eyes. Flesh wraps the skull in creased sheets, congealed strands and rivulets.

"Her name's Serata. That's a common injury she's got." There's no horror in Lila's voice, just rue. "When an epileptic woman tends a cooking fire, sooner or later the flames are going to flicker at a frequency that triggers a grand mal seizure. She falls headfirst into the fire." It burns me to look at her. "Most times her family is afraid to touch her because they think it's possession or a curse or something, so she thrashes around in the coals until the seizure runs its course."

A yellow fog hems me round and thickens until I am peering out of a small clear hole in it. I am weightless; Lila's steadying hand on my arm upends me and I sink slowly to all fours, hanging my head, hands in the dirt. From very far away I hear, "Good, just keep your head down, give yourself a blood shot."

When the faintness subsides I am on my knees on the ground. "Don't worry about it, Ty. Happens to the best of 'em. My first day I passed out cold."

Lila is standing over me with a baby in her arms. "Here's what you need," she says. Quickly, before I can recoil, she settles it in my arms, where the eyes find mine and pop, mocking mine, then soften in cooing laughter. Tiny wet hands wave and bat at my face with an impossibly light touch.

And the microbes and worms slink away defeated. They have lost their power over me.

"Hissi, look who's here, it's the Water Man." Lila elbows me, not as lightly as she means to. "Hissi gave you the picture," she says to me.

"Hello, Hissi"—my voice singsonging out of control—"I came to the camp just to see you."

She sits at a table with a blank page, alone with a dozen kids. Hissi is a frail toddler of six, bandy-legged, scanty hair, all eyes. She ignores me gently, consumed in some memory that arranges her every muscle into a mimetic pose of pure grief. Reflexively I huddle with her, assuming her position without looking at her, and *crack* I'm in the green jungle with my wife's green eyes, bright green, dry and still in a shaft of light. At that instant Hissi starts and looks at me. Our eyes meet, and loss relived is an electric arc between us. She studies me with intent awe, watching what's inside her at a safe remove. She takes my hand and puts a crayon in it. Mimicking Lila's tutelage, perhaps, she guides my fingers and imbues my hand with talent I have never had. Her soft touch stops the muscular tug-of-war that makes my hand jagged and wild. I can draw intricate curlicues, subtle textures, shades and hints of forms.

We are drawing a fireball.

The land here is littered with *dreikanter*, faceted stones. Blown sand erodes them on the windward side until they tip. Then the wind erodes another side. My existence is like theirs. Swirling solitary thoughts ground down the jagged fractures where my wife was torn from me, and slowly wore me away. When Lila came, I tipped and exposed something else. Now camp life flows over me, eroding more. I can feel myself disappear.

First my consciousness collapsed into a self-contained black hole. Now my identity dissipates amid needs that shame my own: Thirst, the need that obliterates all others, multiplied by four hundred throats. Hunger, insistent even in those to whom it has done its worst, the blind, the lame, the slow-witted, the piebald. Sickness—bone infection in mine-mangled legs, sores in the mouth and nose, eyeworms making their slow way across the white.

Each day I watch a new family make a ceremony of death. There is no wailing to the corpse, no silent vigil. The helplessness of a dying man inspires shared labor to lift him, clean him, feed him. His oldest memories well up and regale his family, and he leads prayers as he sees fit, a priest now for life. His delirium renews the family's faith with miraculous visions.

I hood my eyes to dim the sights as the sights dim me.

A tiny hand rests on the shin of a starved old man. The fingers twine in leg hair luxuriant as wool. Hunger has made him too weak to move his legs, and the hair grows undisturbed.

A family turns a woman to air her sores. Her dropsied back holds the imprint of a stone that lay beneath her, and of the hands that move her.

Clinging together, a woman and her daughter grope toward their lean-to in the dusk. Life on a distant river has cost the mother her sight; the daughter is with child, and here in camp night blindness is a sign of pregnancy, like nausea or nesting, because the baby has first claim on the scanty nutrients in a wasted mother's body.

A bashful boy is paraded through the camp by bigger boys. He has become a man: here, where worms throng in your bladder, a sleepy spurt of blood announces puberty.

Their want impels me, simulating will. Their suffering rouses me like pins and needles in a sleeping limb.

There is Serata, the faceless blighted woman Lila showed me. She is draped and decorated with children, child-strewn. One lazes with his head in her lap as she strokes the boy's hair. Two more snuggle at her side. More orbit her in play, calling to her, basking in her. She loves through that scorched mask.

Remembering how I quailed when I first saw her, I feel small. But African tragedy cuts outsiders down to size. Terror comes first. Pity follows in time.

This morning a truck came banging into camp on tired springs, a full load bouncing in the bay clangorous and joyful like tin cans dragged off to a honeymoon. By a fluke it has avoided the various armed officials who wait to levy improvised fees.

The camp has shaken off its lassitude. The truck shivers as they unload it. The shipment is all food, and medicine is needed most right now. Still, unplundered food is a windfall too. Here in the camp, an occasion for gratitude suspends ordinary life as a blizzard does up north. Lila gyrates and hoots, broadcasting elation as volunteers lug sacks to the camp's truck.

In the past month camp life has secured me with a thousand little snares: not responsibilities, since none have been assigned me, but worries. At this moment I am gnawing at the problem of vaccines. The magical solar fridge is malfunctioning. We have no idea how it works, so we cannot fix it. "We'll just have a shotfest," Lila says, "shoot everybody up before the vaccine goes bad."

I have a list of objections, but Lila ignores me and darts toward a naked toddler. She sits in the dirt, perches him on her knees and jounces him, ducking closer, ducking away, faster and faster until the boy is writhing in giggles.

I have run out of querulous steam by the time she returns. Her eyes are shining as she says in a gruff basso, "Malnutrition check A-OK. Playing behavior verified."

A malnourished baby stops playing. It's the earliest of warning signs. Lila is not playing to test this child, though. She is simply playing. Lila can celebrate without dreading the long fall to mourning. I admire that, but I cannot emulate it. I must not be set in motion or the pendulum will swing back to my wife. That fear makes me pull against her joy.

"Crabby today," she says. "Hungry? Maybe we should get some mush into you."

"I'm fine."

"Oh, I see, you're just a wet blanket," she says, and sweeps up another child.

I have ventured farther north than I normally do. One tributary of the buried river flows into Algeria, and I have followed it almost to the frontier. I can't turn back yet, though. I have to see where the birds are coming down.

The black birds rise and wheel in the air, driven off by a rival, and screw up courage to descend again. It must be a feast. The birds are too many for a dead snake or a lost goat. I saw them first, and now I can hear them blustering.

They watch my jeep approach and move off grudgingly. They

have found a Peugeot. It stopped on packed gravel with half a tank of gas and some bottles of water. I could drive it away if I chose to move the occupants.

Three of them sit with glass shards like dandruff in their hair. Their throats are hinged. A single cut bares the flexed spine of each: a man, a woman, and a boy.

Algerians. This is their revolution. The government militias may have killed them as Islamist sympathizers. The Islamists may have killed them as government spies. There is no way to tell. The woman's face has acne—she wore the veil—but the man has no beard. They probably changed sides as required, day to day.

These three must have been desperate, to flee this way. Algerian violence is more personal. It cannot generally be outrun. Think of My Lai massacres every month in an endless chain, each new one avenging the last. The country has guns and bombs enough, but intimate hand-crafted knives are the weapon of choice. The revolution poses no threat to the regime. The adversaries have proven their capacity to coexist.

There was a time when refugees flowed north, from Mali to Algeria. In Algerian camps frightened Tuaregs could escape Muru's black-supremacy movement. Blacks could escape the Tuareg slavers of Inhad's Holy Garrison. But now the flow has stopped. Mali's warlords have cleansed their realms, and Algeria is worse.

It's almost dark. I need to be alone. Capering in the mothers' tent, Lila is practicing keeping me here. Tomorrow she's going to get on my phone with a bishop and hit him up. She is drawing me out, testing her charm.

Why am I so solemn all the time? "I don't like fun."

How did I get into this line of work? "I was a roughneck on an oil rig. I know enough geology to get by, and my stint down south proved I won't fall apart in Africa." I don't fall apart. I break quietly down like a frost-spalled rock sloughing chips and dust.

I must have kept on speaking. Lila cocks her head and says, "Michelle? Who's Michelle?"

I couldn't have spoken her name aloud, just like that. Turning inward, I say, "My wife."

"I didn't know you were married."

"Widowed."

"I'm sorry."

A crack has opened: "She did microcredit. She had an army of local women, I called them the little loan sharks. They would form 4-H-type clubs and lend each one money to buy chickens or a pig. They worked with the clubs: blinker the cocks so they don't fight. Stack the coops on the pens so the pigs can feed on the waste falling down.

"To decide to go one dollar into debt, it's a decision of such gravity. The fear in the faces of these women, and the resolve . . . We're all so deep in hock back home, we just can't comprehend. Every dollar my wife lent changed a life."

I break off, appalled to have spoken of her. I have stopped short of the next question: How did she die? Lila looks at me in silence. She has put all her questions away. What is left in her face is the look you get when you show a child her first scorpion, saying, *Don't touch.*

I still do my own work, but more listlessly than before. I map the unreachable seas underfoot, distracted by too many worries to count. Sunsets flare and breezes cool my skin, but I am ungrateful. I look at the ground at my feet, feel the well running dry. The camp's uncertain future fights my wife's truncated past for my mind. The here and now is put to flight. To return me to the moment takes something strange, or worrisome: something like what I hear now.

In the ravine where I am dowsing, a Harmattan wind is sweeping like a broom, from the north, from the east, from the north again and back, and the brief puffs of north wind carry a sound strange enough to penetrate my cotton-wool thoughts. The sound would not jar in any city in the world, but in the desert there is no reason for a repetitive rhythmic clank. Within it the sound has a cry of almost human pitch that rises and falls again in a split second. Its metronomic regularity could pace a funeral march.

I follow it in the jeep, and the sound grows clearer rather than louder. The anvil chorus caroms between two scarps that hide its source. I thread my way among cobbles strewn in a wash, geared down, fighting the wheel.

The tan hillside changes. Now the creases and outcrops have softened. Blowing sand has worn the rocks to globes on slender stalks. The hills here are crumbling into dunes. My heartbeat converges with the *clank, clank, clank,* thumping a split second after each sound but never quite catching up.

The twin scarps fall away, laying the landscape open, and now I can see the source. This thing will not yield to the haze. It is new here, and the flying grit has not yet polished away its reds and blacks and angles. A top-heavy lopsided tower with a confusing, industrial ugliness, form following ungainly function, it shimmies in the heat waves, quivers at the top. Even from this distance it seems tall enough to reach me if it fell my way.

The monster crawls along a stair-stepped wall that sinks into the sand. It looks like a crane or a pile driver, but it must have a different name because its scale is incomparably larger. From its narrowest, uppermost point hangs a hammer that would dwarf a locomotive. The pilings are skyscraper-tall. They must be piercing rock. This is not exciting, as great works can be. This is frightening, like violence, or like nails sealing a rude carved coffin.

A vehicle approaches from the worksite, moving fast enough to outpace the billowing dust it raises. It is an armored vehicle of a kind uncommon in Francophone Africa: six wheels with six thousand lug nuts each, a boxy proboscis and a thick gun trained on me. I've seen it in my travels in the south and east. The name *Saracen* comes to mind.

It stands off fifty yards away. It changes direction and circles me. It approaches, slowly. "Get out of the vehicle." The loudspeaker does not obscure the white African accent.

I emerge, as ordered, more bewildered than threatened. The thing draws closer and says, "Identify yourself."

I do, at the top of my lungs, feeling that my voice has to pierce the armor plate. "Nationality," it says, and "State your business."

I reply, "Geologic survey for the United States Agency for International Development."

"This is a restricted area."

"Since when? And who are you?" I know every bump in this ground, every puddle buried beneath it. This is my aquifer.

A hatch opens and a thick-jacketed shape emerges, camouflage-clad and vague in the glare. Sunglasses scan me with an affectless insect gaze. "Let's see some identification. Passport."

"I don't have identification," I say. "I've worked here for four years with permission from the government of Mali. This is still part of Mali, right?"

He takes off his sunglasses, lets me see pinpoint pupils in pale blue irises. He puts concern in his voice, but none in his eyes. "This area is a construction site. Like any construction site, it can be hazardous."

"Who can I contact to find out what's going on here? It's not clear to me that your work takes precedence over our program."

"You don't understand," he says. "My options are to remove you or to detain you for questioning. You talk like 'at, you narrow my options."

It goes on that way for some time. Bureaucratic chest-beating is still the same. It concludes in the same ritualistic way. I leave; the guard displays respect.

Back home I bounce a question off the satellite. I don't wait long for the terse reply: *The site is restricted. Herewith contract scope is modified to exclude surveys on property of Timbuktu Earthwealth.*

Each night I return home from the camp to reclaim my privacy, draw energy from solitude. I nap fitfully and wake to savor the quiet. Solitude does more for me than sleep.

I struggle up as the night cold seeps into me. This is when the world sleeps most deeply. I am most alone now. The lifeless darkness frees my mind. At this hour I hear everything that makes a sound. I can hear the smallest puff of wind. I can hear blown sand bouncing off the jeep, a high note rising from a pouring-sugar sound.

That sound, the other one—it is already gone and I cannot tell if it is real, like the wind, or merely there, like the bell-clear sound of my wife's voice waking me. A double clap outside the door, polite and diffident. A Malian caller would clap, not knock. But no one calls on me. The crash of a bandit's battering ram, that could be, but not clapping, not now.

Again. Not insistent, but louder this time. I go to the door without taking the gun. Palms tell more than knuckles on a door, and these hands are no threat.

I open the door on gullies and stones in gibbous moonlight. Opened wider, the doorway takes in the shoulder of a dark slender form standing back from the door, and a sheen on shaved scalp.

"Mister Ty." Bouncing African intonation and a buzz of anxiety, ruthlessly suppressed.

"Fatimatou?"

"I am sorry to wake you."

"You didn't," I say.

"There is trouble at the camp," she says.

"What's the matter?"

"Cholera."

"You need help?"

"We have no more salts."

Cholera is so simple. No one has to die. The sick sip a cup of sugar and salts, and endure, as they endure everything, and live. The ingredients are dirt cheap, almost worthless until you need them.

"I have some," I say, "about a thousand count."

Fatimatou calculates. "That much can save fifty cases or so. It's just beginning: thirty active cases. If we can isolate them and stop it spreading, that might be enough."

I switch on a lamp and beckon her inside. "Let me dig the bag out. I've been lucky—no crud for a long time." In this tiny capsule, storage space is packed to bursting. Unused things must be excavated. With my head inside the metal cabinet I'm blind. Scorpions kink and twitch in my mind's eye as I search by feel through tools, instruments, tarps, and boxes until my fingertips indent powder in a sack. I drag it out and push it up at her.

Fatimatou hovers over me, hugging the sack and framing words I can't anticipate.

"Keep some for yourself," she says.

"I can get more."

She stands without moving long enough to make me think, *Why doesn't she go back?* She keeps standing there and I ask her, "Where's your truck?"

"We're short of fuel," she says.

"I'll take you back."

We get in my jeep. Fatimatou settles in the seat, and for the first time I see the bone-weary slackness in her face and spine. "How long did it take you to walk here?" I ask.

"I started out at dusk," she says.

"You have to get a satellite phone."

"Why? Supplies come when they come. Sometimes once a week, sometimes once a month. Praying works as well as phoning."

"At least you could call me," I say.

She is gauging me in silence.

"Do you need me down there?" My words are sagging with reluctance.

"Yes, we need you." Fatimatou is speaking with care, setting words in place one by one like bricks. "Lila loses hope sometimes. Never for long. I know how to bring her back. Now I can care for her or for the sick, but not for both. Sit with her, please. You don't have to speak."

We move crabwise down the hillside toward the camp. I can't see them dying from above. Dim calm shrouds everything as we approach. When we leave the jeep and pick our way among them, I only see repose.

Fatimatou leads me in loops straight to a campsite among the tight-packed tents where Lila kneels over a glassy-eyed girl. She rises, her knees caked with sandy mess, her brows wringing welling eyes. She jigs in place. This is not the detached compassion of an aid worker. This is a panicky fight against loss of a kind I have never known. Loss to me is numbness, a protective stupefaction sheathing horror. Lila is raw nerves and reflexes, naked pain felt now in alert expectation of death.

She is burping out words and sucking in shuddering breaths: "I brought them here." She shakes off Fatimatou's arms closing around her, stalks in figure-eights. My heartbeat thumps harder, not with fear but with a purely physical resonance that I have not needed, or known, in years.

Fatimatou says, "Ty is here. Get some rest. We will do your work."

I say, "Let's go wash up." She is ready to be led. Her panic is gone now, a trough between crests. I circle her with an awkward arm and she sags into it.

In the mothers' tent Lila curls on her cot. Whatever it is she's looking at, it's not for me to see. She's murmuring into some phantom ear and I'm eavesdropping. "We're not giving them enough water. It's not your fault, your well is a lifesaver. We just can't carry water fast enough. The sandstorms are hell. They have to build shelters."

They use water to stabilize the sand so it will hold sticks or poles. Then they reuse what's left until cholera takes hold.

Lila throws herself into a world where survival is luck, and takes responsibility for it all. This is fate's stronghold. Doesn't she understand that?

She is asleep now, or shutting out the world. I leave her and go out.

Fatimatou is darting among a volunteer crew mixing salts. Her voice is soft, but urgency flows from her taut shoulders and tight grip. "We'll draw more water later. Mix what we have first."

A volunteer says, "Their families can take it to them."

Fatimatou shakes her head. "We have to isolate them."

A young volunteer turns around. "That would be slower than panning for gold. The sick ones are scattered throughout the camp."

Fatimatou's brows slip inward, pained, then settle in resolution. She is yielding to a cruel idea. "We can't move them, but we can move the camp," she says. "They will not like it."

Calling in a piercing tone, Fatimatou gathers a huddle of blacks around her. She speaks in Bambara: *Auye taara na.* She meets objections: *Agni. Unh-uh.* The camp is going.

The group recoils and distends. Their voices join in a noise like a screeching of birds. The crowd grows as more people rise.

She turns to me with her head down, nudging with a shoulder. Lila would hold her to comfort her. "I'm making them abandon these little windbreaks. Not forever, but just go a day without tending them . . ."

I know. The scraps and rubbish will disappear beneath the sand.

Fatimatou says, "This could get ugly. Hunger makes us short-tempered. Especially when it's not too bad, like now."

Fatimatou repeats her flat final phrase in Bambara until it submerges in the crowd noise. She strides to the supply truck. "Ty, take your jeep," she shouts.

Their battery labors and groans. The engine turns over with a dusty cough. The truck jerks, then settles and whines forward. First they call, incredulous. Then they think of being left behind and start to run, or limp or drag themselves. The cargo of the truck is all that keeps the camp alive. She pulls away in a rooster tail of sand, using panic to cut through their lethargy. Only the cholera victims are past caring.

She stops a mile away. The refugees straggle to the truck, shouting and pounding on the cab. It looks as though they will mob her.

She steps out and stands quietly, listening. I see the crowd come closer, craning intently as Fatimatou murmurs. She is insinuating a message: *This is hardship. What we've left behind is death.* The group's agitation ebbs. Gestures lose their force. Slumping, the refugees disperse to find new patches of dust.

Now the camp is split in two, a new and more destitute camp by the truck, and the sick, strewn in ragged rings around unseen taints: cookpots or jugs or spots of sodden sand.

Fatimatou walks back to the sick, leading a handful of volunteers. She sets them to administering the sweet-salty water. Until their syringes run out, they inject it inexpertly into pinches of skin. They grind a cup into the sand near each prostrate figure. Volunteers replenish the cups and wet the mouths of those too weak to drink.

One dies. Only one. They give his cup to a new case, who is saved.

Lila does not buckle again, but Fatimatou takes pains to draw me into the camp. She binds me to Lila and to herself with little confidences, making an intricate rigging of us, each tie tugging at the others and shoring it up, keeping us standing like tent poles in the wind.

Fatimatou tells me only so much. It seems much of Lila's life is off-limits to me. But Fatimatou tells me her own story in bits and pieces over the course of many days.

Her family had a little land and a few animals. They always had enough to help the destitute, even when the gullies grew. For *terjeten,* when friends come to visit and leave with a loan.

Her mother didn't circumcise her. One by one she watched her friends go through it, and she lost them. They were too good for her. The boys wanted her, but not to marry. They rolled her in the mud, grabbed her or ground against her because she wasn't sewed up. Sometimes Fatimatou was grateful even for that. She couldn't find a man to marry. No family wanted her dowry of groundnuts. She'd be lucky to become some crippled man's third wife. She left and went to town.

She went to the university, where she lived in ruined dorms without water or lights and never saw a book. Sometimes she was a whore there, or was raped—the transaction takes various forms. Sometimes she traded things that came her way.

For the days or hours when she could look beyond survival, Fatimatou had another life with the students. She was as much a student as they; no one had books or papers, and she had a careful mind. Most wonderful, and frightening, was the tempting fantasy called *bènbènbèn,* subversion. Her friends at the university talked about politics, who ruled, and why, and how. They talked as though the rulers cared, it sounded crazy, but they met, indoors, then outdoors, in bigger and bigger crowds until the city stopped when they marched.

Then there was fighting, not just with the rulers but with men who came to take what they could find. The worst were the sobels, soldiers by day, rebels by night, the boldest and best armed of the bandits.

After stop-and-go months of casual terror and routine panic, they had new rulers. Not generals or thieves, but wise men like elders. "Elders we have chosen!" She felt like Washington in America.

Sometimes she telescopes the horror of the past two years with her eyes put aside to think: "To choose your ruler makes you proud, too proud. We believed we could tell them what to do, remove them, replace them at will. We marched to get more, and the rulers changed, and changed again. The revolution we started was taken from us. I fled the city . . .

"I found Lila in an oasis. She had many whites with her at first, but they left, one by one. Lila begged me for help: not for food or a loan, but for me to work with her, think with her, learn what she knows. I was afraid. More people came to us as the hungry season set in, until we were too many to be let alone. You have to stay quiet and small."

Now we are jolting toward the well in the truck. A thick translucent dome of haze diffuses the light without tempering it. Fatimatou shades her eyes from the glare and shades me from her eyes. "When Lila talks to you her words come out in a great rush. I think these are things she can explain only to another American."

"Certain things stay bottled up inside you when you're not at home. Some people like it that way."

Fatimatou's eyes are sharp, but they retreat after confirming that I'm speaking of myself. "I think Lila is like that," she says.

Fatimatou must be working on Lila, too. For the third time this month Lila is pounding on the door of my container, yelling, "Hey, Ty." She is breathless when I open the reverberating door. She storms in and says, "Have you got needle-nose pliers?"

I say, "You don't always need a reason to come up here, you know."

Her head rocks back a few degrees. A slow private smile spreads on her face. She sits and stretches against the strictures of my little chair. I sit up on the sink looking down at her scruffy head.

Looking around, she says, "Right angles. You get to miss right angles—isn't that weird? There are thousands of acres for each person here, and we just want to shut ourselves up in something." She lounges in the pipe-and-canvas chair as though it's stuffed with down. All of her physical strength is in her thighs. They swell gracefully from delicate knees. I can imagine her as a girl jock: a striker perhaps, or a miler.

The corners of her eyes droop, briefly; then she pulls herself taut again. She is keeping something at bay. I say, "The camp has another ten minutes before everything falls apart in your absence."

Lila says, "You are not privy to my state of mind, so stop poking around in there."

I get up and grab my glass jug. "I want you to try something—here."

She looks suspiciously at the cup I hand her. “What is it, home brew?”

“Fossilized water.”

She sips gingerly, confines it in pursed lips. She gulps it with an alarmed flash of her eyes. “Disgusting.” She’s holding her tongue up out of the last traces in her mouth.

“Don’t just glug it, pay attention. It’s got top notes of iron and a palatal bite of hydrochloric acid. The nose is faintly metallic without even a whiff of chalk.”

“You’re going to tell me it’s good for me?”

“It’s water. You are the first living creature ever to drink that glass of water. It’s been trapped inside rock since the dawn of time.”

“Didn’t some dinosaur drink it once?”

“No. Not this. This is one thing you can have all to yourself.”

She’s watching, trying hard to see the point. “It’s like if you went back in time.”

“If you were here alone,” I say. “If you were here first.”

“Just waiting for Adam and Eve to show up?”

“Not waiting. Just enjoying the last peace the world will have.”

A soft smile drapes her eyes. “You don’t understand peace. It’s not like water, leaking away. You can always make more. If you make enough to fill up a pup tent and it lasts five seconds, you’re doing good. It keeps you going all day.”

I have struggled in silence with my abiding confusion: What are these people doing here? I can’t question Lila’s judgment, but coming here is insanity. Lila rebuffed my first attempts to probe: *What, this isn’t Disney World? Who are you, the zoning board?*

I learn Lila’s life and times, bit by bit, puffed out in syncopation with the rhythms of labor, like snatches of a sea chantey. She joined the Peace Corps from her midwest cow college and clawed her way into the cutthroat world of relief. When she couldn’t make it into the Red Cross or CARE she bottom-fished among the shoestring church groups, following crises the way migrant workers follow crops. In the sleek stateside headquarters where funds are raised, administrators turned her away, again and again: her training was scanty, her experience was scattershot, her language was a street kid's patchwork of Mandingo, Arabic, and French.

Lila would simply show up at the camp and pitch in. The administrators didn't really care—their grants and appeals consumed them. They know that raising money is the hard part; emergencies take care of themselves. In this way Lila infiltrated Africa. But none of that explains Lila's presence in this dead place.

Fatimatou tells me Lila answers questions in her own time.

And now I am in the mothers' tent, sitting at the foot of Lila's cot. A weak yellow bulb hangs from the center pole, glowing with the day's stored sunlight. Lila has given herself no more space than the six other women who share the tent, but she has a measure of privacy. The mothers speak no English, and they are absorbed in their talk or their thoughts. We excite no curiosity.

Lila reclines on the bed, her fingers interlaced behind her head. Under each arm the hair lies flat in two separate tufts, one on her arm and one on her body. She covers her body tonight, as it is cool.

Lila seems to value the haze of fatigue for its analgesic properties. Sometimes she sleeps through the night, too exhausted even to hear the ripsaw cries of the smallest infants. She is most haggard then. The well-rested alertness is too much for her.

Lila retires before I do, and wakes earlier. Putting her to bed has become my habit, and hers. For me it is a eunuch's ritual, sexless unction for an indifferent superior. She is dozing, but she is telling me the bedtime story. "We came here from Tabankort," Lila is saying. "We were five hundred there."

"You're four hundred now—the other hundred?"

"Dead. One by one, then three at a time, then in dozens. We left some to die when the truck couldn't hold any more sick, don't look at me that way, they were already comatose, you'd have done the same thing.

"For five miles straight we used ramps. Put them in front of the tires, drive six feet and bog down, drag them around to the front again. That's when we started to die. We were living from well to well. We'd get down to literally no water, except what I had stashed away. I had my private jerry can. Can you believe that? I wasn't ready to die with them, like I'm not from here, so I get special survival privileges. So I should live when they have to die."

An upheaval under the skin of her face tugs her scalp and hoods her eyes. "And that was only a minor bout of cowardice."

When her breathing finally gentles, I tuck the blanket around her and work the filmy tepee of bednet under her mattress. There is contentment in the single note she whimpers in her sleep.

I'm alone in the desert, sounding for water. The echoes say it's bone-dry down below. The dunes are quiet today. They wait until I'm straining to hear whispers of water, then they act up and addle my computer with noise.

Instantly wary, intent and staring—at what, I don't know, some reflex took control. Now in the sky to the south I see it: a molehill of flying dust; a convoy burrowing through it, patchy clay-colored stake trucks sheathed with thick tarps. It's coming my way. This sad caravan looks reassuringly commercial, but bandits drive all kinds of wrecks. I reach for my shotgun, cradle it in my lap. When did I last clean it?

The trucks waggle and bound as the sand shifts beneath them. Their forward creep is scarcely faster than the dunes. Time slows to their pace as they approach.

When they pull within earshot an Arab sticks out his head. He's anxious, not con-man friendly as the bandits are. He's just trying to make an honest living. *"Captifs?"* And I see the little black fingers holding on to the stakes in back.

There's nothing I can do. I drive away.

I mention my encounter next day at the camp. Lila averts her eyes. She still thinks she must answer for all this predestined suffering. She says, "Sometimes I think they're the lucky ones."

Slaves have a measure of safety in troubled times. It's been this way for a thousand years. Go over the border into Mauritania and ask any black: he'll say, "Of course I'm a slave, I was born to be one." When order broke down and raiding resumed, the trade routes came alive again.

Lila gouges with a thumbnail at a callus on her palm. Speaking more to her open hand than to me, she says, "With all the raiding, the price of slaves has gone way down. You can get a pubescent girl for fifty bucks now. Sometimes the traders come sniffing around with a wad of bills and an empty truck. There may come a time when my abrasive personality is not enough to drive them off. You think maybe I ought to have a gun to wave around?"

I could give her my gun. I know I'll never use it.

As a boy I hunted, and expertly—but not like my father. He could choose his bird from a flock and bring it down with the tail end of the shot string. We would never find more than half a dozen pellets in a fowl. It wasn't just his eyes, though they were perfect smooth beads that saw impossible things. It was his calm. He could wait until his blood and breath and sinews were utterly still, then, with the twitch of a lone tiny muscle, cause the bird to fall.

His calm never wavered, even when my dog mauled my cousin's face. He got between them quick as a crossbow bolt, with intent eyes and a loose jaw.

My cousin is a man now, ten years my junior, with one closed eye and a smooth arcing scar. He is not bitter. The dog turned suddenly, inexplicably vicious as dogs sometimes do, for a moment, no more.

I begged to be allowed to put the dog down. He was my dog. I took him to the dump with my gun and a shovel after the bulldozers went quiet. He was a German shorthair. When he was a pup I would take him there and he would flush rats for me to shoot, skidding in and out of my line of fire.

I left the gun there, buried with the dead dog. It was seventeen years before I picked up a gun again, and even now I cannot touch a gun without seeing those feral gray brows crumpled with an inhuman purity of remorse.

When I stopped hunting I sensed kindness in my father's calm acceptance. I was his only child. He hunted alone after that.

The satellite phone sits in my hand like a lead weight. I have not used it for more than a year. I send dry text messages to my mother and my father. The messages grow in fits and starts. I write until I blurt a truth. I prune it back and start again, but truth creeps in and spoils my sterile words. The message I'm writing now has been waxing and waning for six months.

But touching the shotgun has made me crave my father's calm. My mother replies to my messages, not he. I need to hear his slow voice and the small smile that flattens its timbre.

The phone is alive. This is his voice; but the incredulous catch in it is new. Nothing surprises my father. Can he really be so shocked to hear his son's voice? And where is his calm? He is crying. Maybe he is changing with age. My long absence makes the subtle changes plain.

Or maybe this is what my absence did to him.

It's still cool at the camp this morning. Too cool. Lila bolts from my side to break up a fight: three boys writhing in the dust. A ten-year-old sits on a smaller boy. Another boy squats there, slapping the victim's head with calm precision.

In most places a disturbance will draw a crowd. Not here. Violence flares and dims as in a charred log. Perhaps the refugees feel the instinctive skittish alertness that those screams evoke, but the response does not attract onlookers.

Two of the Mind Your Manners Men have come loping over, big gentle volunteers who pour oil on troubled waters. They stand aside as Lila reaches down and picks up the older bully by the scruff of a thin shirt. Cords stand out in her muscleless arms and the boy scuffs, sullen and limp. She holds his shoulders, barks in Bambara. She sends him off.

Fatimatou joins Lila and they examine the victim. He tries to rise but lurches crazily and clutches at Fatimatou. She wobbles and braces a hand on the ground, murmuring through pursed lips that touch his face.

Lila says, all control, "Child soldier. One of Inhad's kids. That's one of the tricks they learn: break his eardrums and put bugs in his ears. It's a traditional slave punishment, but there are all kinds of new variants—put in caustics; put in gasoline and light it. I don't know what it is about ears."

Now Lila's hugging herself, twisting gently in place, rocking herself like a baby. If it comforts her, I can't see it in her face. "The Red Cross guys, they call Inhad 'Lord of the Flies' because of all his little wild boys. You can cripple a boy or starve him until he's an imbecile, and there's hope for him. But rear a boy to kill, and he's lost. At some point we'll have to send him away, and he will die."

"You know why we left Tabankort? Why we left a hundred people dead in the desert? We left Tabankort because I knuckled under."

It is another night. Lila is naked on top of the sheet, shining in the day's residual heat. The mothers take no notice. Clothes are not taken for granted here. Muslim modesty has long since been cooked away in this crucible—nakedness is just another kind of poverty. There is nothing sexual in Lila's nudity. Knees up, fingers interlaced behind her head, Lila is cracking open. It looks painful, like the rib spreader used for surgery, and it serves the same purpose, exposing the heart.

"Inhad came to town that day." Lila is looking inward now, her forehead creased into tiny furrows. "He said it wasn't safe there anymore. I had to take the townspeople away. I said, 'Their safety is in your hands, not mine.' Inhad thought about that a little. And he called his men. They ran down a woman, dragged her back screaming—she knew what was happening before I did. They cut her to pieces in front of me. I knew her name, I knew her kids, I knew her smile, and she looked at me before she died like I was her only chance.

"When they finished chopping they kicked the pieces of her into a pile. I just stared at her foot, where it was propped up against her side. The eyes in the severed head were probably looking right at me, but what shook me up most was that foot in the wrong place.

"Up until then I had good luck playing the bigmouth American-aid bitch with marines and blue berets at my command.

Then it hit me—I'm on my own. Ecumenical Alms is in liquidation. No one knows I'm here in Tabankort. Maybe I have some extra food, but that woman and I are just alike.

"Inhad didn't know that. He didn't care. He wanted the townspeople gone, or dead. He would have been happy to kill them himself, but a death march through the desert had some advantages. If he behaved himself even a little, when the multilateral force came it would cut all the deals with him.

"Maybe it was a bluff, killing that woman; maybe if I call his bluff there will be no more death—I remember thinking that with a cool little part of my mind while I fought to keep my knees from letting go.

"In the end it was an easy choice, to kill them myself. It felt so inevitable. Like it's OK, like the whole universe wants it that way, God and nature and all the powers that be.

"So I go to the truck and get in. The wheel burns my hand, and I'm wringing wet within a second, but I'm shivering. Everything we have fits in the truck with room to spare. Just dividing up supplies in my head, I know: one in four will have to die. I'm just hoping the weak ones will die soon so the other three-quarters will live. I start north in low gear. People are coming out of their homes. They know the routine."

Lila's gaze passes through the fabric of the tent. "People started dropping ten miles out of town. The first was Tabililte, one of the volunteers. She didn't get a chance to sell her goat and she kept it too long before she slaughtered it. By the time she stopped watering it, her own dehydration had got ahead of her.

"I was stronger and calmer with each new death, stronger and calmer than ever in my life. It didn't make a difference to anyone, but that's all I could do—be strong and calm."

She narrowed her eyes, fixing on the memory, hardening herself to it. "Not ever again. I won't do their dirty work again."

At night the haze settles and the air stops twisting. The camp is sharper by moonlight. I don't like it. The prospects are too clear.

Fatimatou is still awake. She sits in a circle of young women, playing at subversion in a place where there is nothing to subvert. They solicit my opinions, invite me to pretend with them. I can't.

"Lila told me about Tabankort."

It subdues them, and I feel cruel. "Inhad—that holy lunatic," someone says.

Fatimatou says, "No. He is not insane. He speaks that way to lead his men. Inhad is a trader, shrewd and practical. He trades blacks. He kills only as needed to conduct his trade.

"Muru is the madman. Thank God he is a coward. If he had no rivals, we would soon be living his delusions. Not black supremacy, but blacks and Tuaregs and Arabs and immigrants, all dying together."

On an impulse I have stopped on my way back home. When I was alone here this place gave me solace. But this is too much to ask of a sacred cave: displace the thought of Lila presiding over death, strong and calm.

I stoop to enter a shallow grot in a basalt outcrop. The little cavity shelters in the lee of the Harmattan winds and traps a bit of cool night all day long. Tonight, like most nights, it is warmer than the open air outside.

Inside the grotto is an expanse of incised rock. It shows faceless foot-high hunters with torsos of a bowtie shape and stick legs dangling from mounts that dwarf them. Their world is crudely gouged and flat, without perspective; but if I hold my torch just right the scattered figures show me a hunt with heights and depths and distance and speed.

A line suggests a cliff with large figures on the right and small figures on the left. Hunters drive a herd of beasts toward the edge. The carving freezes the animals in midstride, legs reaching or bunched underneath.

One hunter is caught between the stampede and the cliff. The scratches in the rock show the life and death of it. The horse shies. The hunter throws long arms in the air: in panic, or in a brave attempt to turn them.

I need to see a carving that shows what happened that day. Did the stampede sweep the hunter off the cliff? Or did it part and spare him? On this night the question absorbs me. Did he stand? Did he die? It must have seemed like God and nature and all the powers that be, demanding flight.

I am troubled to find desert thoughts of Lila encroaching on the jungle inside me. It's no longer so lush and so loud when I close my eyes. My dozing thoughts are brown and tan and gray now: the fear in Lila's eyes when she concentrates, and the extravagant way she startles. Her delicate ant's waist and arms of disproportionate strength. The caution with which she speaks of herself, and her headlong dazzling smile, comet-tailed with squint lines at the temple. Her unself-conscious amiable scratching.

Her presence in my mind betrays my wife.

The mothers' tent is crammed with refugees tonight. A dust storm has driven them inside. More crouch outside, faces covered with scraps, palms plastered over eyes, but the sand will find its way in—into the unfortunates outside, and into us. When you blink it feels like gravel gouging glass. Grit mucks up your sweat and adheres to you, cakes on your tongue and in your nose.

I will not be returning to my shelter tonight. The flying grit would destroy my jeep. We feel our way around the tent as though choosing to retire. Soon we will seize up and drop. I trip on a hummock under the blue tarp, break my fall with a hand on my bedroll.

"Hey, watch the mosquito netting, don't snag it." Lila probes it with her fingers. "Shit. Ripped."

"I can't see any rip," I say, prizing an eye open, willing more tears, pretending to look.

"See, there."

"You call that a rip?"

"The bugs will find it, you know that," she says. "We can gang two cots and share my net. Forgive me, I haven't showered lately.

"Come on under." She strips and kneels on her cot to tuck in the netting.

She falls asleep at once. The speed of it is remarkable. It belittles me. I rise on one elbow and inhale the scent of her body. I listen to her breath catch, more with a snuffle than a snore. I feign sleep and roll against her, drape my arm over her. Then I must be asleep, because I'm riding a horse. I drive mosquito-legged children toward a cliff.

I snap awake. Lila is sitting bolt upright in bed, rigid and trembling, oblivious to the lantern I switch on. She gasps with her eyes empty white under half-open lids.

Eventually her body relaxes. She curls into a ball. Quietly as I can I ask, "Is it the malaria medicine?" The best one causes night terrors. I thrash on the floor myself, sometimes.

"Dream. Just stuff that happened today."

Even under the blanket, her back is slick and cold against my arm.

The flimsiest net can be inescapable by virtue of its size. Lila bound me up with the camp: to Fatimatou and to Hissi and the mothers and children and to the few men who escaped conscription or massacre. The net does not stop there.

Something is raising dust to the east. It comes from the impassable *erg*, weaving steadily closer like a tacking sailboat, tracing the contours of the dunes. A hovercraft, ferryboat-sized, painted verdant green with cool blue letters reading TIMBUKTU EARTHWEALTH. Fifty yards away, it curtsies on its skirt and quiets down.

Lila is in front, scenting them, and I can tell she's not going to stop and point; she's going to flush them. I catch up with her.

She says, "Look, a flying saucer come to save us." Lila's elated. She's sure this is good news.

A heavy-looking hatch opens. When he squeezes out the hatch, he's ruddy, blond-stubbled and big in khaki and blue. A broad-brimmed hat tops him off. He clambers down a ladder, turns, clasps his hands behind his back, and waits. I see a smile in the shade of the brim.

I'm hanging back. Lila comes up to his chest. She shakes hands like one of the guys, putting her back into it. Their back-and-forth gives way to mostly him. As she listens, Lila's face goes slack with awe or disbelief. She stands with her arms out from her sides like a timid hint of a hug.

I approach where they huddle in the sun. The man turns to me and sticks out a thick hand. "Bud Van Sickle. I'm with Timbuktu Earthwealth."

"Oh," I say, "you're the guys who own the Adrar now. What's all the pounding about, anyway?"

"He's going to supply us!" She's giddy, bouncing lightly on her toes, nose in the air as Fatimatou creeps closer.

"We're going to take real good care of you until the security situation stabilizes and we can get you out of here. You've been stranded out here long enough." Bud is subtly big, agile and proportional enough to look average from a distance. Up close, he makes me want to back up to reduce him to a more familiar scale. Bud's face is shiny red on the cheeks, like Santa Claus. His eyes do not twinkle, though. They burn steady blue like a cutting torch coming for the next length of pipe in the pile.

Lila's showing Bud around. I see them meandering through the camp, Lila voluble and loud, Bud nodding crisply with narrowed eyes. Lila is loose-limbed, swinging her arms even when standing still, flicking on her grin more and more. She flirts like a man, expanding and taking up space.

I occupy myself with a muddy leak under one of the pillow tanks. The plastic bears the marks of a palm rat's teeth. They learn fast about this big juicy blue fruit. The patch won't take, the sand turns the glue into gum and the acetone reaches deep in my head. I don't catch myself muttering until I've barked out a curse.

I eat dinner with Fatimatou, using the truck's wheel like a bar rail to cock my hips and ease my worn-out back. Fatimatou stands up with me, though she could fold effortlessly and squat in the dust. Lila doesn't come by. This is her spot, too, most nights.

Fatimatou says, "Finally someone is going to open their purse."

"How do you know?"

"I know it," she says. "We will get more than we could hope for. It won't come cheap. I can see in his eyes he wants something too."

"What." I'm clutching the word with my throat, keeping it casual.

"I can't tell," she says. "But Lila will give it to him, whatever it is."

After dinner I walk through the camp, acting out an elaborate sham of checking and noting: *New sheeting for the south latrine. Dig the truck out of the sand again.* I'm preparing to playact for others, but I don't lie to myself. I am looking for Lila and Bud.

I follow a worrisome trickling sound to the curtained shower stall. In the stall I hear the valves opening to spray, then springing shut, again and again. No one takes showers that long. My pulse thumps in my ears as I imagine Lila letting go, squandering water, shedding her brisk bonhomie and turning to Bud with the intensity she reserves for the starving.

Resentment and uncertainty keep me circling the shower. When Lila comes out I'm approaching from an improbable direction, skirting the lip of the latrine. She looks annoyed at me: at my presence, at my spying, I don't know. Maybe I'm kidding myself, but she looks ashamed, too.

My hello comes out mournful in spite of myself. I can feel my mouth work as I grope for something else to say. I feel like a pitiful harmless voyeur. Lila turns aside without a word. I veer away from the shower without waiting for Bud to come out.

When Bud speaks with you he ducks his head as if conspiring. I noticed that mannerism right away. Nonetheless, when I saw him last night, huddling with Lila in just that way, I imagined confidences exchanged, intimacies risked. Bud is ducking his head at me now. Absurdly, I expect morning-after man talk: a wry reference to his conquest, a flash of pride to cut him down to size. But he takes his liaison stoically. A remarkable woman enthralled with him—it's one more situation, objectively noted and assessed. It's none of my business anyway. I know my eyes show the downward arc of my thoughts.

"How's this plot for water?" Bud asks.

I say, "There's nothing here but fossilized water at six hundred feet. There's a well about ten miles west."

"What's the bedrock, all basalt?"

So he knows about my specialty. Maybe Timbuktu Earthwealth checked me out when I trespassed on their land. Bud sees my suspicion in the angle of my gaze and says, "Lila told me all about you. The way she sees it, you saved four hundred lives that she dropped in your lap."

I didn't imagine them talking about me, except in the condescending tone in which people newly intimate reassure each other.

"So, how stable is this stuff?" he says, stamping. "What's the pattern of intrusions?"

"A big vug here and there. Nothing to weaken the overburden, if that's what you care about—you're a miner, right?"

He ignores my question. "Anybody know more about the geology of this place than you?"

"Probably not. There's no reason for anyone else to care. The ore is low-grade and hard to get at. Most of this was seabed up until the Permian era. No oil, though. Just Mali's luck."

He narrows his eyes. "Know anything about the seabed?"

"Nope."

"No oceanography in your background?"

There is something purposeful in his probing. It combines the observant pressure of an interview with sharp leading questions I don't understand. I might think him a know-it-all, but he's too self-contained. I decide to do some probing myself. "You on the exploration end or the extraction end?"

"I'm just kind of a public relations man. The experts tell me the big news and I put it in fourth-grade English for the newsmen and the congressmen."

"So what's the big news?"

He looks for something in my eyes, finds it, and says, "You've got a moonlight job, if you want one. Two hundred K for six months' work. Tax-free, paid offshore into a nominee account. Don't go bragging about it, though."

5

Bud said nothing more about his job. I let the matter drop. Maybe he thinks I'm wrestling with temptation. But this waste is all that's real to me. He can't give me back the one thing I want. Now he's here again and his smile says *All this can be yours.*

"Come out to Timbuktu with me," Bud says. "I'd like you to meet some people, tell them what you think."

"It's not that easy," I say. "I'm posted here for an AID contract."

"Oh, come on, AID needs you to work what, two, three days a month? They pay you what, GS-13?"

"This is the job I've signed up to do. Even if I could run out on my contracting officer, the camp is demanding a lot of my own time. They're in tough shape here, as you can see."

"I promised you we'll take good care of these people."

"I'm not interested. That's what it comes down to. I don't want a real job. I am the wrong guy for you."

Bud moves in close, leans his bulk over me, and says, "You are the only guy for us." He stalks off.

Aid has started to flow: tins of fat and bags of meal, hand-pumped water purifiers with plenty of cartridges, cholera kits. Bud missed nothing: one of the trucks brought crayons just as the last muddy-colored stubs began to crumble in Hissi's fingers. No one in camp can let go of the fear, as yet. They have had lucky days and weeks before.

Fatimatou got a gift of her own. I find her in the biggest of the tents Bud sent. They will use this one to muster volunteers. Fatimatou is cooing over a laptop computer. A baby satellite dish connects it to the world. She has bound herself into some Malian nerve plexus: stacks of messages about what has happened and what is yet to come. Screens that blink with hourly reports of the merest twitch: Inhad's raids, Muru's maneuvers, Bozo's hamstrung response. She barters, bargains, and begs.

Who are these people? Friends from her time at the university or fellow protesters from Bamako. How did she learn computer magic? With a sniff she says, "I can read, you know." She is smiling into the computer, thinking of a time when she was more than a victim. "Bozo says it's a way to whisper when you can't speak out."

"I need this, Ty. I've never needed water like I need this." This must be how Lila looked at Bud, with a crack addict's need that promises sex, love, abasement, anything. She is pressing close, thighs and body, lips parted. I cannot meet her eyes.

"You don't need anything from me. Bud's bankrolling you now."

"We need Bud. Bud needs you."

I snap at her, "I can't hold down a regular job." She must hear my ambivalence. I want to be in league with this mystery man, Lila's guardian angel. To Lila I'm just another decent person, kind by necessity. Bud is miraculous to Lila. I want to be miraculous too. "What does he want from me? What did he tell you?"

"He's going to feed us. Nothing else matters. Ty, Ecumenical Alms sent a courier here today. You know what they sent me? A first-class ticket out for me, and a letter saying we're cut off. No more supplies. Bud is all we've got."

I've consented to talk, but I haven't signed up, not yet. I will go to Timbuktu with Bud, to the representative offices of Timbuktu

Earthwealth, S.A. I will not meet the corporate officers. Bud doesn't know who they are.

Bud takes me south in his Hummer. The seat is a tight squeeze. It feels as if it's designed for an approved bodily position that specifies the required angle of knee, hip, neck, and elbow to the nearest degree. As the seat closes in around me, the route ahead spreads out to a boundless, directionless plane. "Driving sucks out here, but I wouldn't fly a bird. You're asking for it, even if you change out the air filters mission by mission. The Hummer may break down, but at least it won't fall out of the sky."

The road has disappeared. Bud steers by the stars with his satellite receiver. We weave along a red line on his glowing green map console.

I say, "That's not like any navigation program I've seen."

"No?"

"We're a pinpoint on that map. My locator just puts me in a quarter-mile zone."

"This one uses all the V-and-H information, down to the gnat's ass."

But the African satellite footprints always fuzz up the geolocation data—too much accuracy encourages heavy-arms mischief. "I thought that kind of resolution was reserved for government use."

"Depends," he says.

We pass a linear graveyard of stuck and rusting cars. Bud pokes gingerly ahead and backs out of drifts, swearing, but confident and absorbed. "So this is where the road is, big shit. It's ten feet under a pile of rock flour."

"You seem to know what you're doing," I say.

"This thing is pretty forgiving. The components are all up to MILSPECs. It's more than you need for a business trip."

I turn to look him in the eye. The bumpy ride makes me duck my head as if I'm intimidated. "Isn't it time you told me what, exactly, your business is?"

"Timbuktu Earthwealth is a Mauritius-registered offshore company with paid-in capital of forty million U.S. Three Fortune Fifty firms hold minority stakes: Sigdyne, C-3, and Systech."

"Who are they?" Freedom from news has been priceless to me, but these are alien names.

"Beltway bandits. Defense contractors. They like to keep a low profile."

"I thought the defense industry was bleeding white with all this world peace. Where did they get forty million to chip in?"

"Oh, you know how it is," he says. "The technocrats who run these companies, they're like Tarzan swinging from vine to vine. The defense vine breaks, they grab another one."

"And this vine is . . ."

"The peace business. Peace and prosperity. We have a business proposition that will lift Africa out of the dark ages. We're a resource business, but we don't extract, we don't deplete. We add value in situ. Never been done, never been tried. Can't even explain it without a hogchoker pile of charts. I'll just confuse matters if I try. We've got to line up some experts and let them take you along step by step."

When Bud speaks he fills the air with a Harmattan haze of words. "Bud, I thought you explain things in fourth-grade English. Why don't you just tell me what you do in one English sentence? It doesn't even have to be fourth-grade English."

"We hasten the inevitable." Without taking a breath he says, "You ever been to Timbuktu?" and we veer away from my question.

"Imagine a city where gold grows like carrots," Bud says. "Where they use gold instead of iron, instead of wood, instead of paint, paving the streets with it. That's what everybody imagined for five hundred years. It was the most remote place on earth, so no one really knew.

"Finally some Moor made it there. He came back and said, 'There's nothing there, just dirt.' Nobody believed him. Then an Englishman made it. He reported back: 'There's nothing there, just dirt.'

"Same way now," Bud says, "there's nothing there, just dirt. But wait. Timbuktu will finally see real wealth. We're going to make the legends true."

I ask, "Why didn't you set up in the capital? At least that's under government control. Timbuktu is Muru's turf."

"It's peaceful enough in Timbuktu. The Creepers keep the criminals in line. It's Third World at best, but so what? We've got satellite phones, solar arrays, generators, reverse-osmosis machines. We wet-lease a cargo plane for weekly supply runs. We've brought all the infrastructure we need, which is everything. To look after it all we retained Janissary Systems, a security outfit. They're the best."

"Janissary—the mercenaries?" I have little current knowledge of the world, but Janissary has long been a household word on this continent. Janissary spawns subsidiaries like a barracuda spraying milt. Each subsidiary takes a share of some mine or oil field or industrial complex that Janissary has rescued from terrorists, or rebels, or strikers, or local pamphleteers. Each subsidiary is said to be worth a billion dollars and a thousand African lives.

Bud switches on the radio—not the BBC, but an English-language satellite broadcast. Instead of Beeb-style African pulse-taking we get talk radio. This is a sky-high soapbox for angry old men. They rage at the New World Order, whatever that is. Maybe they mean Bud.

We roll into Timbuktu in twilight. The skyline is free of grandiose rich-world pride: just modest stucco lumps and a few obscene socialist erections, tasteless gifts graciously accepted. The streets have no curbs, and cars gently plow sandaled crowds. Patches of concrete mar the packed-dirt roads like scabs. Shallow, insidious potholes ease you into oncoming traffic. Mired with the clapped-out motorbikes and trucks are Mercedes sedans, dirty, dinged, but unmistakably new, with assaultive horns and seismic stereos. Their drivers flail out the window, rattling quarter-pound gold bracelets in frustration.

When the horns let up you can hear generators humming in all directions, spotlighting luxuries on pedestals in shops, painting restaurants with neon. In front of a mobbed casino a laser light show paints rainbow colors on arcing fountains of precious water. Beggars crowd a cordon at the casino's exit.

"Look what we've done," Bud says. "We haven't even begun to throw real money around. Wait until the project gets under way."

Bud turns the Hummer through a gate in a twelve-foot cyclone fence. A small fleet of trucks is stabled there. "We have to walk from here," Bud says.

We set out down a street you could cross in two strides. No kids throng us. As we come in sight they disappear between *banco* houses that look like the bucket-shaped mounds kids make at the seashore. The domed clay bread ovens beam heat at us and stir the dust above them. Glistening women tend them in graceful slow motion.

Bud turns, bumping into me and enveloping my shoulder in an apologetic hand. "This is us, here," he says. It's a great limestone tomb of a house, all slabs and pilasters. It squints at us from little hatches of windows, shuttered tight, and a door of basket-weave ironwork with modern glass inside. The door swings open with silent greased reluctance and splashes me with refrigerated air.

Inside it's all cybernetic modernity except for the undulant stone walls and floors. In the room's far left corner, a puck-shaped core of granite shims up a computer desk shaped like an artist's palette. This kind of barren neatness means the men in charge are obsessed with computerization. Or with security: to my right, adjacent file drawers show two rows of combination locks, rough and red like a mother dog's teats. A magnetic sign on each reads LOCKED.

"See that vase?" he says. "Chinese. They dug it up right here. It cost me thirty dollars. It's a piece of history. There really was a time when Timbuktu wasn't just dirt. The bazaars held goods from China, India, Egypt, the islands. They supplied the world with gold.

"But now gold is a glutted commodity. The mines are exhausted or unproductive or just lost in the sands. It's time to stop taking wealth out and start putting it back."

Dinner steams in copper pots on a limestone table. I am sitting opposite Bud. We are six feet apart, with a bigger expanse of stone table on each side. The walls are bare white like the table. Something about the echoes from the high ceiling makes Bud's voice jump around as he speaks. He must know this place and its acoustics—he smiles as I blink at the remote whispers. Night air flows in through tiny window gratings glowing blue-gray from the eastern dusk.

Locals wait on us. They watch silently from the corners when Bud leans back, and they slip out of the room when he leans forward in a portentous pause. Bud's conversation is a Morse code of rambling travel stories and quick confidences.

Bud is leaning forward now. "Everyone is on board. The Ex-Im Bank is financing engineering costs plus a twenty percent contingency. Commercial banks are begging for a spot in the syndicate, but we have all the funding we'll ever need. People know this is a project that can't fail. ECOWAS, the West African community, they gave us a ten-year tax holiday. They can't collect taxes in rebel territory, anyway. Still, it was a nice gesture.

"OPIC is trying to sell us political risk insurance, but there is no risk. The Organization of African Unity is backing us. They smell the money in it. OAU is the tinhorn dictator's union, Local 12. We pay them off, but we pay them off at prearranged rates. It's not extortion because they know we have more and bigger guns."

The help come to whisk away plates as Bud's voice rises and drawls. He cuts to a customs horror story: ". . . and this asshole's pointing to the national hypodermic needle sitting in a bottle of bleach. Cholera shot, my ass, this is a stickup. He wants a few bucks. So I tell him . . ."

The staff disappears and he sharpens up. "The African Development Bank wants in: they're pitching transport projects, water projects, solar-energy projects. They don't understand that we fly it in if we need it. Just like in Saudi before the Gulf War. You can't eat their food or drink their water. You can't even breathe their air. Everything comes from home.

"Like this authentic African dinner," he says. "The couscous and the dates are from California. The goat is from Carolina. The peanuts are from Georgia. U.S. exports from the congressional districts of the House Foreign Relations Committee. That's one thing I learned: grease the skids."

Bud's lack of urgency unnerves me. If Bud's hiring me or part thereof, I want to know what I've got left. "So is there something I need to sign, some employment contract, consulting agreement—anything?"

Bud snorts. "Paperwork? What are you, nuts? Here's your two hundred K." He smacks a card down on the table—a black charge card with electric blue print: ETHERBANK. That's all.

"It's in there. Just stick it in any teller machine. It's blinded digital currency drawn on a pooled Panamanian clearing account. Don't bother to report it to the IRS. They won't know what you're talking about."

"What if I can't do the job?"

"We only want you to be yourself."

"I need to know what I've signed up to *do*."

Bud's amusement is an upwelling of affection. "You're a man in a hurry. I like that. We'll be in a hurry soon enough. You can take one night to kick back."

Bud submits to a mighty yawn and a salivary gland sprays a tiny arcing jet. "I'll tell you what, Ty: this traveling wears me out, the squinting, the tension of always being half-stuck. Why don't we just turn in and meet up tomorrow afternoon? Sleep late. Take a stroll around town if you're a glutton for punishment. In case you're feeling ambitious I'll give you a little file to read. It will give you all the background."

6

My room holds hanging rugs, piles of cushions, and an old bronze torchère lamp. Waving me into it, Bud says, "Do you need a mattress?" The wrinkles on his forehead say I won't get one tonight.

"This is fine," I say. Once I am shut inside, the fuzzy cavern seems boundless, like the out-of-doors. Bud has given me a pale leather portfolio with intricate tooled scars. It's got papers and a boxy lump inside.

The rugs sop up the crackle of paper as I root through it. The light on the paper is a dingy orange smear. Nothing to learn here: just access logs, nondisclosure agreements, cautionary tales and rules.

The lump in the folder is a book-sized plastic case with a few buttons and a screen. The screen shows a document, one page at a time. You page through the document by clicking the buttons. I'm dipping into it, trying to piece it together. It's some kind of dossier: a dry announcement like a Wall Street tombstone; reports, articles, proposals. What's it to me, though?

IAEA

International Atomic Energy Agency

RFP 665/HS

The International Atomic Energy Agency solicits preliminary proposals for permanent nuclear waste storage. Proposals must demonstrate methods and procedures that can accommodate high-level nuclear waste from any UN member nation.

Respondents shall undertake to accept up to 58,000 Metric Tons Heavy Metal (5.8×10^4 MTHM) in the form of KBS spent-fuel canisters or containerized vitreous nuclear waste.

Proposed repository sites will sustain a localized toxicity index of 10^{15} after 10 years, and of 10^{12} after 400 years. Sites must tolerate heat generation of up to 500 kW per hectare at the repository site.

Respondents must hold IAEA harmless from all damages due to toxicity or heat.

Timbuktu Earthwealth
Timbuktu, Mali

Proposal: Permanent Nuclear Waste Storage for the International Atomic Energy Agency (IAEA)

Executive Summary. We are Timbuktu Earthwealth, a consortium of African governments backed by the world's most technologically advanced private companies. We came together to meet IAEA's urgent need as expressed in RFP 665/HS. We have developed a waste storage method with unique advantages. Our proposal meets all IAEA requirements. In so doing it redresses the long-standing development handicaps of the world's poorest continent.

We propose to site a disposal facility in waste lands of the Sahara Desert. We will excavate 319 disposal cavities in geologically stable bedrock. Each cavity will contain up to 200 metric tons of spent fuel or vitrified nuclear waste, sealed for all time in an impervious lining: 80 cm of isostatically compressed bentonite. Our proposal will isolate the waste at least 500 meters below the earth's surface.

Several nations will participate in this effort, and benefit from it. South Africa will bring its engineering know-how to the southern Sahara. Tanzania, Kenya, and Morocco will supply bentonite. The Government of Mali will use its rich petrologic resources in a new way: as profitable dump sites. Our proposed site minimizes disruption of existing populations: the surrounding areas support fewer than one person per square kilometer. We selected the site to ensure unmatched geologic stability: all sites are deep within the African Shield, a vast mass of Precambrian rock that has lain unchanged for billions of years.

Timbuktu Earthwealth undertakes to accept nuclear waste for $52 million per MTHM. This is affordable for the developed world, and it will quadruple per capita incomes in the Sahel.

This project permits the developed world to assist Africa without subsidies. It makes effective use of necessary environmental investment, and it promotes African development by putting Saharan lands to their best and highest use.

Minatom
Moscow, Russia
RFP 665/HS

Proposal to the International Atomic Energy Agency (IAEA) for the Permanent Storage of Nuclear Waste

Executive Summary. As manager of Russia's nuclear waste, Minatom is taking care of civilian fuel and surplus weapons material. Minatom exercises jurisdiction over much land affected by Soviet nuclear accidents. We control large tracts in and around the Ural Mountains amounting to almost 20 percent of Russia's land area. This land is waste to us for the foreseeable future. To put in a storage site the opportunity cost is nil.

Russia has comparative advantage in handling nuclear materials, due to the large size of the Soviet stockpile and prior accidents caused by the Soviets. Minatom benefits from Russian military and civilian experience in nuclear waste disposal, incineration and entombment.

Russia ~~now~~ already stores most of the world's nuclear waste. We propose to consolidate the rest in Siberia. Our approach will minimize the cost and risk of transport.

Our proposal is fully compliant with IAEA requirements. Minatom undertakes to accept up to 58,000 (fifty-eight thousand) Metric Tons Heavy Metal (MTHM) in the form of KBS spent-fuel canisters or containerized vitreous nuclear waste.

Minatom's storage sites will tolerate a localized toxicity index of 10^{16} after 10 years, and of 10^{13} after 400 years. Storage areas will bear 1,000 kilowatts per hectare at the repository site. Minatom and the Government of Russia will hold IAEA harmless from all damages due to toxicity or heat. As a bonus we will also indemnify IAEA against loss in transit, explosive release, or long-term teratogenic consequences.

Minatom offers waste disposal at a fixed price of $30 million U.S. dollars per MTHM, exclusive of transport costs. We offer these very favorable terms in view of Russia's current economic exigence.

The Authority
Kingston, Jamaica

Proposal for Permanent Nuclear Waste Storage

Overview. The International Seabed Authority (The Authority) is the United Nations agency charged with stewardship of the world's subsea resources. The Law of the Sea Treaty established The Authority to manage and coordinate the resource-exploitation activities of treaty signatories.

Under the leadership of Alain Theriault, The Authority has developed the world's first seabed control regime.

We propose to use Authority resources for nuclear-waste disposal. Specifically, we offer the abyssal hills in the stable central region of the Gulf of Guinea. This site is vast, with essentially unlimited storage capacity. It is remote from all human activity. Its extractable mineral resources are negligible, and it is biologically barren. The seabed is earth's largest expanse of fallow land. Under The Authority's impartial guidance, the world will use the seabed for the collective good of all nations.

The emplacement site is covered with 100 meters of red clay. The high sorption qualities of this material make it uniquely effective for radionuclide retention. The clay's compaction increases with depth, so we can attain any desired level of stability by burying the waste to the appropriate depth.

Our proposal is simplicity itself. We will drop darts into the seabed from surface ships. The darts will penetrate the clay to the ideal depth; free-flowing surface clay will quickly seal the impact point. Self-contained instrumentation in the darts will monitor their condition and report by extremely low frequency telemetry. Buried at sea, nuclear waste will remain beyond the reach of terrorists forever.

We offer safe, permanent waste disposal at a price of $60 million U.S. per MTHM. The implied total disposal price of $3.5 trillion is a small fraction of world GDP.

The complexity and scale of this project demand an unprecedented degree of international cooperation. Success is imperative for environmental safety and for geopolitical stability. Who can ensure success? Only The Authority.

The dining room is featureless in predawn half-light and glaring incandescent patches. The chairs are gone. Roused in the dark for a stand-up meeting, I shift on my feet alongside the marble table. I feel as though I'm struggling up from a deep sleep, which surprises me. I must have nodded off reading the files, but the night felt like skittering thoughts, not dreams.

A woman stands at one end of the table, hands clasped behind her in a vaguely martial at-ease stance. She is to brief me. She's a miracle-worker from Planning, Bud says. She has some fey name that doesn't catch in my mind. Her short dark hair is a tidy mass with no stray strands. Her nose has been ruthlessly cut to a juvenile size. Her face is the color of skin but eerily uniform, even under her eyes and at her temples. The same remarkable makeup trick has polished the surface of her face to the smoothness of a precision bearing. Her shirt and pants give off a blue-gray silky sheen, darker below the waist. They do nothing to dissemble her body: falsified bosoms, prolate in shape, and an unnaturally tiny waist. The result of all this vivisection stirs me and jars me. What must needy hands feel like on the sutures and swellings and stretched flesh and thin stiff scars?

A penlight laser pointer rests on the table's edge. It slips to the floor and she picks it up, squatting with a grunt. She is corseted. Before I left for Africa the television thronged with women like her: computer-generated women. They had the same exaggerated sexual cues and surface perfection. They came from computer games to become artificial television personalities. I assumed they would become more lifelike. I never expected real women would become less so.

On the table behind her, a small projector dwarfs a tiny computer. She turns the projector on and an outline appears on the white wall, orange on dark blue. She flicks the penlight to underscore the top line, but my eyes are locked on her. Something glazes her eyes as she starts to speak: nerves? "Mr. Campbell, we are pleased to welcome you to this important initiative." No, not nerves. She's reciting boilerplate by rote.

"We have confidence in your absolute discretion. Please note that confidence differs from trust. Our confidence comes largely from our procedural and technical antidisclosure measures." She meets my eyes. "In lay terms that means shadows, snoops, and eavesdropping devices.

"Commit the following to memory. Take no notes. Speak of this information to your project officer, Bud Van Sickle, and to no one else."

She smiles and her face flexes without creasing. "The millennium has brought political stability and wholesale disarmament in all the places that matter. But all this peace, love, and Kumbaya is not without its price. Disarmament means nuclear waste. Nuclear waste means disposal, and disposal, that's a hot potato: Where to put all this waste?

"The International Atomic Energy Agency has been forced to arbitrate. They know this is suicide. There's no way to satisfy everyone, and everyone is passionately involved. If you're not fighting over the money in it, you're screaming bloody environmental rape." She is quite an orator, prowling the room, modulating volume and tone independently from one word to the next. But she is playing to Bud, not to me. She pauses for barely perceptible gestures and nods. He controls her as though she has a joystick. "The energy agency wants to form a panel of independent experts. The experts will choose among the competing proposals. That way the agency can point to a scapegoat if there's any trouble."

Bud mutes her and seamlessly breaks in. "What's all this to you, Ty? We're going to put you on the panel."

Now I see. It all comes together with a solid clank like leg irons. Bud wants eyes and ears on the panel. I never really formed an opinion about industrial espionage and its practitioners. It always seemed less glamorous than the foreign-agent sort of spying but also less perfidious, just more dirty pool in a nasty sphere where ethics don't apply.

She says, "Your fellow panelists will make it sound ever so civilized and objective and scientific. Don't be taken in. There is far too much at stake to keep it clean. Only the winner survives."

She turns and points with the red laser dot. "Minatom is desperate for funds. Their scientists live on potatoes they grow by their leaky waste dump. If they don't get the contract to take the waste, their choice is stark: find new jobs—in North Korea, perhaps in Iraq—or wait for the winter and freeze."

The red dot drops and jitters somewhere else. "The Authority is living on borrowed time. The U.N. won't get their American dollars unless they gut their white elephant agencies, and the Authority is the whitest and most elephantine of all. The headchoppers and efficiency experts are circling like vultures. To ward them off the Authority needs a raison d'être: a massive seabed dumping contract."

"And how about Timbuktu Earthwealth?" Bud turns and asks it for me. "We're insolvent. Unpaid interest mounts. Our loans haven't been called in only because we've borrowed too much. We'll take two big banks down with us if we don't get the work. Don't sweat it, though. Problems like that are above your pay grade."

The woman says, "Don't worry if the proposals set your lips moving. The scientific bumf won't matter a pin in the end. But you have to know the people inside and out. We don't want insight, that's for amateurs. We want telepathy.

"We'll fill you in on the people and their little fiefdoms. Just the essentials, of course; the rest you'll have to get yourself by eating, drinking, or sleeping with them—whatever it takes."

My hermit's life ended months ago when Lila came, but this morning marks my first return to society as I remember it: hierarchy, subordination, constraint. Bud is my boss now, unsmiling, staring fixedly into my eyes. Eyes of any kind are hard to meet after my long solitude, and I sense an unspoken rule that I must cede a bit of my free will each time I look away.

Timbuktu's spacious headquarters feels like a cell. I can't sit still. Bud must have noticed—he has taken me out for a morning walk.

Bud leads me down into a terraced garden, a series of nested holes that cut a stepped cone in the earth. We sit at the bottom, in the smallest circle. If this were Dante's hell, the most treacherous damned would go down here, but this circle is more dispiriting than awful, well suited for dispassionate technical corporate wrongs. The air is calm but cool, with a faint smell of urine. Ropes of green algae drift in a pond full of wrigglers, and flowers wrestle gamely with weeds. The locusts are torpid and lonely.

Bud asks, "Any questions?"

Lots. "Why me?"

"The Atomic Energy Agency needs experts to pick a dumping scheme. We think you're uniquely qualified. You would be the panel's expert on the geology of the Sahara. You understand the people there and what they need."

"But you are an interested party," I say. "How can you just choose someone to be on this panel?"

"We're not choosing you, we're suggesting you. Someone else will choose you."

"You sound pretty confident of that."

Bud just looks at me.

I am irritated to find myself stammering. "The file. Something's not—the file has all three bids in it. Aren't those bids sealed?"

"Of course they're sealed," Bud says.

"Then how did you get the copies?"

"We broke no law," Bud says. "Every bidder collects competitive intelligence. We just do it better." A mosquito lands on Bud's arm nose down, ass up—the malarial kind, slavering lethal parasites. Bud flexes viciously, crushing it with a big smooth bicep. It had a lot of blood inside.

Lila's appeal has indentured me, but I still have to live with myself. In the desert I honed razor-keen ethical principles. They never lost their edge in use—it's hard to do wrong when you're alone. They were my wife's principles, not mine, but I took them when she died. I protected them with pristine isolation, honored them with tranquil courage in my fantasies. This is the first real test. I'm too weak to make a choice, so I appeal to Bud for help: "So this is on the up-and-up?" I need to hear him say yes.

"When you take the broadest view, you'll see this is the right thing to do."

Ty the hermit has been retired. I am being retooled for intimacy with Bud's rivals. The woman from Planning is introducing me to them. Now she calls them the targets. I am back at the marble table. This time I am permitted to sit. Evidently she is not. She stands, lightly touching the photographs projected on the wall. Bud is a silent presence.

A grainy photo scowls on the wall. "First, Alain Theriault, chief authority figure at the Authority. The Authority is not as Orwellian as it sounds. Granted, they enforce the Law of the Sea. But look closer: Who signed the Law of the Sea Treaty? Only poor little landlocked countries. The signatories have no money to get at the seabed. The wealthy countries refused to sign up. They didn't want this Authority nattering about.

"America hobbles the Authority by squeezing the U.N.'s budget. The staff can't do much but shuffle aides-mémoire around. That hasn't stopped them from setting up a plush office in Kingston, Jamaica, but Authority headquarters is a bureaucratic backwater—a dumping ground for the U.N.'s black sheep. The only chap who's not outcast or unknown is the director-general, Alain Theriault."

She gives the photo's cheek a backhand pat. Thick artificial nails click on the wall. "Theriault is a French Tom Swift, with a fetish for grandiose inventions and a Eurocrat's yen to run the world. He's a graduate of ENA, of course, the charm school of the Gallic ruling class. He made his name in R31, the industrial-espionage labyrinth; he perked up mundane commerce with bugs, blackmail, honey traps, and dumpster diving. Later he ran an emergency relief effort in Burundi: emergency food for the tall people and emergency guns for the short people.

"Now Theriault has reached the pinnacle of his career. He is building the ultimate symbol of Gallic virility: the free-fall penetrator."

The photo changes—not to a portrait, but to an aerial photograph of some industrial complex. This target seems to be faceless. "Minatom has a different plan. They want to bury the world's waste in their own backyard. Classic Slavic masochism: 'We are the most radiologically buggered country on earth. Give us your waste, we can take it.' Minatom is hopelessly outclassed. However. They have made an uneasy alliance with Ushi Lassen." The speaker's most significant glance. "Yes, that Ushi Lassen: eco–sex kitten, breaker of balls. Beware."

I have never heard of this Ushi Lassen. They haven't bothered to provide a photo.

She says, "That's it then, a three-sided battle royal: Timbuktu Earthwealth. Russia and the Greens. France and the Authority. With you as referee. Don't let us down."

As though I'm a chip plugged into a board, burned in and tested. And why not? Bud seems to have eliminated the human factor, at least among his staff.

Bud is ready to sum up. His female avatar has stopped speaking and fixed me with a level gaze.

"How are we going to win this?" Bud asks. "What distinguishes us from our competitors? We have feelers out, controls in place. We leave nothing to chance.

"Positive control," he says.

I am left alone each evening to memorize background files. The detail only aggravates my culture shock. Closeted with Bud's electronic dossier, I pinch buttons with my thumb, paging back and forth, but tonight it won't add up. I'm ignorant of Bud's business and profoundly out of touch with his world. My remedial education must encompass the better part of an encyclopedia, but also advertisements not obtruded, words not debased, cultural junk not dumped on me. My mind is insufficiently littered.

Here is a photo, easy to look at, something to seize on. This face is familiar. I never pinned a name to it, but it has arrested me before, maybe on some newsstand back home, maybe glowing on a television screen. So this is the enemy.

ATTACHMENT G:
SELFSTYLE MAGAZINE

Ushi Lassen,
Fashion's Quisling

The former most beautiful woman in the world. The woman who brought nipples and vaginal clefts to mass-market lingerie ads. You may remember Ushi as she looked in frilly knickers. You may recall her downy abdomen surmounting Times Square, her lintless innie navel dominating a world like the great crater of Mars. If you do, don't mention it. Ushi is the supermodel who bolted the runways at the top of her form and joined Greenfleet.

Ushi's modeling assets resist comparison. She's six foot four or so, and maybe has a touch of acromegaly, because her cheekbones are remarkably angular, even by the standards of the modeling agencies. She's the scary kind of pretty, with her powder-blue eyes and purply black hair and toothy smile. She's more a silent-film star than a model. Ushi was never one to be cool and lovely. She specialized in miming emotions: wistful, frightened but resolute, bereft, horny. "Nobody does horny like Ushi," says Tamara Lea of the high-powered Penta agency. Ushi has a thousand walks, too. She has a timid walk that makes your heart go out, and a reckless defiant walk and a wary walk and lots more.

When Ushi abandoned modeling she had three or four years left in her face. Dropout though she was, she had put by a tidy sum, so she gave Greenfleet money as well as time. She bought them a tall ship; not a very tall ship, but a genuine schooner from the waning days of sail. Mangling her history a bit, she fitted it out with crow's nest, carbide cannon, and Jolly Roger. Corny but effective, especially when she mounts the crow's nest or gangplank to do her Saint Joan face at some smoggy port.

As a model Ushi's life revolved around cosmetics. When she abandoned the mannequin's life she rejected them, vehemently, in reaction. Nonetheless, as her approval and Q scores climbed, marketeers hounded her for endorsements. Ushi had no agent to protect her now, and the petitions exhausted her. One merchant in need of a glamour-girl pitch tried to strong-arm her with breach-of-contract litigation. Ushi decided to teach him a lesson.

With cameras rolling, she brandished a paint pot and said: "This product is evil shits, formulated to enslave you. Don't buy it."

The merchant, a genius, produced the commercial untouched. In four weeks brand share rocketed from 6 percent to

24. Ushi received her fee, and as an extra thumb in the eye the manufacturer loudly donated a share of the profits to Greenfleet.

With their windfall profits Greenfleet bought a barge to ply Europe's canals. Now there was nowhere for landlocked polluters to hide. But the experience chastened Ushi. Revered though she was, she was misunderstood. She took to tacking a bemused excursus onto her prepared speech, *Perhaps we should think about what we give up to get things. . . .* A little Thoreau, a few snippets of Epictetus out of context. Trite stuff, tired since the days of the desert hermits; effective only because it's Ushi saying it. Over time her meanderings crystallized into the concept of the waste strike, fighting words Ushi never used.

Depending on who pays you, you think the waste strike is either "economic terrorism" or "the most powerful form of social resistance since Gandhi developed *satyagraha*." The think tanks' term for it is *political asceticism,* to distinguish it from religious asceticism, which is not revolutionary. The waste strike, by contrast, is decidedly revolutionary. Consumption is mostly waste, you see. Demonstrators simply cease to consume. They give up whatever they choose. An anarchic boycott results; organized action is not required. Ushi's prompting and pouting sets something in motion that even she can't control. The thing becomes a grand competition, and Ushi's ports of call teem with consumers that could outrenounce a monastery full of Trappists.

Within 90 days, job losses start, first in retail and later in manufacturing and services. Idled workers cut back and compound the austerity. Liquidity dries up and the free-fall slump lasts for months.

Traditional Greens are dubious. They don't see that Ushi's mopping up much effluent with her waste strikes. Ushi dismisses them: "They are searching always for the plume of smoke. Our aspirations get polluted first of all."

Ms. Lassen declined to be interviewed by Selfstyle, *calling it "obscene female mind-control propaganda."*

"Roll the dice."

Two fours. In the shivering hours after midnight I am playing games with Bud's artificial woman. This crude old-fashioned board game will train me to serve on the bid-evaluation panel. The panel must choose a dumping scheme in accordance with World Bank rules. Along with the other panelists I will comb through the proposals of Minatom, Timbuktu, and the Authority. We will judge them according to hundreds of precisely defined criteria and rate them with tick marks on forms. We must be prepared to explain and justify our ratings.

As judges of a contest with trillion-dollar stakes, panelists must expect bribes, extortion, leaks, protests, and political meddling. The identities of the panelists are secret, but Bud has pierced the veil. Others will too. The pressure will not take long to mount.

I advance my marker, a spindly plastic pawn taken from some other game.

Smiling brightly, she reads from the board. "A prostitute is at your door."

"Who sent her?"

"Choose a card."

Bud has subjected me to a series of all-night "tabletops." Some of these exercises are like computerized tests. Others are deadly serious playacting, improvised debates and confrontations, moot inquisitions, audits, or investigations. I am practicing to detect others' dishonesty while concealing my own. Bidders and panelists will attack from all sides, but I cannot take a purely defensive stance. I may have to persuade or suborn other panelists. I can't throw the contest to Bud by myself.

"Go to jail." She slaps my wrist. "The Authority's boss is partial to blackmail. So watch out for prostitutes, watch out for gifts. As an American you are vulnerable to the Foreign Corrupt Practices Act."

My two-hundred-thousand-dollar charge card smolders in my hip pocket.

Ushi may have looks and brains and fame. Theriault may have a world bureaucracy at his command. But Bud has a secret weapon.

It presents itself on the screen of my electronic tablet, modest and cautious and appalling.

DISCLAIMER

The attached Custom Consumer Profiles are prepared for Timbuktu Earthwealth, S.A. Custom Consumer Profiles, Inc., makes no representation regarding the accuracy of these profiles. Profiles are extracted from multiple on-line sources. They use detailed data on individual consumers' purchase decisions. By linking each purchase to the emotional content of the advertising used to sell it, they interpret consumption patterns as a detailed projective personality test. The statistical validity of such methods is firmly established, but in individual cases a small probability of error always exists.

CUSTOM CONSUMER PROFILES, Inc.
Insight • Understanding • Control

Now every advertisement is a Rorschach blot, tailored to a specified weakness. Each time you succumb they learn a little more: a secret shame, an irrecoverable loss, a rankling humiliation, a scornful voice in your head. You imagine that you make a choice, but you are lured by your inadequacies and trapped and bottled for inspection. The bottle holds you and a very few others who share your precise constellation of fears and wounds and empty places. The meaning of your purchases is secret: you have no right to know. That information is the property of Custom Consumer Profiles and its select clients.

This is more powerful than blackmail. Blackmail is crude coercion. It allows the victim to retain his adult identity and his dignity. With these state-of-the-art psychographic profiles Bud has the knowledge he needs to manipulate you or to destroy you.

Seeing these powerful people stripped bare makes me want to go back to the desert and hide. No one can escape this new science: every move winds you tighter in its coils. I've lost my virginity to this perverted alien intimacy. I wonder what they know about me.

Consumption-based profiles of Ushi Lassen are relatively scanty—she uses a range of privacy-protection services. She appears in only forty-six databases. The databases characterize her with moderate confidence: the probability of incorrect profiling ranges from 7 to 12 percent. But then, her secret weakness is easy to spot.

Hypochondria, spawned perhaps by a childhood visit to a sick relation, but clearly sustained by neglect at a vulnerable age. She lives in fear of something inside her, ghastly and repulsive, hidden for now. The threat of our disgust hangs over her head all the time. Her beautiful body, her hold on us, turned pulpy and rancid, or monstrous and lifeless, decaying before death.

She tries to defy the fear with pitched public battles and thrill-seeking publicity stunts. These inure her to danger, but not to disease. Her bravado does not protect her. Ushi can feel strong, but never safe.

Theriault's profiles are quite consistent. An enthusiastic consumer, he appears in 272 databases. The databases categorize him with high confidence: the probability of incorrect profiling ranges from 1 to 4 percent.

Who knows what made Theriault so brittle? Some kind of abuse, perhaps, endured but not transcended by a mind too young for it. For whatever reason, Theriault seethes with humiliation. Time and again it pulls him inside, where he is pleading or weeping, pants down or beaten, helpless or publicly mocked. All the power in the world won't salve the raw places.

To contain the corrosive effects of his pain, Theriault has constructed a cocoon. It exalts him and abases others. He sits at the top of a rigid hierarchy, remote from others who might challenge it. He dominates his insular world, peopling it with inferiors, demanding public acknowledgment of his superior intelligence and admirable character.

Who would think it's all there to read in his handsome jewelry and clothes, in the understated furnishings of his flat, in his refined taste for wine.

This must be a press kit of some sort. The words are vague and stirring, the numbers round and awesome. The charts have tick marks on the axes, but no numbers. The maps are colorful cartoons showing great crosshatched clouds of safety, but no dump. The project is floating in the clouds. I need to moor it.

I get up off my back and open the door. Bud is right outside, pondering the screen of his computer workstation. I put a question to him when he finally turns: "Exactly where do you plan to dump?"

"I'll show you," he says. He intones commands to the voice-activated computer. The screen goes brown with a map of Africa, landmasses first, then borders, then cities, and finally crumpled textures showing hills. A pattern of red dots appears, creeping outward from a central point to form an ellipse.

"You know where that is," Bud says.

Yes, I do. "Now I see why you brought me here to tell me."

"The location is strictly confidential. It is a Timbuktu Earthwealth commercial secret until the proposals are unsealed."

The pox of red dots covers the refugee camp.

Bud gives no orders. His sentences are declarative, not imperative, and his tone is mild. Bud has broken me to an obscure routine with hints and frowns, training me to read his face. Last night Bud signaled a breakfast meeting with an eyebrow, a word, and a wave. Rising at five, I waited an hour for him and now Bud and I are alone together at 6:15 A.M., spooning yogurt at the big marble table, drinking sugared tamarind juice.

Bud says, "It's time to go back home."

"Back home where?"

"The States," he says. "It's time for you to learn your role."

"Didn't you explain my role?"

"You're playing a part. You have to be convincing in it. You need to learn a lot more to be credible as an expert, and you need to learn a little more—not too much—about where you fit."

"I have to arrange some time away from my AID contract."

"Not to worry. Here." He takes a printout from his pocket. It's an E-mail to me, complete with verified digital signature, from my contracting officer at USAID. The subject: Hydrologic Survey Contract 06-234.

I've seen that header dozens of times. The words underneath are mostly familiar contract boilerplate. But they won't come together on the page. My eyes get stuck on a word, hop over a line, bounce forward and back. I'm trying again from the beginning. *Just look at it, get the sense of it. You don't have to believe it.*

It says my contracting officer expresses his appreciation for my responsive and diligent assistance. *OK, sure—*

In accordance with clause 16(a) of my Basic Ordering Agreement with USAID, my contract is terminated for convenience.

7

Bud has given me tickets to Washington: inconspicuous coach seats. We will fly out of Bamako days apart and meet discreetly at a private location.

An unstoppable beast from the company fleet drove me from Timbuktu. The driver was local, polite, but closemouthed about his employer on the long ride to Bamako. He played games with the baked blown-out tire scraps on the paved stretches, artfully gunning the engine to send them flying. He reveled in the megawatt air conditioner, freezing my face with arctic blasts.

Bamako announces itself with stop-and-floor-it traffic swathed in leaded-gas fumes. Beggar hands and heads probe the windows at every stop. Sewage oozes through the gutters and spurts up from bald tires as trucks ream the streets.

The short walk to the hotel door is a gauntlet. Hands dart out from the press of the crowd, frisking, tugging anything of value, two hundred hands to your two. The driver's brandished rubber truncheon scares no one. They drone, *You my friend, you my friend. . . .* The shoeshine boy has smeared a handful of shit on my boot. It cakes the laces. The driver's baton taps the little boy's shin, and he yells. A hand, having found my money belt, rakes gently at my shirt.

My new friends fall away as we enter the hotel—the bellmen

here are known for their thick black sticks. Inside, I am instantly oppressed by low concrete ceilings, mournful dark wood, and indirect, bashful light. This tells me what to expect: a crumbling Soviet monument with concave mattresses and grisly food. The staff will dole out hand towels, soap chips, and toilet paper in sheets, gratuity by gratuity. Malaria thrives in the potted plants, AIDS in the cheerful lethal whores. Unprotected sex costs more: nine bucks.

The city is a roar in my head after the desert's silence. Incessant horns, clanking and chugging construction, slamming doors, fights among the predators outside. I sleep without dreaming in the din. It is an unexpected kind of peace.

Some experts say any phobia can be flooded away: claustrophobia, acrophobia, agoraphobia. If you're fearful of snakes, just handle one. The shock overwhelms you, your fear pops and disappears. I have spent years hiding from mankind. Now I'm flooded, waiting for the shock to crest.

This plane is the polar opposite of my desert isolation. The head in front reclines into my face. Thighs and shoulders hem me in. The man by the window with the upset stomach slithers around my legs. Stooping under the bulkhead he breathes apologies on me and joins a queue that snakes past our seat.

The tiny plane on the movie screen stands still south of the Azores. In another four minutes it will hop ahead half a length. Arrival time at Dulles International Airport is twelve hours and forty-two minutes from now. Hundreds of hops.

I used to be able to sleep on planes. Now consciousness closes in like a tourniquet around my head, cutting off sleep. My thoughts run faster and faster in an ever smaller space. If I close my eyes my ears betray me, magnifying booming laughs and improbably animated conversations, sleepers smacking lips and tongues. My nose betrays me with exquisite sensitivity to wisps of intestinal gas, expanding fourfold at cabin pressure and mixed by tiny swivel-nozzles into a miasma of manioc, couscous, sheep's curd, airline food.

A soft fat Arab encroaches on my left shoulder. A pasty-faced banker snores on my right. My every move impinges on someone else. This disquiet is more urgent than hunger or thirst, no less urgent than asphyxiation. They're sharing and fouling my air and my space and my thoughts.

I am clutching at thoughts that might take me up. My wife is gone. My work is gone. My new occupation is not real to me. But I can fix Lila in my mind and see the way her gaze sweeps the camp, tripping over children, stopping short at squabbles, widening in fear. I can see the wonder in the Africans' eyes when she lets go and exults in the American way, with shoulders, not with hips. I can watch her athlete's body make a game of work.

She puts me to sleep before I can savor her.

Dulles is mobbed—not with people, but with televisions. It used to be you could hide from them by standing, but now they yammer at you everywhere. Is the whole civilized world like this now? Television everywhere, crowding out thought, demanding attention? The whole world flickers and shouts at me: signs, screens, terminals, loudspeakers. I stare at faces, trying to see what happens to a mind when it lives with this bedlam, but I see no distress. Do their minds get callused from this rubbing raw?

In the Adrar my senses sharpened to offset the calm of my life until I could hear a thousand tones in a gust of wind and see the sunlight changing minute by minute. Here I am caught in bickering and fighting and flight in a stroboscopic rush, yammer, yammer yammer brightdarkbrightdarkbrightdark. This must be what insanity is like. No voice in my head could be worse or more unstoppable than this. The voices are telling me to want more things and note more things, yanking me dizzy and immobile until someone takes me by the arm and says, "Are you all right?"

I thought I was returning to the world of men. This is the center of some hive, and I'm squirming with the packed pupae.

My eyes seize on a promise of relief: a water fountain. I embrace it, cocooning my head in the soft light from brushed steel, wasting great glassy splats of water and drawing the endless plenty into me.

I cling to its solid curves as the water grows painfully cold. Water, abundant and untainted. It used to mean *You're home.*

The man has a card that says CAMPBELL. He has been waiting with uneasy patience. "Trip OK?" He listens in watchful silence for my answering grunt.

He takes me to a waiting car, drives briskly through a maze of turns. We are in some kind of futuristic business terrarium. A single mind has arranged every detail to simulate the effects of nature and autonomous free choice. Even the loneliest roads have arrowed ramps and chutes and special bulbs on all the traffic lights. On these scientific byways sidewalks would be anachronistic and absurd.

We coast to a stop beneath an office shaped like a spacecraft. The cars are sparse on this level of the parking deck. We've pulled alongside an identical car: four-door, dark blue, tinted windows. Bud is at the wheel. I slide in alongside him.

Bud and I crawl away from Washington on Route 7. To my right a tall truck lags and leads as if tethered to us by elastic cord. A van in front blocks the view ahead. Private cars seem even bigger than they used to be. This is like the traffic I remember, only more spasmodic. But the landscape is unrecognizable, full of shapeless interlocking Lego-set dwellings chained and tiered and stacked in hives, and incomprehensible stores in Fisher-Price baby colors, poignant and sinister like the outsized toys in a leukemia ward.

The packs of cars stretch out. The landscape is benign again: it has settled down to hedgerows, fields, and wooded hills. The sun is different here, duller. It enters your eyes politely, from above, not from everywhere as the hazy desert glare does. The roads are older out here; they wind among the rolling hills without a lot of up and down. Bud doesn't slacken his speed—he seems to be testing the car, feeling for the point at which it starts to skid.

I'm unused to being a passenger. I feel edgy and out of control. And the solid car's mild understeer is nothing compared to my hydroplaning life. I say, "I'm going to get destroyed on this expert panel. I don't know the first thing about nuclear-waste disposal. Doesn't that worry you a little?"

"Not a problem," he says. "We've created a virtual expert. You will step into his shoes. The U.N. bureaucrats are searching the Internet for 'nuclear-waste disposal methods: selection criteria.' They'll find twenty papers in precisely that category, authored by you. Your reputation will precede you. Actual experts will lose credibility if they admit to being unfamiliar with your work. No one will contact you until you make the shortlist. By then your credentials will be fully backstopped: you'll have credible references to vouch for you and a shell think tank where they answer the phone 'Dr. Campbell's office.' "

"*Doctor* Campbell? What is this, impostor training?"

"Relax," Bud says, "it will work. We've done it before. Scientific interest communities meet mostly on-line. The experts read a tiny fraction of the research papers on offer. The U.N. bureaucrats are hopeless laymen. It's easy to keep up. We'll spoon-feed you in an environment with no distractions."

"What else am I expected to do?"

"Just do what comes naturally. That's all we ask. We're going to put you in charge of the world. You'll be making decisions for everyone on earth. When you give a man that kind of responsibility, you can't tell him what to do."

"So I can be a model of civic duty except I'm entirely full of shit."

Eyes on the road now but louder, Bud says, "This a terrific career move for you. Six months from now your life will *take off*." He zooms the car, showing me how it will be. "You'll be bruited about for all kinds of appointive jobs. You'll write your ticket: government, industry, Wall Street. The money we pay you will look like pocket change."

He thinks that's what I want. "Here's your magic credit card. Get somebody else. I'm out."

"Calm down," Bud says evenly. "You can't make an informed decision to back out yet. When you reach that point, you're free to go."

"Until then I'm what, detained? Who do you think you . . ."

The grade steepens and Bud slows to a retiree's pace. The road rounds a hill, revealing a fence. A sign reads U.S. GOVERNMENT. The fine print underneath lists lots of reasons to go away if you're just curious. Two big Detroit sedans swoop by. Their drivers wear broad-brimmed hats like state police, but the cars have no state markings; no markings at all.

"Welcome to the most exclusive hotel in the world," Bud says.

As we pass through the gate, hills and trees hide the fence. We've crossed some frontier, but we're not inside, we're simply somewhere else. Bud is blurring at the edges too, like a ghost or a spook. I try to squint him into full view. "Are you working for the government?"

"I told you, I work for Timbuktu Earthwealth, *Société Anonyme*. Don't ask me that question again."

8

As they let us in, step by careful step, Bud explained, but not nearly enough.

This place has a name, not Camp This or Fort That, like it looks, but Bear Mountain. This is where we prepared for the dark age that would follow World War III. Very biblical, not just Armageddon but the time of troubles too—Christians had the president's ear.

We set up militias and they played Mad Max: bunkers, martial law, guerrilla resistance on Main Street, USA. Then came the millennium and nuclear disarmament. We dwindled to a hundred missiles and a few dozen megatons. Global throw weight has declined by 95 percent. We couldn't destroy the world if we wanted to.

We had a place to hide and no apocalypse to hide from. But Bear Mountain abides; its privacy is suited for the most delicate matters. Disinformation. Cover-ups. Training for our less presentable allies.

Bud flashes a plastic pass. A guard nods and another gate retracts. An old worn mountain rises in the distance behind a windowless one-story cinder-block box.

I enter the box behind Bud. It feels like an aquarium, with a lugubrious pop-eyed guard moving slowly behind a wall of green glass. Following Bud's lead, I put my passport on a Plexiglas turntable. The guard pulls a lever to bring it to him, sealing it in behind the green glass wall. He studies my young little picture and my browned face. I flinch from the intimacy of his look, but he is unembarrassed. He nods and puts my passport out of sight.

The door buzzes and clicks with a billiard-ball sound and we pass through. Behind the guardhouse a valley sags out of view under the mountain's weight.

Another guard drives up: same broad hat, same broad car. He stands up straight and Sirs us. Bud has him drive us down a steep road lined with dorms: one-story, cinder block, spray-painted federal blue. We stop at one near the end of the line and the guard hands us each a key.

The door is thick steel with a single face-sized window. A mesh of twisted wire strains the view through the pane. Inside, a central corridor runs the length of the building. "Come on in my room for a minute," Bud says. "I've got a bottle of bourbon in my duffel bag. You're going to need some background. Not too much—just a word to the wise."

Bud works a stout sticky lock and pushes the door open. The room has dark abrasive carpet, a white ceiling with little whipped-cream peaks, a narrow bed, and a boxy dresser. A tiny gooseneck lamp burns on a desk in the corner, painting the fake wood top with a jaundiced ellipse. Trash cans flank the desk; one says DUMP and one says BURN. Two chairs, suited for the third degree.

Bud swings his duffel onto the bed. His hand spears into the bag and draws out a bottle. He spins a chair to face mine. He's looking at me with the kind of unsettling ambiguity that shows only in pale blue eyes like his. It looks like confusion or hostility and I'm sure it's something else.

"OK, listen up," he says. "This is Africa 101. You see two basic situations in Africa: chaos and hell. Hell is when someone's in charge, and chaos is when no one's in charge."

I get it: "You've never lived there, have you? You never bought anything in a store. You never ate a meal at an African's home. You float over it in your climate-controlled hovercraft like little green men. When you touch down you say, Take me to your leader."

I see anxious concern in Bud's face, but no doubt. He is appraising me and finding me wanting. "You live in Africa. You're too close to it. You don't have the big picture, the geopolitical picture. You're going to have to grow into this role." He slumps in a silence that's comfortable for him until my mind wanders. Then he resumes my lesson.

"OK, hell. Easy to handle. We perfected our methods with the new Africa policy in the late nineties. Dictator's acting up? No problem.

"Step one: make a portentous announcement: *We are not ruling out any options.* Something like that. Step two: give Janissary a confidential contract, and watch the dictator die of one of those heart attacks. We did it in Nigeria in '98, we did it in a couple other places, and that was enough. After that, all we had to do was raise an eyebrow: General So-and-so would call a snap election, repatriate a billion dollars, whatever we want. We got the dictators to the point where they wouldn't take a leak without our OK.

"So hell is easy. Chaos, that's tougher to deal with because no matter who you make die, nobody notices. We tried dipping a toe into chaos once or twice: in Somalia and in little Congo. Fiascoes, both of them. But we learned.

"The main thing we learned is, don't just go in there and stand around. Do some make-work."

I wave my hands to stop the flow, shake my head. It takes me a second of silence to gather my thoughts: "You're telling me a trillion-dollar contract is just make-work?"

"I'm not saying make-work is unimportant. It's critical. When people see work going on, they gravitate toward it to see if they can cash in. Not by working, of course—by letting you get something done, for a price. By doing work you can attract the more enterprising locals and pick them off one by one. See, the enterprising ones are the dangerous ones. Next thing you know they'll be shaking you down, or shooting you up.

"It doesn't matter what the work is, as long as it's done with showmanship. Secrecy, vague announcements, on-again off-again. If everybody's milling around some construction site, jostling for a knothole in the fence, you're safe. Curiosity can make wars stop."

"So, to you, the biggest civil work in the history of the world is just make-work. What's your real work?"

"Hold that question," Bud says.

My impostor training begins the next day: three weeks of briefings in darkened rooms, scrawling notes by the light of glowing charts, drilling questions and answers with scowling men in threes and fours whose words outrun my thoughts until I answer by reflex.

Fifty-eight thousand metric tons heavy metal: nine-tenths of mankind's destructive force, Hiroshimas everywhere, the planet blinking like a field full of fireflies. Five hundred kilowatts per hectare: the warmth of today's winter sun. Toxicity index, ten to the fifteenth: you could drink this waste if you diluted it, one part waste to 1,000,000,000,000,000 parts water.

Through the brief grateful nights I dream of radiation: dry scalding particles drifting in clouds to be borne on the skin, swallowed with food, or drawn into lungs, the three pathways. Pathways, a sylvan garden term for the entryways of ionizing death. In my dreams I slog down garden paths with death clouds in pursuit. They're red like the atomized blood from a gunshot wound.

Yes, bury the waste and dream of it. That's the only way.

When the man named Joe shuts the projector off, pink and purple ghosts float before my eyes. Joe's barked questions demand an intensity of concentration that binds my chest in bungee muscles, plucks my neck cords guy-wire taut.

The day's lesson is over. The struggle to burn it into my brain backward and forward, as required, that is tonight's work. By now my mind's impermeable as the concrete grout that seals the Yucca Mountain prototype site. I float out of the room in a fog, head down.

"Good work, Ty." Bud's voice, behind me. "You deserve a catnap. I'll call you later in your room."

My room is identical to Bud's, only left is right and right is left. I stretch on the bed, deep breaths wringing tension from muscles as if my ribs were a washboard. I enfold myself in thoughts of Lila nude on her cot: brown shoulders, white hips, blond calves.

The phone wakes me in stages, ring by ring. Knowing where I am, that's the last stage. "Come on over," Bud says.

My footsteps resound in the painted concrete hall. The building has a duck-and-cover solidity that recalls civil-defense days.

Bud's door is ajar. He fills his room. His dreadnought boots rest toes up on the bed. His body is far away in the desk chair. He waves me to the bed and I flop on my side, propping my head on one hand.

"Look at you, lying there Mauritanian-style. The Africans will love you, the way you've gone native."

I'm not giving him anything: not hostility, not curiosity, not anxiety. Bud just smiles and waits in the silence, making it clear he can't be drawn out.

Finally: "My compliments. I'm told you've read all your journal articles. Don't worry that you don't understand it all. You'll be fine if you learn it by rote." Bud stands up, stretches and swells. "I want to show you something."

We go out of the building and take a walkway downhill. Distant ambient light hides the stars. The air tastes like mist, not dust. A cement stairway forks left, toward the mountain, and we take it down. The stairs end at a low-profile bunker. "Into the bowels of the earth," Bud says.

A guard inside the bunker herds us through a sequence of doors: we're locked out, then locked in between, then locked in. The featureless concrete corridor ahead slopes down and curves out of sight. Fluorescent lights buzz overhead. At the end an elevator slides open for us. The ride is very smooth—I can't tell if we're going up or down.

The elevator opens on a colorless corridor. It feels like we're underground, or in a vault. The doors are shut and locked with keypads. At the far end one open door leads to a small anteroom with a desk. Bud sits behind the desk and motions me to a chair in front of it. A steel door at Bud's back has a keypad and a face-shaped cage.

"We're coming to decision time," Bud says. "Any reservations?"

Where to begin? "Let's say I pass as an expert, Bud. People might assume I'm too biased to sit on the panel. They'll know I'm passing judgment on a nuclear-waste dump in my backyard."

"To gain influence on the panel you'll have to play to your strengths. You're studying water and desertification. Play to that and you can win acceptance as a Green. Looked at another way, you spend most of your time caring for African refugees. Play to that, and you can gain the panel's trust with your cultural sensitivity."

"I don't know if that will fly," I say. "I'm a *toubabou*."

Bud shrugs. "Being white can be an advantage, too. If people see native Africans on the panel, they worry about their, ah, susceptibility to corruption."

It's better to have a white Western panelist on the take—no one will expect that. Bud sees me holding that back and he doesn't like it, even if I keep it to myself. He has made it clear that a particular attitude is required. Cynicism is to be reserved for our competitors.

"We'll do a lot more role-playing," Bud says. "When we're finished, you'll have a better feel for the internal politics of the panel."

But I have to test the proposition that Bud owns me. "What if I came to favor Minatom's plan, or the Authority?"

"You do what you think is right," he says. "When you know all the facts, I will trust you to do the right thing."

Having suborned me, he trusts me. I'm fighting to come to grips with the breathtaking arrogance of it. Maybe he's trusting to the slow step-by-step process he used to cut me off from my livelihood and my tenuous ties.

I can't tell what's showing in my face, but Bud is ready to pounce. He leans over the desk. "I'll tell you why I trust you. For the past nine months, you have had three to five companions every minute of every day, steaming open your E-mail, reading your memos as you type them, listening to you say *Fuck* when you stub your toe. Your name appears in, let's see . . . four hundred and twenty databases, of which sixty-two are confidential and secure. There's a man named Bill—he doesn't have a last name—he told us that. Bill told us where you keep your money, how much you've got, what you spent it on eight years ago and what you spend it on now.

"You have a record at the MIB," he says. "You don't know what that is, do you? That's the Medical Information Bureau. That's where your physical and mental frailties are tabulated for future reference. Remember back in 'ninety-nine, that burning sensation you had when urinating? We know more about how you got that than you do."

He grips my forearm. "You'll be pleased to know that you are, by the standards of the people who judge these things, a solid citizen. You are not wicked or nuts. Your vices are not statistically significant. You are thrifty and loyal and true."

"You can't root around like that unless I sign a release. And I didn't."

Bud waves that impatiently away. "We had to vet you. Otherwise I could not show you what you need to see. I could not tell you what you need to know. You are now one of the dozen or so people in America whose word we trust. Only one thing remains: to give your word, to assure us that you will never repeat what you learn here."

He reaches into a drawer and rattles papers at me. "You will note that this document does not rely entirely on your word. It also invokes several key provisions of the National Security Act so we can lock you up in ADMAX if we even *think* you might talk. If you read and sign this document, we will step through this door and into the cockpit of the whole world."

To sign the form, I only have to contemplate the alternative: reconstruct a life from scratch. USAID doesn't need me anymore. I'm worse than useless at the camp; Lila needs me here with Bud. And I've severed all connections to my previous life. I've driven off my friends, and my family despairs of me.

My freedom lasted only as long as my solitude. Now I'm a stolid ox yoked to the windlass of a well, trapped in a circular rut. Domestication, patient and resistless: at no point could I have refused or turned back. To balk is futile.

Bud turns to the door and hunches over the keypad. It takes him some time to key in the code; either he's fingering with care or it's a long sequence. He puts his face in the cage and holds it there. Whatever's behind the cage likes his face; the door clicks and Bud swings it open.

The only light is a blaze of color from the far wall. Squinting, I see it's frosted glass: a room-sized rear-projection screen.

"I built this," Bud tells me. "It was my last job before going to Timbuktu."

A workstation sits on a semicircular conference table. The keyboard is shaped like an airfoil. A blower whooshes in the computer's works; hot air flows off souped-up chips. The big flat monitor mirrors the maps and charts on the wall. Bud sits down and taps.

"My system tells you all you need to know to run the world. You can do anything with this map, see? I can go up high, see the whole world. I can zoom in, see into your backyard if I want to. Best of all, it does intelligence fusion. I want to use force, I look at the world this way: troop movements, political instability, civil disturbances, new gravesites. I want to throw money around, I look at the world another way: currency reserves, foreign debt, current and capital account balances, growth rates." He's making icons and multicolored glyphs come and go on his map.

Bud is warming to his topic. "You just want to have a quiet weekend at Camp David? OK, let's just check and see if you've got anything to worry about. We roll everything in together: trade, stability, violence, ideology." Now each country glows green or yellow or red.

"The system lets me worry more or worry less. I can color a country yellow if it's the least little bit troublesome. Or I can set the system to be less sensitive and flag only the most extreme problems. Watch, I'm making it less sensitive: one by one the pesky countries are blinking out, from red to yellow, from yellow to green.

"See, now I've turned the warnings all the way down. I don't give a shit. As far as I'm concerned the world is all clear, one big green light. . . . Almost. The whole world is green with one country glowing red like a hot coal, even when I'm trying my best to ignore it. What the hell is that?" He turns and stares at me. "What in God's name is that place?"

I don't need to answer. That place smolders just over the horizon from the camp. I would often think about the killing there and how close it comes, not in fear but in dry stubborn rumination as though the prospect of my slaughter were a geometry proof.

"That's Algeria, Ty. Algeria, the second biggest country in Africa." He wiggles a mouse and we dive down until Algeria blankets the wall. He taps and gravestone icons grow. Violence shows as animated flames. Algiers is surrounded by a ring of fire. "Algeria has chewed up a hundred thousand lives in its Islamic revolution, and it's not finished yet. You can slit throats or get your throat slit. It's that simple. Soon nobody will be left but the kids who grew up raping and slitting throats and slinging babies against the wall. Algeria has raised a generation of serial murderers. Soon they'll be in charge.

"When the dust settles, the new regime will make the Taliban look good. And look where they are, Ty. They're nestled up against Europe's soft underbelly: the bent officials and mafioso of Corsica, the Arab underworld of Marseilles. Terrorists will come trickling through, then streaming through. It will be no use hiding the explosives and the weapons of mass destruction. They don't need that crap. They'll come unarmed and buy a gun, or a linoleum knife or a claw hammer or a sock and a bar of soap. They'll settle in your hometown and kill a family every night for Allah. Just like they did back home, they'll break in at night and kill you in your bed. Look into your eyes to show you how much they like it. They'll keep doing it until they get caught. It's beyond ideology now, beyond religion. It's simply who they are."

Fatimatou has kin in Algeria. She would speak of fixed abodes, prosaic worries, birth and marriage as well as death. I wish she were here to tell me if this is more of Bud's big-picture geopolitics. All I know is Bud believes it. He is scared.

"Algeria's going to pop like a boil," he says. "All the pus building up in there, it will splatter all over the Western world. Terrorists will ooze into Europe and into Russia and, from there, into America. It will take three years, max, before terror comes into our bedrooms one house at a time. We might not even notice at first. This kind of terror looks almost like crime.

"Let's change the view to a topo map," he says. North Africa turns brown and crumples into relief. Algeria's stoplight glow dims to a ruddy tinge.

"Look at that knob of rock down there at the southernmost point of Algeria. That's your turf, Ty. You know that place like the back of your hand, right? I'll bet you never looked at it in quite this way.

"The Adrar des Iforas could be a handy staging area for a multinational force. Our dump site will have paved roads and runways, satellite shots, supply depots, access control."

Bud is bending over me, whispering. "The Adrar des Iforas is the panic button of Africa. If we push that button in time, we can prevent a worldwide wave of terrorism. We can stop a Pan-African holy war. That's why we'll be dumping there." He stoops down to get face-to-face. "When Timbuktu's plan is selected."

He's cross-eyed close, paying out words like fishing line, alert for any twitch: "Now you know why we're in this together. This is what's at stake."

It's not dawn yet, and the pink eastern clouds don't light up the hillside. Bud and I lie facedown on a sloping pile of sandbags. We're staring down a hill into piles of crumbling concrete. The concrete has no flat surface, only treacherous jagged rubble. Rusting rebar pokes from crumbling slabs. Small-arms fire twangs and cracks in the ruins. Figures creep and scuttle through the dust and smoke. This is a training session of a different sort, meant for others, not me.

Bud presses a matchbook into my hand. "Don't take this outside the gates," he says.

I turn it over. It shows a gold silhouette of a bear rearing up inside a black half-oval. The dark shape curves over the bear's head like a dome.

"Bear in a cave mouth," Bud says. "Guarding its lair. It's not smart to poke around in a bear's cave. Bear Mountain is the inmost recess of the bear's lair. This is the training camp of what we call the Home Guard. Our last line of defense. Also sometimes our first line of defense."

Bud is briefing me into something: "We disbanded the state militias when we stopped preparing for all-out nuke war. But we kept a few of the stars and put them back to work as the Home Guard. Now we've got two teams, company strength. The Red Team does terrorism, the Blue Team does counterterrorism. The Red Team does urban guerrilla warfare, the Blue Team does search and destroy. The Red Team does covert logistics—that is, smuggling—and the Blue Team does interdiction. They keep each other sharp."

Bud is drawing with a finger in the sand. "Understand? One team is expert in stabilizing a country. The other team knows all about destabilization."

The noise stops and white suits converge on the ruin. They carry out a body on a stretcher, but no head.

"Happens twice a month, at least," Bud says. "They tell the trainees, Don't sweep your teammates. They're blue in the face from saying it, but that's the hardest thing to learn."

With the dead man removed, the noise starts again. A ripping sound draws my eyes to a wall that patters smoothly down to earth.

"See what I'm saying, Ty? We can use the Red Team and the Blue Team to train selected allies. If we want them to take over, the Red Team shows them how. If they're already in power, the Blue Team helps them stay there. As the State Department is training them in democracy and pluralism, the Home Guard is shaping up their military. We get friendly faces in the ranks.

"It's called IMET. International Military Education and Training. It's the new wave. It means we have the world's best capability for fighting proxy wars. If public opinion won't countenance a military operation, no problem. We just use the local talent.

"We may never fight again," Bud says. "We've perfected the art of proxy war."

Finally it is time for my valediction. In the shade of Bear Mountain I pick at my food in a squat glass-and-girder cafeteria. Bud eats quickly, with rhythmic stabs and cuts, and tucks his food in a cheek to talk. Like a hospital cafeteria, this is a place you go against your will. Only a crisis can drive you to such a place: injury, illness, national security emergency.

It's an alien place. An American meal on a tray, with glutinous gravy and lumps of meat but no grains. The indoors, too big after my desert hermitage, and the outdoors, too small, cropped by windows and crammed with trees. The light, too bright inside and too pale outside. Bustling figures, jarring and uncountable after the isolation of the desert and the languor of the camp.

But a green print dress on a small fair form, that is too familiar. It doesn't recall my wife, just the feel of our severed tie. Bud's words are trickling into me. They register long after I hear them: "You were a desert hermit, renouncing the world. Well, now you're back. You're in the very center of the world, the hub that everything turns on. The things we do change maps and governments and lives all over the world. We've never had this kind of control. We can speed up change or slow it down, whatever's best. We can reach into countries where we wouldn't dare send a force. Do you see what I'm saying?"

"Sure," I say, or maybe think.

"You're going to sit on a panel that will change the world. You're not just cleaning up waste. The decision you make will change the landscape of Africa. It will put a stop to more suffering than you can imagine. No more camps like Lila's camp, Ty, think of it. No more needless death.

"If the world disgusts you, change it, help us change it. You can't run away. We're in the cockpit, keeping the world on course. Without us it will crash and burn."

Bud flew me to Vienna in a business-class cocoon, and I have settled into the effortless nonlife of a plush hotel. The International Atomic Energy Agency is a short walk from here. The evaluation panel meets ten steps down the hall.

If a medieval hermit returned to his society he would find life as he left it: the same manors, the same hovels, the same cathedrals bound together in immutable hierarchies. He would have nothing to learn or forget.

It's not that way for me. While I covered my eyes in seclusion, my world hid, condemning me to hopeless hide-and-seek. The cities and buildings are only hiding places: the real world is banks and courts and bodies and forums that keep out of sight and entwine and tug. If I had all-seeing eyes like Bud's, this new world might look like an orb web, crossing at a million angles, touching at a million points, delicate but inescapable.

My new world is the panel where Bud planted me. I sit in a cold-gray hot room with five others. The long black table has a sharp edge that digs into my forearm. Water pitchers gather beads of condensation. Green-tinged light comes from everywhere and nowhere. A glass booth in the corner wheezes ozone-scented air and computer sounds.

I am part of this panel, but the others seem like a new race with a secret language. Half their words are alien—not foreign, but new and unknown to the world outside: MEGA, EXIM, COFACE, OPIC, JEXIM, in a language that dictates words be spelled with alternating consonants and vowels. A language of letters mixes with the first in a kind of patois: syllable-syllable, letter-letter-letter. A number-letter language gives us thousands of ways to say no (eighty-six stroke Dee four, UNC 38).

A pink-and-white blond woman sits at my left. Next to her a tall man sits in my peripheral blur, charcoal brown and silver. An Indian man of a leathery brown sits across the table next to a straw-colored man from Asia. At my right elbow is a young woman from the South Seas. Despite their different skins, they speak these languages. They have the same brisk way of speaking, the same small smiles and knowing eyes.

The Polynesian-looking woman comes into focus first. She is called Faye. Her cheekbones lie deep beneath her rosewood face, but her body is slim. She has a tiny flared snub nose. Her hair is shoulder-length, brown, with sunbaked rusty red strands here and there. She has a slow, low-pitched voice and a heavy-lidded smile, but she can turn to you and siphon your thoughts almost before you speak them. She growls her R-sounds, as Americans do, and there is something northern in the drawn-out foghorn sound when she speaks *abowwt* this *owwtcome* or that *towwn*.

As I listen to them and absorb their meaning I begin to understand. These people are bargaining. They could be haggling in Bambara over the price of a hen.

"OPIC will insure the project for country risk, but only if Sigdyne gets fifty percent of the engineering work."

"No one else can do that work. Sigdyne will get it all."

"Give Plenum a contract to process the waste—that's twenty billion dollars."

"Africa has to be included, that's what it comes down to. Sink it in the Gulf of Guinea, bury it in the Sahara, I don't care. Africa has fifty votes in the General Assembly. They will block any plan that shuts them out."

"Russia could pull out and turn their waste into MOX, you know."

"They don't dare. That's been tried. MOX is a terrorist's dream."

The black man is the next to come into focus. He seldom speaks, but the haggling stops when he leans forward. He is tall with a sprinkling of silver hair. His name is Sam. "Get the gnomes," he says.

A button is pressed, words are murmured, and a door shuts in the glassed-in corner. The far wall lights up with a picture of a crystal ball.

Faye nudges me and whispers, "It started as a joke, but people think of it that way: the Crystal Ball sees all, knows all. Twenty thousand interlocking equations. It vacuums in data from everywhere. You could kill a forest printing out the software code."

Just as Bud has his cockpit, our panel has a Crystal Ball. We steer the world to cross-purposes, equally omnipotent. There must be dozens of such confident cabals independently running the world, all-knowing and oblivious to one another.

"Let's do some what-ifs," Sam says. A map of Africa takes shape.

The Oriental man speaks, a stern look melting into a deferential smile. "Try it the Authority's way. Put it in the Gulf of Guinea."

The map blinks colors and patterns. Faint arrows weave a mesh from place to place. "The balance of trade will cause problems. South Asia will want compensation."

"You have the same problem if you give it to Minatom."

They paint the Earth and paint over it, fill it and empty it dozens of times. I am resting in a silent pause when Faye turns to me: "What do you think, Ty?" All eyes are on me, and my mind is blank.

"What about sharing the waste around?"

"It's all or nothing, I'm afraid," Sam says. "The nuclear powers agreed not to scatter the waste. It's easier to choose one site and write it off."

So the contest is winner take all. The room subsides into a long silence. Faye luxuriates in it, but the pink-and-white woman turns her eyes down to a page of neat notes, writes intently and scratches out.

Sam breaks the silence. "What's Timbuktu's schedule for Mali?"

"It's a five-year project," Faye says.

"Let's see what happens if we speed it up a bit."

Each country changes color, second by second, from blue to green or from yellow to orange. Faye asks, "What's that shimmering?"

"Billions of dollars are sloshing around. Economies have to adjust."

"But if it's an adjustment, it should settle down. Why doesn't it?"

"Try slowing the project down."

"Don't bother, we can't," Sam says. "Every year you stretch it out, cost overruns compound themselves. You have to dump quickly or not at all."

"We need to find out what that shimmering means," Faye says.

The Asian man says, "Ignore it. It's probably just a bug."

"It doesn't act like a software bug," Faye says. "It acts like Africa would if it went out of control."

We're taking a break in the lounge off our conference room. Most of the panelists finger telephones with lonely intensity. Faye relaxes expertly. She sprawls on a leather couch, drinking a cup of coffee that seems to have a soporific effect. Her slow low voice glides from word to word and calms me.

Her eyes can take on a trancelike fixity. Looking around she says, "I don't belong here. I'm not a bureaucrat, I'm not an expert, I'm not even a Green."

Each evening Faye has sketched me a bit of her life. Her reminiscences leave big coy gaps. I suspect she's leaving out the best parts.

When she was a little girl, floury stuff drifted down over the islands. They only got a little bit. Other places got more. Faye and her girlfriends scraped it up, mushed it up with water, made cakes and pies for their baby dolls. Later they learned it was sawdust from pulverized trees. It didn't look like sawdust. It was ground up so fine, you couldn't tell it was wood. So fine it could fly for hundreds of miles. It came from the French nuclear weapons tests on Fangataufa. Fangataufa is still on the maps, but you wouldn't see it if they let you go there. It has crumbled into the sea.

God knows what that did to her inside. Ever since, she's been behaving like she's got six months to live. She doesn't work too hard. She finds rich eccentric patronesses with flaky little foundations. They give her grants. In this way she became a newsgroup agony aunt for combative pacifists.

Faye studied physics in Canada and bounced to the forefront of one of the disarmament groups. They were not much more than a social club: barn dances, pilgrimages, bike tours of missile silos, vigils. "The worst was Peace Camp: we might as well have been Girl Scouts making s'mores."

She fell in with a delinquent faction that liked to get themselves locked up. They would lie in front of trucks or paint graffiti on the giant NSA golfball antennas. Faye didn't see the point of getting caught: "You don't scare anybody singing folk songs in jail." So she took up satellite spoofing. It's like hacking, only you diddle with the airwaves instead of the Internet. It's not so hard; a field-tunable radio base station costs a few hundred thousand U.S. Faye knows heiresses who will bankroll the purchase. You set the gizmo to a satellite's frequency and tell it what to do. The hard part is the social engineering. You need to make friends who will help you with the protocols and codes. Faye and her buds were good at that. They made cartoon doves appear on a U.S. early-warning radar. They flashed a DISARMAMENT NOW banner on some Royal Navy computer screens. They picked the easy targets: the National Guard, the logistics agencies—any little thing creates a stir.

Faye is the panel's mascot. The nongovernmentals trust her, whatever their agenda: Amnesty, Greenfleet, Ploughshares. A tiny kid from a tiny country, she's spunky and unthreatening and devoid of malice. Her presence on the panel shows just how patiently the U.N. listens to the little people. The gray Vienna bureaucrats congratulate themselves for their daring, but they know no harm can come of this. This Faye is not the kind of power broker Ushi is. She's just a prankster.

The panel is about to reconvene. Sam takes me aside in the conference room. "You're something of a rockhound, aren't you? Maybe you can tell me what to make of this." He gives me a crumpled sheet of paper.

PROGRESS REPORT FOR ■■■, ■■■■■■■
TIMBUKTU EARTHWEALTH PROPRIETARY

Name of project: Demonstration Shaft 3
Location: Approx. 120 km. south of Tessalit, Mali
Dimensions: 3,412 feet, 16 feet 9 in. diameter
Design conditions: Lateral pressure 40% of overburden weight. Hydrostatic head 750 feet

Contract type: Cost plus fixed fee
Stipulations:

- Monthly disbursement, 10% retained until completion
- Changed-conditions clause
- Disputes resolution in accordance with standard General Conditions

Project cost to date: Estimated $28,105,212 / Bid $46,405,390
General contract mods to date: $30,785,298
Subsurface-related overruns to date: $29,340,571

Current month

The original program plan was based on freezing systems to control face instability of pervious ground. Ultrasonic readings indicate multiple windows in the freeze wall caused by dissolution of combustible gases. Compressed-air techniques will be necessary.

The project must now budget for airlock and compressor procurement. A hyperbaric worksite requires decompresssion time, cutting productivity by 50%. Airlock access and egress will retard operations, and all equipment will require enhanced spark-proofing.

The full cost implications cannot be determined until subsurface evaluations are complete. Costs will depend on detailed measurements of density, permeability, shear strength, and grain-size distribution in the rock matrix.

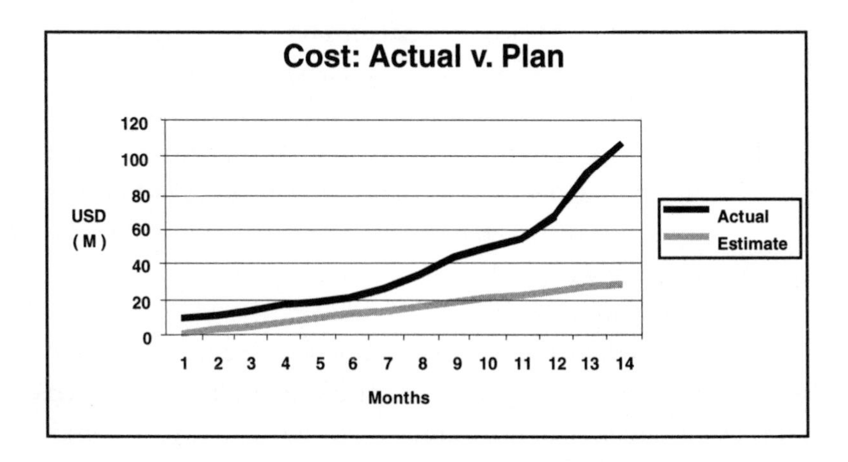

"All it means is they'll go bankrupt if they get the work," I say. "The nuclear powers will have to bail them out."

"It's like that for all the bidders. What about the safety implications?"

"Let's submit a question."

"We have to be circumspect," Sam says. "We can't act on the basis of misappropriated trade secrets. And you have to consider the source."

"Who's that?"

"Ushi. She showed up at my hotel room last night, very cloak and dagger."

"Ushi, in the flesh?" My designated adversary.

"Unmistakable, despite her blond wig. Incognito is not her strong suit." Sam preens, momentarily starstruck.

"How did she get the document?"

"She told me a concerned whistle-blower risked everything to leak it."

"She must have some connections."

Sam smiles. "Greenfleet has been known to do a bit of hacking, or now and then something more hands-on. Rumor has it Ushi likes nothing better than to tag along on a second-story job."

Faye has taken a shine to me; nothing sexual or romantic, just some odd need for affiliation with another outsider. She pairs off with me for dinner, which I prefer to eat alone in my room. When I state a preference for room service, she calls from the balcony afterward. Gregarious people mystify me. Perhaps they appreciate my silences—silence still comes naturally to me.

Silence, yes, but not attention. Faye gives and takes with her eyes to connect, but she cannot reach me. Attending to her words is like climbing out of a deep hole. By the time I poke my head up, half her words are past, and I must piece the sense together from a sentence's end and its pitch.

". . . it's not like the old days, when you could trot out a lawyer and carry the day with old-fashioned debate, with logic and rhetoric and sweeping gestures. Now models run the world. I don't mean gorgeous models like Ushi Lassen, I mean computer models—my equation is bigger than your equation, my charts can beat up your graphs."

". . . I was on Mururoa after the French nuke tests, counting tern's eggs. The radiation was plinking at my DNA, knocking it loose. I was trading my life bit by bit for those stupid eggs. One egg, one, one, one, two eggs, two, two, two, two, for hours. Two eggs, that's as high as I got."

Past midnight, but I have yielded to a nagging idea. I get out of bed to make some notes. I walk down the hotel corridor to our lounge and stretch out on the overstuffed sofa. When the thought lets me go, I hear movement behind the door to our conference room: unstealthy creaks and thumps. I open the door. The room is dark except for the glowing crystal ball on the wall.

The Crystal Ball grows land masses and becomes a globe. Faye is in the booth, her face reduced to a shine on one cheek. I duck through the door of the booth and prop my backside on a desk behind her. She cants her body intently at the screen.

She touches the keys in a tentative way, and Africa begins to shimmer in colors that change too fast to name. They pause briefly in a deep violet, swing back through the spectrum, and pause again in rusty red, all in a second or two.

"Pretty sight," I say.

"It's driving me nuts. If it's for real, it means waves of booms and busts."

"Don't worry about it," I say. "That's never happened. It can't happen."

Faye says, "How do we know? Nobody's ever poured this much money into Africa."

"The gnomes know the Crystal Ball better than anybody. What do they make of it?"

"The gnomes can't explain it," she says. "They think it's a bug in the Crystal Ball's software."

"You don't believe them?"

"It doesn't matter whether it's a bug or not. The computer code inside, everybody uses it. The data, it's all the same data from the same think tanks and agencies. Governments make rules with it. Investors bet their life savings on it. Look." Faye's hands dart around the computer keyboard. Africa flutters, then flickers, then blurs with stop-and-go booms and busts. "I put this much money in Africa, and the economy goes out of control. I see this happen, and I know everybody else will see it happen too. Everybody will act on what they see, and they will make it happen. This is a self-fulfilling prophecy."

Faye is watching for comprehension or resistance. "It's like the mind of the world. A shared perception that lets everyone act as one. Do you see what I mean?"

"This isn't real," I say. Lila's world, that is real. *Hunger, thirst, necrotic flesh. Your wife turned inside out before your eyes. This flickering screen is a troubled night's sleep from a big, late meal, a well-fed world's bad dream.* "If this were real, political stability would go down the tubes, too. Does the Crystal Ball show that?"

"Political stability? You can't show that. I wish you could."

"Sure you can, they—" I catch myself on the brink of yammering about Bud and his top secret cockpit.

Faye has a tiny smile and narrowed eyes. "Who does that?"

I feign confusion, scowl my way out of it, and shake my head. "Sorry, got mixed up."

Faye drops her question, but she looks at me with interest. "It would be great to have something like that. You could just sit there and run the world."

Like Bud does. I try to make a wistful face.

"Make everything turn out OK." She swivels the chair around. With one hand she plinks absently on the keys. "Wet dreams. The most you can hope for is something like this: getting a God's-eye view. Watching it all happen, feeling bad about it, knowing the reasons for all this suffering."

The rainbow colors flicker in her eyes.

Here in Vienna I'm no longer under Bud's thumb. He still owns me, of course, but he can't commandeer my mind. The frantic pace of training helped attenuate my grief. Now, though the letup is slight, the grief has begun to seep back. It fills all the interstices: in bed at night, in the bathroom, in the long arid stretches of deliberation.

Maybe news from Lila would help. I'm first in the meeting room this morning. I compose an E-mail for her, the kind of anodyne pleasantry I send to my parents. I crack a few jokes about my situation, but I'm not interested in reporting—I want to hear back. I want to know about Fatimatou's ingenuity, Hissi's drawings, Serata and the children who romp unseen around her. And I want to know all about Lila.

The response takes a few days to come. It has nothing I want.

Aw, come on, Ty, it can't be that bad.

On this warm evening Faye and I sit on the balcony of her hotel suite. The moon is a streak on the Stadtpark pond. Faye sits curled on a springy metal chair with a big blunt fuming in her hand. Now and then she stops speaking to let the dope go to work in her lungs. When she speaks, it's all shimmering maps: "We can't ignore it."

"It makes no sense, Faye. Can't you just shrug it off?"

Her eyes widen with the importance of what is coming. She says, "That's the whole point—*it makes no sense.*"

The chair sways as she leans my way. "Confront the paradoxes. That's the main thing I got from physics. Think about physics enough, and your mind breaks open. You have to go through it, experience it. Then all of a sudden you know what moves the world."

"So what moves the world, Faye?"

"Things you can't understand," she says. "I can't explain it. I can only give you an example."

"So give me an example," I say. I'm steeling myself for a pothead's rant about tiny solar systems in each atom of my fingernail.

Faye says, "Have you ever heard of Bell's theorem?"

I have not.

"It's not really a theorem," she says. "It's the way things are. It's called a theorem only because nobody believes it. Nobody believes it because it's not possible."

"What, the theory is wrong?"

"No," she says, "it's absolutely right—just impossible. Quantum theory predicts the impossible. Then we see it happen, every day, in labs all over the world. I'm not talking about physical impossibilities, like flying elephants or headless men. I'm talking about logical impossibilities, experiences that make a mockery of your mind. You can set up an experiment and prove that the predicted result is impossible. Logically, mathematically, you can rule out the predictions. Then you perform the result and the impossible happens."

So that's it: Faye's a mystic. Her mind is full of ineffable physics and math. To communicate with the laity she has to speak in riddles. She is trying to initiate me into mysteries. I can see her frustration.

"Einstein proposed an experiment. It was just a thought experiment—you didn't have to go through with it, the result was so obvious. His argument ran like this: 'Look, let's say you do umptyump, the theory predicts umpety dump, and *obviously* that can't happen.' So with simple common sense, Einstein disproved quantum mechanics. He reduced it to an absurdity.

"Well, someone got around to trying the experiment for real—and damned if the impossible didn't happen. It's not just that God plays dice with the world. God picks up the dice and rolls a one, or a thirteen. You check the dice, count the dots on each face and it can't be. But it is."

Faye soaks up cannabis with her rib cage expanded. Leaking out just enough breath to speak, she says, "Sure, the Crystal Ball's predictions are illogical, impossible, absurd. Just don't tell me it can't be happening."

The International Atomic Energy Agency is holding a closed-door conference in Vienna. It has been arranged in strict secrecy to limit attendance. Politics will not intrude, for once; this is to be a free exchange of ideas among experts, reasoned and objective.

Today is the day, but the start of the conference has been slightly delayed. Looking out a second-story window, I see crowds of demonstrators surging in front of the marble hall. Greens spatter phosphorescent paint, Africans sing and sway. Effigy skeletons bob on sticks, demonic Uncle Sams swing from poles. Two women stretch a banner showing Russia bisected north to south by a red gash. It reads TWENTY PERCENT OF RUSSIA'S LAND UNLIVABLE. Behind the bare trees in the Stadtpark pond, hundreds of candles drift on tiny rafts. The demonstrations snarl traffic on every street in sight. A limousine rocks in the midst of a swelling crowd.

Faye and I turn from the window to the dim doorway of an ornate auditorium. The gilt-and-plaster ceiling and the red-curtained stage seem remote from our concerns. Opera or symphonies would resound in here, but the ancient space threatens to swallow the thin sound of our science.

Most of the seats are occupied. We take places in the center of the third row. The voices blend in a solemn hum.

A man appears at the podium. He is narrow, with a spherical

head bisected by a perfect part. Silence creeps back from him like rising water, until the last bass voices are stranded and hushed.

The round-headed man speaks in a south Asian accent of musical intonations. Interminable acknowledgments and thanks. Defining and delimiting. Lots of road maps showing us the way. Faye fidgets in the seat next to me. "They can barely speak English," she says. "How do they learn to string clauses together like that?"

The round-headed man makes endless introductions. He ekes out a ragged tattoo of increasingly grudging applause. One man is always the last to stop clapping. We can't see him, but we hear him cupping meaty palms, distinctive as a voice, *pock-pock-pock-pock.*

The podium stands in a pool of light, alone in the universe. Figures do not move to it; they appear there.

Bud appears. He will be speaking for Timbuktu Earthwealth. The great proscenium cuts him down to size, almost. He pitches his voice slightly lower as he bends to the mike, fatherly and reassuring. He describes his project with paternal pride: Pan-African participation, Pan-African growth, African self-sufficiency, and an end to foreign aid.

"Our plans are based on an econometric model." Bud's voice has slowed to help us along. "Two hundred equations, each linked to all the others. Two hundred variable factors encompassing the developed world's economies as well as those of Africa. We would only confuse you if we showed you the thicket of equations we had to solve. We can suggest the rigor of our methods with a simplified diagram of the economic relationships."

A slide snaps into view. It teems with lettered boxes, large ones, tiny ones, stacked or nested. All are hatched with Day-Glo orange or blue; they set the eyes pulsating with moiré effects. Each box stands for a critical factor: copper exports, machinery imports, wage rates, income, shipping capacity, on and on in a blur of words as meaningless as crowd noise. Lime-green arrows snake everywhere. Ripples course along them, pulling the eyes this way and that like a dozen hypnotists vying for your attention.

Bud's words console us in our confusion. "No human mind can comprehend all these relationships together. But with our computer model, we evaluate them all with perfect consistency. Let's consider what this model tells us. First, we will look at the benefits in objective terms." New graphs and charts, colorful, three-dimensional, trending ever upward. A burst of words, a wave of the hand, and we hop to the next chart. "Our intervention analysis shows the Sahara, before and after. But we can't know what it means unless we put a human face on the benefits. Before."

The projection screen cuts in with an audiovisual tour of hell: starvation, mayhem, and disease in sharp clinical focus and direct-flash freakshow contrast, linked in quick flicky cuts that shock without touching.

"And after." Bud hymns the virtues of the wealth to come, and the screen smiles on groups of mugging kids, high-spirited and alive, and family tenderness. The music makes your eyes wet even if you fight it.

"No computer model can weigh the importance of this change," Bud says. "It takes human hearts and minds. Africa understands the value of this approach immediately, intuitively. A village elder in Mali described the project in traditional terms, terms we can all understand." I've never seen Bud smile that way.

"Timbuktu Earthwealth's disposal complex will be an oasis: an oasis of opportunity, an oasis of hope for a better life. Life in the Sahara has always been shaped by oases. Now we can nurture a new one and change millions of African lives."

Bud has retired to polite applause. Alain Theriault materializes at the podium: black hair slicked back, black eyes sunk deep in his head. He is powerfully built, with a long torso and short legs. His tailored black suit teases the eye with tiny pale flecks. His knuckles are too big for his big hands.

Theriault disdains to orate. He speaks in casual and understated tones. To Theriault, public forums like this are a sign of botched deal making. He will condescend to persuade, but not to a crowd like this. He introduces a multimedia presentation, then slinks aside.

He has chosen a sensory assault. An animated presentation blooms in color, and abruptly we are flying over an ocean, descending over sleek ships plowing high seas. Six-track sound tickles our ears rock-concert loud as we fly toward the ships and dive beneath them.

Now we are underwater, looking up at the ships' hulls. Great bays in the hulls whine open, disgorging needle-nosed canisters that streak down past us. We follow them vertiginously down. The canisters land with satisfying thuds, raising little plumes of mud and disappearing forever. Transmitters in the canisters reassure us with slow signals; the rumbling bass notes shake our seats. The screen cuts to consoles of dials. Needles sway gently and readouts hold steady, in control.

The screen darkens, and Theriault glides back into the pool of light. He says, "This project will require international cooperation on an unprecedented scale. The stakes are high and the risks are real. We must choose wisely. The right choice is emplacement at sea, within the framework of the United Nations and the Law of the Sea Treaty."

The door bangs open behind us. Chants rise in a syncopated roar and police are barking. The light of the door silhouettes a heaving knot of protesters. Feet pound down the aisles. Acrid wisps make my face crunch up.

Glop comes down all around. Faye shrieks. It slithers down my neck and oozes on my suit. Faye combs it from her hair with clawed fingers. It's a bright green polymer with a snotty consistency, slimy but not liquid. "Fake toxic waste," Faye says. "You know Ushi's behind this."

The disturbance is rolling down the aisles. The protesters aren't playing dead for the police, they're scuffling in the dark. Faye is collecting a blob in her lap as she grooms herself. Her heavy lids have parted and her eyes are strikingly bright. They glitter in a way that cuts me off from her.

She takes a handful, twists around, and flings it.

Raus! Out. We both jump. *Polizei,* fed up. Faye's mouth gets very small.

The cop collars a man behind us who has risen to his feet. "But I didn't—" They hustle away as one.

Faye is more furtive, less impulsive now. She's aiming with gleeful random malice. For the first time I see her as a born leader: impresario of middle-school subversion, egger-on of dim acolytes, unsung hero of a thousand food fights.

She's drawing return fire now. The slop is pelting me too. The auditorium is out of control.

The disturbance has been contained. We have been granted a brief break to freshen up. Bud retakes the podium. He stands and waits for us. Then he turns to the screen without speaking. Timbuktu's logo flashes on the screen.

Faye nudges me with her shoulder. "When do the Russians get to say their piece?"

Not yet. Music swells: *Thus Spake Zarathustra*. The projection screen fills with a picture of Earth from space. A voice as deep as a giant's booms through the speakers: "The Authority has an intimidating name. The U.N. power structure backs it. They offer a simple plan. We can watch the waste drop out of sight and hope to shirk the costs. But the costs are inescapable, and the whole world will bear them."

The globe changes subtly in the starlit blackness. Vaporous trails appear, tracing currents and winds. They writhe and pulse like globe-girdling smoke rings. "Think of the heat from this nuclear waste: five hundred kilowatts per hectare. No one will feel the heat, the Authority says; their dump site is barren of life.

"But what surrounds the hot clay of their disposal site? A vacuum? No. Solid rock? No. The sea.

"The hot clay will disrupt the great abyssal current called the gyre. Heat it, and it will rise and disrupt surface currents that determine the whole world's weather.

"To predict the effects of such a change is the most difficult question in all of science. It takes all the power of a supercomputer. We cannot explain our methods in the time we have today. The complexity of our computer models is difficult for laypeople to imagine. Complex as our models are, they predict clear and unambiguous consequences. Grave consequences.

"Watch as we compress years of global weather into minutes." On the screen a globe sickens. Green land turns brown, brown land turns white. At the threshold of hearing, wind howls from the speakers all around. "Heating the seabed will mix more nutrients up into warm surface waters. Gigantic algal blooms will put the greenhouse effect into reverse. We will have another ice age, only a little ice age, God willing, but twenty percent of the world's cropland will be left barren. The trade winds will parch Southeast Asia to desert. Drought and frost will drive a billion people from their homes."

Faye stirs alongside me. She raises her hand, diffidently. When she has the floor she ducks and shuffles. "Your model of the ocean, how does it work?"

Bud says, "That's a very complex question—"

"My question is actually pretty specific," Faye says. "Are you using spectral methods?"

Bud straightens up, his eyebrows hop. He was expecting a puff-ball question from this little Kewpie doll. He says, "No. This is what's called a Lagrangian model. A La-GRAN-gian model. It's based on the most advanced techniques. With spectral methods you have to cut the earth to bits and track each one. That's crude, brute force. With our Lagrangian model, we treat each major cyclone as a single element. Each one interacts as a whole with all the others."

"Very nice," Faye says. "What are you assuming about changes in the rate of diffusive exchange?"

Struggling hard to condescend, Bud slows up and gives her a kind smile. "Even with the most advanced models, we have to ignore that. It's an imponderable."

With an upturned girlie intonation Faye says, "I don't know. I'm no expert, but you're heating up a lot of water. Who knows how fast it's evaporating? You could get significant changes in heat uptake."

She's talking with her hands now, bouncing and waving: "Now, as I understand it—correct me if I'm wrong—most times weather is flat. It spins horizontally like a turntable. But you get little turbulent knots inside that roll in three dimensions. And changes in heat uptake can turn those little knots into big knots, you know?"

She's whipping her hand in circles, showing us. "In that case Robinson's conditions apply, right? Small-scale uncertainties infect large-scale air movements. Then your predictions are good for maybe two days. How far out do your predictions run?"

"Twenty years." He says it without moving his mouth.

"Did you say *twenty* years? Wow, that's a long time. Wow. Twenty years." With a shrug Faye sits down. She flicks her eyebrows at me Groucho-like.

Bud has turned in desperation to a ramble from some kind of professor, an epic of *if you will* and *as it were* and no question in sight.

The crowd's growing restlessness does nothing to discourage the professor. But an abrupt silence turns him around as a woman stands up, and up, and up, transfixing the crowd, glowing in a spot, causing a murmur to swell and crest with the shushing sibilance of the chorus: *Ushi*.

Her dark woolly sweater is bedraggled with beads of slime. She bears the indignity with touching pluck. Handed the microphone, Ushi gathers herself in the silence for long seconds. Then she speaks in a tiny fluty voice, audible but soft enough to demand silent, breathless attention.

"Timbuktu Earthwealth promises an African oasis. An oasis of money. Yes, Africans can see Timbuktu's project in traditional terms. Those who stand to get rich will see an oasis. Others will see a different feature of the Sahara.

"Look closely at Timbuktu Earthwealth. Who are they? The military-industrial complex. The arms merchants. Times are hard for them now; there is not enough war. With no terror or chaos to feed on, they swarm toward the money in disarmament. Swarming and stripping the life from the land, this is nothing new. The Americans of Timbuktu Earthwealth, they are another plague of locusts.

"Locusts behave just so. When drought threatens starvation, the locusts converge wherever food remains. They consume every scrap of green before moving on. These new locusts will not destroy one season's crop, one patch of cover; they will poison the earth and keep it barren for centuries.

"Do not abandon Africa to the locusts."

The silence is absolute. Ushi cradles the microphone, with her head bowed. Then a solitary pair of hands claps doggedly. Other hands join in ragged syncopation. Then more applause pours in, a great swelling wave that catches me up too, and Faye. All around me I can feel the same stinging palms and shining eyes turned toward Ushi, who raises her head to listen. She has filled this gilded space with the right kind of Sturm und Drang.

We are spent. The little round-headed man waits in silence. Now eyes begin to turn to the rear, toward a thin arm that rises as if tugged from above.

Lila. *How did she get here?* I must have said it aloud. I hear Faye say, "Who is she?"

The vibration we feel is not stage fright; Lila is not here with us. She envisions a camp and brings it here. She reaches for thin shoulders we can't see as she peoples the camp with names and faces and stories and memories and aspirations, all lost in a desperate needy now. With offhand mimesis she clings to life with them.

She pulls away from the camp, stops speaking in visions, and says a few words: "I know who Timbuktu's partners are: Sigdyne, C-3, Systech. Sure, they're greedy death merchants. Sure, they're only in this for the money. But they're all we've got, back at the camp.

"It's not a good life we have at the camp, but it's life. Without Timbuktu Earthwealth, we will die. Babies first. You have to let them die—hunger blights an infant for life. Their mothers will give them all the love and care in the world, but no food. We don't waste food at the camp."

The round-headed man is taking much too long to break the silence.

The conference has ended and the Authority is hosting a reception. A waiter brings a silver tray of caviar tarts in reach. I snatch two.

Lila squares off in front of me, cutting me from my herd like a steer. She glances at the caviar with affectionate contempt and says, "I hear you're going to decide who dumps the waste."

"The Atomic Energy Agency set up a selection panel. I'm just one of the members."

Lila's undertone blares, "It all depends on you. We're going to lose everything if you don't help us. Greenfleet has been pissing on Timbuktu's plan for months. The Authority has experts and consultants sniping at it. And now Bozo is having second thoughts. I'll bet Theriault is leaning on him."

Bozo is the least of Lila's worries, I would think. His legitimate democracy is far from the camp. The refugees are sandwiched between warlords, Muru on one side, Inhad on the other. Lila never used to notice who's in charge. "Since when do you follow politics, Lila?"

"Timbuktu's project is pure politics. And Timbuktu is our sole supplier now. Like it or not, they own me and everyone in camp."

"And you really think Timbuktu will pull the plug if they don't get the disposal contract?"

"You know what's at stake," Lila says. "You know better than anyone—you've seen the bids. What are they worth—billions, right? Without your help there *is* no Timbuktu Earthwealth. The backers will pull out in a heartbeat."

The people around us have paused to listen. They look on and meet my eyes with queasy sympathetic frowns. This Lila person is uninvited.

"Ty, please. Give them what they want."

Lila has moved on. Bud glides into the awkward little hush she left behind.

"Mr. Campbell." Bud smiles warmly into my eyes. "Want to play hooky and take a walk in the Stadtpark?"

Bud squires me out, laying hands on shoulders, waving clipped greetings. People are watching us leave together. "Bud, is this a good idea?"

"Don't worry," Bud says. "Everybody figures I'm kissing your ass. They don't know I'm your paymaster."

We veer away from the park, circling and backtracking—to shake off tails, Bud says. My soles are wobbling on the stones of the Graben, where we walk through the late-afternoon shadow of the cathedral. The shops are clearly desperate from Ushi's latest waste strike. Some have resorted to discounting.

Bud stops by the Roman ruins. We are standing over a pit dug to excavate ancient stone foundations. Bud props his backside against a rail at the pit's edge and looks out across the square. Without turning our heads we can see if someone comes within twenty yards. No one will eavesdrop.

Bud says, "Lila did a nice job in there, didn't she? People say she's a loose cannon, but I knew she would make a splash with that wild-eyed prophetess act."

So Bud flew her in. "I don't think it's an act, Bud."

"Well, if she's not acting, she's the only one. All this posturing, the razzle-dazzle debate, it's just for public consumption. We have a deal. Minatom will withdraw their bid and, shortly after, the State Department will coincidentally announce a big new aid package for Russia. The Authority, they'll just fade away. They can't do a thing without multilateral credit, and we control that. Their only hope is an appeal to the U.N., a Security Council resolution mandating we do it their way. But that's not going to happen. Russia will veto any resolution. All you need to do is give us your objective scientific seal of approval."

"So Russia just rolls over, huh? Did Ushi help cut this deal?"

"We're dealing at the highest levels. Ushi has no say in this."

My hotel suite overlooks the Graben. The other panel members stay in adjoining suites. We are all within steps of the conference room where we work. The security staff sends curious guests away. I live on room-service breakfasts, working lunches eaten in, and business dinners. I seldom notice what I eat, although my fare varies as it never did in the Sahara. I've hardly seen Vienna, and this suits me. It is a gray city, the color of a bureaucrat's suit. The streets are gray. The masonry is gray. The river reflects gray sky as it flows between gray concrete banks.

I will enjoy some brief escapes: the panel needs someone to inspect each bidder's demonstration site. I am elected. Alone among the panelists I have dug holes and read cores and wrestled gushers. I will submit incisive trip reports to be swept instantly aside in the panel's give-and-take.

Here in Vienna I do nothing myself. Everything depends on others' concurrence or approval or cooperation. In Africa I did only what I could do alone. Now I am jointly, infinitesimally responsible for everything. Our work is all maybe-this-if-maybe-that or maybe-not, an imaginary trickle of agreements and consensus. It evaporates faster than water on a black desert rock, and we broker new agreements, forgetting the old ones.

I would like to fix a pump or fetch water or sprinkle lime on shit. Now I'm just sweeping fine sand that creeps back around me.

Our panel has adjourned for the day. Today's debate was like a lovers' quarrel in an adopted language, flaring tempers hobbled by the need to think. I am blurred from the session, all hot eyes and slow ears.

"Ty." Faye is coiled on the couch. "Did you see it today?"

"See what?"

"The shimmering on the map."

"No."

"It wasn't my imagination." She says it insistently, as if I doubt her.

"I wasn't looking for it."

"I still can't figure it out," she says. "I've been poking around on the think tanks' Web sites, looking for something that might explain it: theories, experiments, anything. There's a paper in the archives of a think tank in town. It reports on an experiment with the Crystal Ball, or something just like it: what if this, what if that.

"I went to talk to the author. It was very nice and courtly until I asked to see that paper. Then he looked at me like I had snakes for hair. He wanted to know, How did you find out about that? I showed him where I found the abstract: on a little Internet backwater that probably gets two hits a year. When he saw it there, his jaw dropped and his face got white. He deleted the reference on the spot and then he kicked me out."

"It probably has nothing to do with shimmering maps."

"You're right," she says, "but I have to find out. Can you help me get that report? Do you maybe know somebody?"

"I've spent the last four years in absolute solitude," I say. "You're in trouble if you're counting on my contacts."

"Well, please try to think of something," Faye says. "That report is important. I can feel it."

The plane is banking over a mottled turquoise sea. The leather first-class seats are mostly empty. Jamaica is too hot this time of year, unless you can loll in the chilled air of the Authority's headquarters. They have summoned me to listen and learn.

The Authority is what its name suggests. It resides in a cool graceful building with contemptuous guards. Their windows face the sea, not the shanties of Kingston. They draw in visitors with smooth efficiency from plane to car to portal past polite and conscientious gatekeepers. I am expected; this is the first of the bidder demonstrations.

Theriault's white-walled anteroom has no coat rack or rest room. The hushed bustle of the office flows smoothly around me. The anteroom is not conspicuously opulent; this, I surmise, is not frugality but logic. The Authority under Theriault has no outsiders to impress. It works independently of the wider world it controls. The office speaks of power: not popular support or earned responsibility but an old-time Third World gift of fiat and kibosh.

The waiting room has ganged chairs of blond wood with removable cushions. It's mildly institutional, somewhere between a doctor's office and an airport. A man walks into Theriault's office. His forehead is sweating in the air-conditioned cold. His gaze darts, and his hair is unruly. He radiates anxiety. I wonder what the emergency is.

I'm kept waiting another twenty minutes, and in that time I see two more of Theriault's subordinates come and go. Both have variants of the same syndrome. He must recruit people who scare easily.

Theriault comes out to meet me, warm and dignified in his silky suit. He squires me in with a hand on my shoulder blade.

"Cigarette?"

I decline.

"Good," he says, "I abhor the habit." He lights one. "I regret that I have no cannabis to offer you. A lapse of hospitality on my part."

"What?"

"Your evening recreation is an open secret. I'm sure none of the panelists would begrudge you a little relaxation."

Bewilderment bunches my face up and slows my thoughts. "I don't smoke cannabis. I don't smoke anything."

He exhales ostentatiously away from me as though the jet of smoke will stay right there. "Here we take a sophisticated view of the matter. This is Jamaica, after all."

He must be referring to Faye and her pot. Maybe he's got me under surveillance.

"No puritanical Americans here," he says. "Back home, perhaps, illicit drugs could compromise you, but not here."

He's hinting at blackmail, the prick, stressing his tolerance only to point up the contrast with U.S. law. He smiles. "In my view, cultural sensitivity demands gracious acceptance of hospitality in all its forms. Have you tried *miraa*? It's an African drug. Kenyan. Nothing like it."

Looking hard, I say, "Oh, that's right—you're an old East Africa hand. Burundi, wasn't it? How are the *genocidaires* these days?" I get up, excusing myself.

He acts like he runs the world, too, but his little hermetic office world does not matter in the desert.

Theriault seems unfazed by my tantrum. He makes a point of watching closely when he talks to me, but he treats me with the same superficial politesse. In any case, the time for informality is past. They are briefing me into submission. Twelve hours each day, colorful images snap remorselessly into focus on the screen, one after another. Lunch rolls in on carts, but Theriault and his earnest scientists ignore it. They take me through their scrupulous selection process, showing me hundreds of possible sites, proving theirs is best.

I start out making notes, hoping to impress them with the quality of my mind ("slide 34 is inconsistent with slide 242C") but there are no inconsistencies, only subtleties that surpass my understanding. I stop squirming and submit to the force-feeding.

Not that my education is monotonous. They lead me past wave tanks with HO-gauge geysers and quakes. They bring mud pies of glutinous seabed muck so I can feel its felicitous properties. They show me seismographs and rainbow-hued sonar panoramas. There is little to see; the sea floor is calm there, in the Gulf of Guinea, and flat, with gentle ripples like dunes. They show me countless graphs of cost and benefit and effectiveness. Their plan is costly, but beneficial and effective.

At noon on the fourth day the room brightens. The authorities rise in unctuous pride. They present me with a certificate attesting to my enlightenment and a foot-high stack of sea-green binders.

Theriault says, "You will be seeing the other proposed sites, and we do not underestimate the importance of firsthand inspection. We recommend that you see our site too."

We flew to Tenerife and embarked on an Authority vessel. It's a seagoing tug, I'm told, converted for research and support. The only conversion I can see is the brass-and-mahogany decor in Theriault's quarters. Now, sated with dinner, we slip toward the Tropic of Cancer in the dark. The waves nudge us side to side. I sit with Theriault in the officers' mess, sharing a bottle of his Armagnac.

Theriault watches me with arched brows. "Your colleagues on the panel seem to hold you in high esteem."

A couple of times in my previous life I've fallen for this trick: flatter the guy and get him talking. It fails now not because I'm wary but because the esteem of my peers is valueless to me. "I'm sure my colleagues aren't saying much about the work of the panel," I say. "That's strictly confidential."

"Of course," Theriault says, "but people trust one another at this level. You have clearly won the trust and regard of all the panelists—with one possible exception." Theriault shrugs his brows. "But that's just politics."

Theriault's good: tweak my ego and pique my curiosity, and try to learn something from my questions. But he has not reckoned on my apathy.

He tops up my glass. Theriault has been inhaling and moistening his lips rather than drinking. I would drink if he did, but boozy conviviality is clearly not his goal.

"I trust you're doing your spadework," Theriault says. "For example: have you asked Timbuktu Earthwealth who their local partners are? Do you know? The government of Mali doesn't support them. They may have to get in bed with some unsavory characters."

His pupil-less eyes are searching my face. "Or maybe they don't need local partners. They have thugs from Janissary Systems to intimidate the locals. Have you met any of them? Animals, all of them. The higher up they sit, the worse they are. There's one in particular. His forehead slopes like a caveman. Sometimes he goes by the name Mumm. He's the worst of them."

Theriault puts his glass aside and leans forward. "You'll hear a lot of bluster from Timbuktu Earthwealth. Don't let Bud Van Sickle fool you. Timbuktu Earthwealth is stymied, stopped dead."

We have reached the dump site, where the disposal ship waits. It's a float-on-float-off tramp steamer, scabby and overburdened—I can't see the load lines on the hull. This is the first sign of budget constraints I've seen.

I'm with Theriault and some crewmen in the bridge of the Authority ship. It's reassuringly ugly and utilitarian after Theriault's tug. The wind lops the crests off the waves. A feeding frenzy agitates a patch of sea to port. Theriault has been walking me through the disposal operation. The ship unloads by squatting in the water. The stern will submerge, a well will fill, and the penetrator will float free. Most of its volume is air. The crews will let water into its void tanks to sink it.

A voice squawks from an intercom grille in the bulkhead: "We have company."

Theriault lifts his head and says, "This is a restricted dive site. Get rid of them."

"We've tried, but they're here to interfere."

"Who is it?"

"It's *Simpleton.*" Ushi's eco–pirate ship. Greenfleet is here.

A mate points out the tip of *Simpleton*'s mast, pricking the horizon like a sewing needle. Almost imperceptibly, the crow's nest rises into view.

Theriault is squeezing his binoculars. "Look at all the cameras," he says. "If those were guns, she'd be a dreadnought."

The captain says, "It's not their style to stay at telephoto range. They'll probably send a Zodiac full of protesters."

"If she comes within a thousand yards, I'm going to seize her."

"Ushi's aboard. She hailed us herself," the mate says.

The pause that follows has not run its course before we hear three booms in rapid succession. "Toy cannons," says the mate. "Three quick reports—that's a distress signal."

"Don't do anything high-handed," Theriault says. "Take her at face value as long as we can."

The captain raises Ushi on the radio. "*Simpleton,* do you require assistance?"

Ushi's lilting Heidi-voice: "All earth is in distress. You are endangering the maritime environment in contravention of the Law of the Sea Treaty. You are violating your own charter."

Theriault grabs the mike and says, "You are approaching a restricted area. Do not enter the area demarcated by our buoys."

Ushi signs off without comment. *Simpleton* furls her sails and drifts in the distance.

It is time for Theriault's demonstration. We will observe from the bridge of the Authority's ship. The penetrator has floated into view, a big needle half submerged. They must have ripped the guts out of the ship to make it fit. They have flushed the void tanks in the nose, and the missile is swinging down, held at the surface by the aft air tanks. Streamlined as it is, it will disappear with hardly a ripple.

It feels like we're sinking, but we're not. The stern door is open and the deck slopes now: 4 percent trim, noticeable, but not hazardous except in heavy seas. The trim gives the boat a slushy waggling motion in the swells. The crew will seal the stern and pump it out before they drop the penetrator.

Theriault's snarl turns me around. Two Greenfleet Zodiacs are approaching. One carries Ushi and another woman; cameramen follow in the other raft. "Get a duck down there *now,*" Theriault says, and a crew of four rushes it over the side.

The Authority raft is on its way out to intercept them. It buzzes like a wasp, raising spray in three-foot swells. It's coming full speed, and one Authority crewman has a nasty-looking grapple out. The women doff their slickers and plop overboard.

The Authority sailors are at a loss. Underneath their slickers Ushi and her sidekick have swimsuits, air vests, and diminutive tanks. They sink with mask and fins in hand. The other woman has a video camera in a Plexiglas box.

Theriault roars into the radio. "Follow the bubbles. Stay on top of them."

One of the crewmen slashes Ushi's raft with the hook, and the outboard's weight swamps it. "They can't go far," the radio says. "They only have pony bottles. They've got twenty minutes down, at most."

The Authority crew putts tentatively back toward the ship. The sailors are squinting down, looking for the divers. "The bubbles are very diffuse. They must be deep. That's good, it cuts their dive time."

"Don't let them approach the ship." Theriault is seething.

"Not much we can do now." The speaker distorts the sound of a crewman snickering through his nose, and Theriault's look says someone will pay for this.

Trailed at a distance by the Greenfleet camera crew, the Authority's raft moves out of our sight beneath the rail. "They went under the hull."

Theriault replies, "Get to the penetrator and watch for them." His raft buzzes toward the stern in response.

"One's up, filming, thirty meters off"—then the engine drowns him out as they go after her.

"Did you pick her up?"

"She's down again."

Theriault says, "What are they doing?"

From the radio in Theriault's hand we hear, "Wait. Something just surfaced. A nine-inch plastic tube."

The raft buzzes over to it. "Papers. Some kind of legal bullshit."

"Who does she think she is? *We* administer the Law of the Sea." Theriault's face is a dark strangled red. I imagine he doesn't have much experience coping with public defiance, here in his element. Heretofore he's been salving obscure insecurities with his King Neptune act. Now, in his first real exposure to the glare of publicity, it's all falling apart.

From the raft, "They're moving."

When the Authority raft comes in view of the bridge it's darting erratically. Theriault yells, "What are you doing?"

"They split up."

"Get the one with the camera," Theriault says.

Under someone's breath but clear through the mike we hear, "How the fuck do we know which is which?"

"I said, Get the one with the camera."

The remaining Greenfleet raft is keeping well away.

From the radio, "She's up, her air is gone."

Theriault demands, "Which one?"

"Can't tell. She took a breath and went under again. She won't get far that way."

The other diver has surfaced in the distance. The Greenfleet raft is closer, and the Greens scoop her up.

From Theriault's crew, "They got the camera."

"Leave Ushi. Get them," Theriault yells.

"The Zodiac is too far away. They'll outrun us. We should pick Ushi up and see if we can get them to come back."

But the Greenfleet Zodiac heads full throttle back toward *Simpleton.*

"They're leaving Ushi with no air and no buddy."

"You had better rescue her, then." Theriault's voice has returned to normal, except for an ominous vibration in the lower registers.

A mate says, "Put some chum out. She'll pop up if we draw a few sharks." I think he's kidding.

I see Ushi's head come up. The Authority raft is a few yards away. It rears up and shoots over, hits her as she jackknifes for a surface dive. They grab for her legs. She kicks free and slithers down, but one sailor comes away with a fin.

Ushi is popping up in unpredictable spots, but she must be

winded. She can only swim a few yards between breaths. The raft runs at her when she surfaces, cutting the outboard at the last instant.

The Greenfleet raft has come back. The two rafts are facing off, watching to see where Ushi comes up next. It will be a race to pick her up.

Ushi surfaces a few yards away. The Greenfleet raft darts toward her but Theriault's men bump them and box them out. Her snorkel sucks air a bit too long. The Authority raft skids and rocks and Ushi slides into it headfirst, kicking and thrashing. Through the mike we hear her choking and coughing, Theriault's men yelling as they pile on, *Go, go, go, go,* until the outboard drowns it out.

Greenfleet has a Web site, of course. It tells their side of the story. One link is a thick sans-serif headline that screams, U.N. FLOUTS LONDON DUMPING CONVENTION, and for the specialists, endless paragraphs of closely reasoned legal argument.

The site has a link in the shape of a bull's-eye labeled TARGET: EARTH. It shows seaquake isoseismals rippling over the dump site and submarine volcanoes lurking to the northeast. It shows forty-seven species of seabed prokaryotes. Gory animation subjects the bugs to the mutagenic properties of ionizing radiation. Taking a leaf from Bud's book, it shows the Benguela Current before and after dumping: cold and strong to begin with, then curling in feeble eddies.

It has a picture gallery: penetrators in port, winched to the vertical, looking nasty and ballistic. A grainy blowup of a phallic business end ready to penetrate. The tiny Greenfleet raft bobbing under the prow of Theriault's ship, porpoises abaft in innocent play. The Authority vessel has been digitally retouched, darkening it to a menacing Deathstar hue. The sea takes on the brilliant reefy blue of travel posters.

Best of all, concerned citizens everywhere can click on a streaming video link and watch Ushi crash the demo in near-real time.

Television networks are scrambling to keep up. They compensate by airing the dramatic bits with their most obsessive attention.

The video starts with Ushi and a small fair woman, viewed from the other Greenfleet raft. The smaller woman sits at the tiller. Ushi's sitting at the prow, seasick in the swells—she turns from the camera to heave demurely over the side, then splashes her face with seawater.

The Authority raft is bearing down on Greenfleet. The camera cuts to the women as they shrug out of their slickers and slip overboard. We're underwater with them now. Ushi is porpoising, fins together, arms trailing, flexing her spine to swim. The hull of the Authority's ship looms ahead. Ushi folds and dives under it. She pushes off the keel, and the camera zooms in on it. Rust and barnacles hint at neglect and hidden weaknesses. The camera rises with Ushi's bubbles until it breaks the surface. It pans along the hull.

The snarl of the Authority's boat grows louder. The camerawoman tracks it as it comes around the stern. Big men with black watch caps bellow down and grab. She doesn't sink out of reach until the raft is a few feet away. When the camera goes under we see the raft from below. The propeller freewheels lethally.

Now we see Ushi in her virginal white swimsuit. Immersed, her hair is a wild black mop. With a slightly stagy flourish she produces a plastic cylinder and lets it float up from her hand. She watches it rise out of view. The camera zooms in to her mask. She's trying to put up the Saint Joan face, but something is tugging her eyes askew: a joyful and faintly demented glitter. It's a shame they can't show Theriault fuming on a split screen.

The camera follows Ushi as she porpoises down and out of the ship's shadow. Now it looks up at a menacing shaft. The penetrator hangs there as though it could drop at any time. You want to yell, *Get out of there.* A wide shot shows how it dwarfs Ushi. If it went down now it would suck her fathoms under in its wake.

Ushi is moving again. She grays and dims as the divers split up.

Now we see it from the Greenfleet raft. Ushi breaks the surface and gasps a few breaths. Her legs slip away as the Authority raft bears down. She surfaces and sinks again. Each time she comes up, the Authority raft is closer. She can only poke her head up for a quick breath and sink. The fourth time, the raft strikes her head, ducking her in midgasp. They pull her aboard and fall on her. The raft returns to the Authority ship, and nothing can be seen of Ushi until she is hauled up hog-tied in the raft, hair in her face, coughing and choking in the grip of black-clad men.

"Flood the tanks and drop it," Theriault says.

"Are we sure no one is down there?"

"Two came and two left," Theriault says. "Drop the penetrator."

No splash, just a burp and a ripple.

"Twenty knots. Thirty knots, forty. Sixty knots, ninety knots. . . . Impact." I feel a little shudder.

"Well within CEP."

That's good, I know, nice and accurate. As they have explained to me, CEP is circular error probable, ballistic-missile talk for accuracy. Dr. Strangelove would be proud. Theriault barely notices, though. Ushi spoiled it for him.

I say, "Where's Ushi?" I have determined to make a stink.

"We're putting her in seclusion in the infirmary."

"I want to speak with her."

Theriault says, "Wait. I'll get you an escort."

"I want to speak with her alone. I don't want her intimidated by the presence of the people detaining her."

"Ushi, intimidated? When has Ushi ever been intimidated?"

"No escort."

"Under the circumstances, we can't leave anyone alone with her. She is too vulnerable."

Theriault promised me an escort two hours ago, and I'm still getting nothing but doubletalk. I go down to the infirmary. It's locked up tight—I can unfasten the watertight dogs but the door itself won't budge. I work my way around the locked room. I keep to the left wall, trying more doors. Fluorescent glare zings off steel fittings. The thin ridged carpet is dark and damp.

I turn a corner and pull up short before a buzz-cut crewman with a banyan trunk of a neck. His shoulders block the narrow corridor like a cork. He's one of the men who took Ushi in. "Are you medical staff?"

I'm too startled to be uncomfortable with the lie. "Yes."

"Where's your I.D.?"

"In my quarters, sorry"—and I catch a wave of bullshit, briefly my old self again—"Her monitor beeped me. I hope she hasn't swallowed her tongue. We sedated her quite aggressively."

He looks uncertain. "I have to call."

"Right, call, but let me in there right now, *now*."

He's fumbling with the keys. When the door swings in, I push through it. He peers anxiously past me. Over my shoulder I snap, "Don't gawk," and close the door behind me. A dizzying smell of acetone and diesel fumes.

Now I'm standing rooted, staring at Ushi wrapped up like a mummy on a metal bunk, strapped down and thrashing, on the edge of hysteria. Her eyes are big and pink and wet. She takes brief, shallow breaths, then gulps air uncontrollably.

"Let me out, you are trying to kill me."

"I'm an independent observer," I say. "I'm with the Atomic Energy Agency."

"Stay with me. They are drugging me. Needles every hour. Skin patches."

The dogs squeak in the door behind me. Theriault enters with the guard, who's waiting elbows in, claws out.

"What are you doing here?"

"Evaluating the condition of your detainee," I say.

"They are trying to choke me." Her voice rises to a shriek. "Make them *STOP*!"

Theriault's voice has that ominous buzz again. "She's under medical supervision. You are subverting our efforts to care for her. I don't have to tolerate this at sea."

"Who wrapped her up like that?" I ask.

"That's a cold sheet pack. It has a harmless sedative effect. The more she struggles, the warmer it gets."

Theriault sits on the bed and brushes the hair from her face. "Ms. Lassen, please."

She spits in his face, thwacks a big defiant viscous one, and Theriault recoils. She shrieks, "Poisoner!"

"Why don't you just send her back to *Simpleton*?"

"Get him out of here," Theriault says, and the hand on my neck feels like the clamshell on one of Bud's steam shovels, then I'm skimming down the corridor in a half-nelson and a hammerlock, and the guard is cranking my elbow to steer. He throws me in my berth, where I'm kept until we land.

Later they slide a report under my door. The demo was a success, of course. Penetrator casing intact. Telemetry functional. Impact well within the CEP. The report even has a heading entitled "Stakeholder Participation and Protection." That means roughing Ushi up. She's back on board *Simpleton* now. Theriault is through with her.

Success or failure doesn't matter, though. Theriault is simply entertaining an insignificant technician. The success of his plan depends on power brokers, not experts. On the panel we will rate his disposal plan according to strict rules, filling out prepared checklists and feeding them to computers. Forms for Theriault's technical acumen. Forms for his experience and capacity. Nowhere on the forms will there be a box labeled "Egomaniac mad scientist."

Theriault granted me no more audiences. He had taciturn flunkies put me on a plane to Vienna.

Now I'm back, writing up a trip report for the panel. I'll report to Bud in person. He has left me an encrypted E-mail summoning me to Safe House B, north of the Danube. It would be an easy walk from the hotel if not for all the ducking and weaving and waiting and watching he lays out step by step. I appreciate his caution better now. Theriault's watchers are out there somewhere, waiting for me to do drugs with Faye, or worse.

The safe house is a small apartment in a high-rise. When I get there Bud is flicking a black light into nooks and crannies. He unplugs the telephone and motions me to a small square dining table. He sets his elbows on the table, looking ready to spring, and debriefs me on the trip. I start with Ushi's stunt and Theriault's response.

"I'll tell you," Bud says, "Theriault's a pro: psychological pressure applied to her weakness. He used the stink to get at her hypochondria. I'll bet she could feel the lung cancer growing."

"So he contrived those diesel fumes and chemical smells?"

"Did you smell them anywhere else on board?" Bud is smiling in honest admiration. "Nice touch, the cold sheet pack. Morbid, morguey, don't you think? Cerements of the grave and all that. Attention to detail, that's the key."

"Why? Is he that vindictive?"

"Teach her a lesson," Bud says. "Ushi's broken now. She won't mess with Theriault again. He probably extracted a lot of intel about Greenfleet's plans."

"But the Authority is getting reamed in the media worldwide," I say.

"True," Bud says. "Ushi won that round on points, no question about it."

"She's got guts."

"You read her profile, she's a counterphobe. She has to pull stunts like that to control her fears. She runs her whole life to protect herself from disease." Bud watches his hand do some martial arts contortions, locking the fingers to make a rake, a blade, a wrench, a club. "She's lucky she took on the Authority first. She learned her lesson, no harm done. If she tried to fuck with Timbuktu Earthwealth, there would be no psychological patty-cake. She would be a very sorry girl."

12

Ushi has not said a public word about her treatment on Theriault's ship. Perhaps she's ashamed of the weakness it exposed. The public sees her as a fearless crusader. Ushi broken by a stinkbomb: that would spoil the picture.

Back in Vienna, our panel has been languishing. The fight for the waste goes on in obscure world courts: the Authority enjoining, Minatom appealing, Timbuktu Earthwealth objecting, principles and precedents squeezed silently through unknown tribunals like a rat inside a snake. The sense of it all disappears bit by bit, digested in decisions and appeals and reviews. All we can do is wait.

Not everyone is standing idly by. In the papers Faye picks up rumblings:

MALI WITHHOLDS APPROVAL OF DISPOSAL PLAN

BAMAKO, MALI—The president of Mali rejected an act of Mali's National Assembly, delaying a controversial plan to set land aside for a nuclear-waste disposal site.

Mali's President Aras Bozo announced the decision in a radio address. "The plan at issue will affect Mali's territory for a thousand years," he said. "In a matter of such importance, the people of Mali must decide, directly, after careful public deliberations." Bozo stated his intention to conduct a referendum on the disposal plan.

"Refugees have settled near the site," Bozo said. "A mishap at the dump site would threaten their safety. Local instability increases the risk of an accident."

The corporate consortium hoping to carry out the disposal plan reacted strongly to the announcement, calling it a "shakedown." B. D. Van Sickle of Timbuktu Earthwealth said, "Mali is holding out for more money. It's that simple." By Timbuktu Earthwealth's calculations, the plan would make Mali "the Kuwait of Africa," with the continent's highest per capita income.

Speaking from his headquarters in Djenné, military leader Mansa Muru denounced Bozo. "Bozo is weak. He is fit only to govern a nation of powerless beggars. His mongrel clique prefers starvation to prosperity, charity to industry. Bozo is a cancer, sapping Mali's lifeblood. He must be excised with the knife." Muru faces international charges of war crimes and genocide, but he has established control over a large territory in southern Mali.

The panel is in session but I've slipped away. I've gone off to a bench in the Stadtpark to call Bud. He wants to discuss these ructions in Mali. The wind is boisterous and Bud's emollient voice is soft. I'm grinding the handset on my ear to hear.

"Don't worry about Bozo," Bud says. "Instability in Mali is not a factor."

"I don't know, Bud."

"We've got Mali fully pacified."

"Tell the warlords that."

"The warlords don't scare us," he says. "We're going to show the flag. Meet us there. We'll give you a tour of the emplacement site.

"We want to pay Lila a courtesy call," Bud says. "Maybe you can get there a couple days early and soften her up for us. We have to bring some Janissary people along for security. She's not too fond of them."

⁂

Packing up my suite to get the sleepout rate, I'm diverted by Faye's knock. "Where are you going?" she asks.

"Back to Mali."

"Be careful, Ty. Sam says the government is on shaky ground. He thinks Bozo has made some powerful enemies."

"Like who?"

"He didn't say."

"If Bozo's government fell, it wouldn't change things at the camp. The warlords control the north anyway."

"What if the warlords came to blows? The camp is right in between them." She stands tall as she can and frowns, a mother hen.

"Nobody's going to start a fight," I say. "The balance of power is rock solid."

Faye says, "Watch yourself getting there. The airport in Bamako gets shelled sometimes. The bandits are worst in government territory."

"I'll have an escort of Janissary goons courtesy of Timbuktu Earthwealth."

"Pressures are building up there, Ty. That place is getting touchier by the minute."

I wonder what it looks like from the cockpit.

Faye needn't have worried. I flew into Mali on a Timbuktu Earthwealth plane. My Range Rover bears the magic word *Janissary.* Bud paved the way.

I am back. The earth yields in a familiar way as I dig the door out of the drifts. My home is undisturbed inside. It has escaped ransacking. Inside it is just as I left it: not straightened, like a house, but packed, like a suitcase. The windows' glaze of tiny scratches is worse than I remember.

How did I live here? I can't even sit down. The place is a tomb, lifeless and desiccated and full of *gōn gōn*. When they say ashes to ashes and dust to dust, *gōn gōn* is the kind of dust they mean. It's the opposite of life.

The tape has released Hissi's flower drawing. When I pick it up it leaves a dustless rectangle on the floor.

The drive to the camp seemed to take a long time. Finally, here it is. Seen from above on the hillside it looks like a camp, with tents and tanks and currents of calm activity. It has grown. It still sprawls without bounds, not ending but fading to haze. Now, though, the shelters seem more tightly packed.

Lila's frisking toward me. The sight of her is no more vivid than my thoughts have been. I'm congealed in an incipient embrace, and my eyes are incongruously moist. Lila is intrigued. She clearly sees something new—glum silent Ty as a mawkish oaf, I guess. She puts her hands on me and waltzes me around: "Look. Do you believe it?"

The camp is no longer on the edge. A truck arrives weekly with food. Sometimes it brings relief supplies: Lila has a Rubbhall now, an inflatable warehouse stacked high with cholera kits, vaccines, tents, tools.

Lila completed her playground and painted it in garish emergency colors. When a shipment brought hoes, Fatimatou diverted one of the well tubes to moisten a patch of sand. The able-bodied climb the hill to groom the struggling shoots. Some of the refugees bought hens from the traders who skulk in the buffer zone. The camp is worth trading with now. Some of Bud's shipments bring cash, and the peace is such that coins and notes have their uses.

In every country, no matter how torn, long hours of normalcy remain: not plenty, or even security, but the precious luxury of routine. Here in the camp, those hours have stretched to weeks.

Bud has arrived at the camp. We sit at a fiberboard table in the new mess tent. Lila has interrupted her rounds to entertain Bud and his entourage: a freelance geologist and a driver from Janissary. We eat cafeteria-style from portable steam tables, with a choice of porridge or couscous.

The geologist has a skinny neck and a big nose. He likes to call things "professional," meaning good. He clearly spends most of his time in the office, not the field. Bud's driver sneers at his plate. The faces he puts up make his neck muscles ripple.

Lila says, "Look at that body. For exercise he rips pagan babies limb from limb."

The driver grins, and it is clear from Lila's face that she has tried and failed to provoke him. Bud says, "Lila, Janissary keeps the roads clear for you."

Lila says, "Clear except for the human road kill."

I say, "The food has improved." They're ready to stop sparring, and their eyes snap onto me.

The geologist sniffs the electricity in the air and plunges ahead. "So who is Janissary Systems?"

"We're a security firm," the driver says. "We specialize in large-scale jobs. We can secure anything from a factory complex to a border. We've got five thousand employees on retainer, and we call them up as needed. We have forty million dollars in net fixed assets."

"Fixed assets?"

"Weapons," he says.

Bud says, "Janissary recruits retired military from the world centers of excellence. South Africa, Britain, the U.S."

"And Pakis," the driver says. "Their number one export, soldiers of fortune. These aren't mujahideen wildmen, either: Paki mercs are professionals. I'm sure you've noticed that the influx of refugees has slowed. That's because of us. We've taken down all the checkpoints, neutralized the gangs and the rebels and the rogue army platoons."

Bud breaks in. "Have you talked to Mumm? He wants to know about those bandit attacks in Kidal."

At the mention of Mumm the big soldier stops and stammers and all but crosses himself. "Mumm? I've, ah, been reporting to Mumm regularly. They're briefing me on all his current concerns."

Bud has tidied up the wolf-pack hierarchy of the table. He takes control of the conversation again. This is odd. The Janissary man doesn't fawn like a hireling should. Bud seems prickly and defensive. Are the warriors and technocrats at odds? Who's the boss?

"Get the camcorder," Bud says, and soon we're posing, pointing at a map. The gratitude in Lila's face is real. I'm nodding gravely, the perfect shill, as Bud addresses me: "I'm here to tell you there's no worry about country risk. If the IAEA executes a contract with us, we are going to strike out the force majeure clause. We don't need it, because nothing can stop us. We'll get the job done, no matter what."

It is cold in the desert at night. We are sitting in front of a fire, Bud and I, Fatimatou, and a few of the women. It's an African kitchen: a pot on three rocks. The fire is a red glow hugging charcoal and acacia twigs. It glimmers up and out of a shallow pit, flaring orange on our faces when fat drips or sap catches. Everything else is outside the fire's reach, even the ground beneath us, and the darkness negates it all.

Bud is a genial folklorist here, holding forth on what it's like in India, in Myanmar, in Afghanistan. He speaks mostly to Fatimatou, who translates for the women in quick wry undertones. Now Bud is telling us about a Chinese banquet at which the diners scooped brains from a live monkey's skull. Bud was not there, but he heard about it. Every Western expat believes this story with a catechist's calm faith, but I have never met anyone who personally ate live monkey brains. Of course I do not point this out. It is not my place to puncture Bud's tame rational scare stories. When you pilot the whole world from a computer console, as Bud does, you understand everything. The unknown is a rare treat.

Serata appears above us. A boy is leading her gently into our little cocoon of light. The jumping shadows of the flames set her scars in motion, but the firelight is no threat to her now. Though she is still epileptic, the flickering light will not make her fall again. She is blind now, and does not resonate to the flames as she once did.

The refugees do not pity her. Serata is revered in camp. Falling into the fire, she lost everything. But she gained something, too, they say. They smile when I ask what they mean: a European wouldn't understand. An American? A can-do rocket-ship American millionaire with his freezer and his big car most certainly would not understand.

But now Bud understands, a little. He sees a blind woman bound up in a stiff caul of roasted flesh, and he is shaken. His cockpit illuminates the whole world; but Serata is outside the cockpit's little pool of light, in the vaster gloom.

Bud is ready to sign a trillion-dollar contract and toss aside the force majeure clause. He promises to handle acts of war and acts of God. But now it is dark and Serata presides. She left her body and passed through fire, relinquished her eyes and here she is, rubbing her hands, cupping the chastened warmth.

Maybe there are things even Bud can't control.

It's day, and Bud has mastered the desert again. We are skimming over the dunes in Bud's big hovercraft. We sit belowdecks in a roar of compressors and rushing air. We are going to Timbuktu Earthwealth's demonstration site twenty kilometers north of the camp. Bud has brought his geologist, along with Lila and Fatimatou.

I have not been at this spot before. I could never have come here alone. We are crossing a sand sea with great swells and secret depths. The hovercraft floats on it. I can imagine diving in it, swimming in it, drowning in it. Thrown overboard out here a man would sink and die. This sea is more limitless than the watery kind. Not even a horizon bounds it. A ridge rims it in the east like the last glimpse of land. In every other direction the world's edge melts into shimmering heat.

Bud spends most of his time on the satellite phone. The hovercraft is loud, but Bud bellows, so I hear snatches over the roar. "Stay in the background. Support only. . . . Make sure you don't cut off his exit. . . . Has Mumm seen the plan?"

The hovercraft settles in the dunes. I step out of the hatch and the heat presses in, squeezing me dry, drawing off my sweat. Maybe I've forgotten what it's like, but the heat seems worse: airless and awful, like the pain of a burned hand all over with nowhere to recoil. Vienna must have softened me.

Bud says, "Can you think of a better place to put the waste?"

At this moment I cannot, because I don't believe in hell.

Bud is comfortable in the role of guide: "This is small-scale proof of concept work. Eventually we'll need hundreds of pits. Now we have one pit to show each stage of the project. This one shows the first step. Those piles interlock at the edges. We drive them in a ring to make a deep cylinder like a tall tin can—it's the only way to keep the sand back."

A mechanized sledge hangs from a gantry crane, bigger than my home but tiny up there. The thud of the pile drivers slaps my feet. "Those piles are only temporary. We're just going to yank them out again. That's a twenty-seven-ton hammer; but deep as we can drive, it's only the beginning. When we drive a ring of piles and empty it out, then the real digging starts, down in the bottom of the pit."

Bud points with his chin. "See that mirage?" It's a sky-blue blob floating in the yellow haze. "A thirty-acre solar furnace. That's where we get our power. Later on we'll top that up with gas-fired capacity and Algerian gas."

Fatimatou says, "What's the chance the desert will recede and give us back this land?"

The geologist bounces his Adam's apple. "You'll be safe thinking of it as desert for the next thousand years."

If I'm posing as an independent expert, I might as well act the part. "There's water down below," I say. "How do you plan to keep the waste from leaching out?"

"We zigzag past the water with steep-decline shafts."

"But that's the trickiest way to dig," I say. "You hit the strata at an angle. The ground over your head can be half rock, half soil. You're begging for cave-ins that way."

"We're using all the most advanced techniques," Bud says. He smiles indulgently at my performance.

"You have to be drilling through wet ground at some point."

"We shore with concrete grout specially formulated for this project."

"Can I go down and take a look?"

"No," Bud says. "Absolutely not." He's glaring at me, reminding me I work for him.

"What's the problem?"

"We're using machines as much as we can, to minimize the risk. The shaft is not designed for sightseers. It's hazardous down there."

I sleep at the camp now, in the boys' tent. Pranks, snickers, and yelps wake me up every night, but I have no desire to fishtail up to my box in the hills. I'll be back in Vienna soon enough, with my private shower and suite.

Bud has gone back to Timbuktu. In his last few days here he seemed impatient to leave. He spent most of his time on the phone.

Nothing remains of Mali. Mansa Muru ousted Bozo in a bloodless coup. Ingeniously, Muru installed no successor. The National Assembly remains, terrorized and inert, waiting for a sign from Muru.

His rival Inhad did not react; Bamako was the government's last redoubt, an insignificant enclave on a silty river. Muru's Creepers crept softly in: no looting, no rape or massacres, just a few discreet disappearances. To some the very discipline of it seems suspicious: dark rumors circulate of white advisers.

Bozo reportedly escaped into the Central African Republic. He has protectors there, it's said. In better days he brokered a brief peace for them. Still, the world may never hear from him again. He's gone to darkest Africa, twenty-first-century style. It's an easy place to vanish in. No government to register foreigners. No bank drafts or credit to leave a trail, just barter or foreign cash. No rich-world journalist or diplomat will follow him there. The outside world is waiting for the unrest to burn out, and waiting patiently, mindful of the last illusory peace, which swallowed up an oil field, a World Bank mission, and a host of expats including my wife.

I wish Bozo well, but I have no hope for him in the jungle.

13

I am returning from a trip to the well. The ground is subsiding and the flow is getting sluggish. Soon we'll have to beg Bud for a new water supply. With the water in back, the truck is none too stable on the hill that overlooks the camp. I should be watching the clinometer. But something odd is happening down there.

From the hillside the camp looks like an anthill gouged with a stick. Strange trucks cluster there, intact paint glinting under dust. Figures flow among them and into the camp, clumping and breaking up, bearing bulky equipment that dwarfs them.

I pull into camp, skirting the commotion. Lila is standing by, speechless. Fatimatou has her hands on Lila's shoulders. I get out and walk toward them with my eyes on the invaders. Fantastic explanations waft through my head: *Some new sandfly fever broke out and the CDC's here. The receivers have come to seize the last assets of Ecumenical Alms.*

The crush of visitors slowly resolves itself. A dozen whites aim video cameras. More pale faces mill around them, pointing and arguing. Women with clipboards shout hopeless instructions.

Then the mob quiets all at once. It tightens like a knot. I go over to crane past their shoulders. The interlopers are looking inward toward a single point. I come within ten feet of them before one of the clipboard people says, "Stand back, please, we're filming."

A bearded Brit is confiding with a microphone in plummy tones. "The homeland of the Peulh is a harsh land, an unforgiving land."

Lila's voice: "Homeland? You think these people *live* here?" She has come over. Fatimatou is beaming scary outrage from widened eyes, but I can tell she doesn't know what to think yet.

The clipboard woman shushes viciously.

I ask, "Who are they?"

"We're filming a documentary for Greenfleet," she says.

Lila says, "I don't want to burst your bubble, but this is not their homeland. This isn't anybody's homeland, except for this white guy here." She cocks a thumb at me. "Why don't you shoot Ushi hugging him?"

I wheel around. "Ushi's here?"

"Oh, put a sock on it," Lila says. "She's past her prime."

"What's she doing here?"

"How dense are you?" Lila says. "She's trying to romanticize the camp, mobilize the tree-huggers to fight Timbuktu's dump."

The clipboard lady pushes into the film crew's midst. A chorus of voices: . . . *Not a homeland? Ach, was . . . Wanderers, then, some goatherds. Pastoral lives, good . . .*

The crowd parts for Ushi in bush hat and desert camouflage. Her indigo hair flares beneath the hat, and she flushes in the shade of the brim. Two boys follow her, sharing the load of a leather duffel.

Lila says, "Look, she's got native bearers to carry her cosmetic case."

Ushi looks at me, places me. Her eyes flick down as she smiles. She seems abashed. "Lila moved me with her words in Geneva. I had to come and see."

Lila takes Ushi's elbow and says, "Sure, we'll show you what matters here." Ushi seems startled to be taken in hand, but she is pliant and curious. The camera crew falls in behind them.

Lila tows Ushi around a rock outcrop. Ushi has only seen the ambulatory refugees, the ones with energy to gather round. Here we are among the real victims. A woman reaches out to Lila with worm-bloated elephantiasis hands. Lila genuflects and gives her a deft hug. Ushi blanches and stumbles. Her face can flash emotions like a heliograph, and now it signals her horror of contagion.

Lila's gaze sharpens. She could not have known of Ushi's hypochondria. Ushi gasps at the stained bandages on a woman's arms and legs. Her smile becomes a rictus and her eyes glaze.

"Welcome to Africa," Lila says.

Ushi's face looks like it did on the ship. She's immobilized again, but not with restraints. Lila says, "You can sell this separately as a bloopers tape."

A bullock-sized bodyguard says, "Get away from her."

Lila bellows, "This is *our* camp!" The bodyguard grabs Lila. Draped over the bodyguard's shoulder, Lila rears up like a rattler and shouts, "Your boss is a real trooper." More bodyguards close ranks around Ushi and rush her off to one of the trucks.

The bodyguard sets Lila down next to me. Lila stamps on his shin. His face twists up with the pain, but he wrenches it around to make a look of slit-eyed menace and centers his weight in an ominous way. Lila's yelling pure indignation with incidental words. Hunching submissively, I interpose myself, murmuring in Lila's ear. "You got Ushi right where it hurts," I say. "She's a hypochondriac." I don't tell her how I know.

"Then tell her, Stop posing with yucky savages. This is not her kind of place."

I go to see Ushi in her trailer. I try to talk my way past officious gatekeepers. My voice rises, and thick bodyguards lower like thunderheads until I hear Ushi's voice.

"Let him in." Her voice is like bagpipes set down, wheezing without energy.

Ushi droops over a cot, looking as weak as she sounds. A few fine lines sweep out from her eyes and down. Her skin's gray cast submerges the contours of her famous face bones. For the first time, she seems human.

"It happens to everyone," I say.

"It is different for me," she says. "It is my weakness. Sometimes I think it could kill me."

"Same thing happened to me. I almost passed out. A classic panic attack." I'm speaking in a rush, fixing her, hosing her down with comfort.

She silences me with a look. "I wish I had her strength."

"Lila's pushing her strength to the limit, most times."

"I need that kind of strength."

Maybe not. The following day I see her alone with Fatimatou, holding on for dear life, trembling, crying-laughing as she squats with the sick in the dust and the feces and the flies. She is trying to flood the fear away. This is counter to her profile. The profilers' motto doesn't seem sinister now. It seems naive. Insight, Understanding, Control? Not with guts like that.

The winds are kind this morning, whisking away aerosols from the latrine where we are working. Lila is plowing the trench under with the truck, which we've fitted with a sort of snowplow attachment. Bud's latest gift was a toy-sized backhoe. I am translating its instruction manual to a group of volunteers so they can dig a new trench.

The truck falls silent. I turn toward Lila's scuffing feet, approaching from behind. She takes my elbow and says, "Look. Ushi's found a guru."

Twenty yards away, Ushi is sitting at Serata's feet. A microphone boom hangs over the melted head as it quivers and bobs.

Lila cocks her head, pleased despite herself. "She's working on her squeamishness. I'll give her that."

Ushi is relaxed today, loose-jointed and smiling as she greets me. She stops, her entourage milling behind.

"How's your new girlfriend, Serata?" I say.

"Ah, Ty." Ushi takes my arm, not flirtatiously but to communicate something that outruns her words. "Serata is a wonder. She has a natural courtly courtesy . . . it's more than courtesy, it's kindness. You can't help sharing her delight when she hears your voice. She catches you up in her enthusiasm for whatever she's given, even if it's the same lumpy powdered milk she gets every day. Even here she is totally content."

"Crippled as she is, she would never have survived unless she could reach people in a very unusual way."

"But it's not just the survival tactics of a helpless woman. Everyone here reveres her."

"She symbolizes something for them, maybe."

"She could be a symbol for us all," Ushi says. "I want to make a series of television spots. We will show them over and over, like commercials. They will show the world the power of her contentment."

Ushi looks toward the ravaged woman sitting in the dust. "Some little girls were singing, and I saw her smile. Imagine the strength of a joy you could read in that face."

Several days of filming have passed in peace. We've begun to ignore the cameras and crews. Ushi's taking care not to blaze too brightly. I never would have thought she could blend in.

This morning some excitement has drawn me to the eastern end of camp. A few of the first-to-know are hurrying to the big tent, where they muster volunteers. Inside, the refugees are pressing around a television.

Lila collars me, squeezes me. "Look, it's the first TV spot. Serata's a star."

Fatimatou whispers, "Serata heard my voice on TV and called to me. She thought the TV was me. Then she heard another voice and said, Who's that old woman? It was her own voice!"

Serata is cackling, rocking with delight.

On the screen is Ushi's face, rapt and adoring, close as in the moment of a kiss. The camera cuts to Serata's hands, each patting and stroking the fingers of the other. Serata's hands are not scarred. In the camera's soft focus, the bloat of beriberi looks like the plumpness of a gentle grandmother.

Her words trickle over me, translated in Fatimatou's lilt.

Can you put it in your belly? If not, it's a mirage. We must all farm, nomads and settlers alike, sorghum in the clay and millet in the sand. Keep animals, too, goats and sheep and cattle, so if the one dies, the others might live. And each year, sell half, so we need not fear the death of those, at least. Stay put, don't roam for fodder; even in hard times you can get crushed cottonseeds from the oil makers. It's not so hard to find cooking fuel. The shade trees are dead, but acacias thrive, light on your head and good for charcoal. Plenty is a matter of clever cookery. We can eat tô, *dough in cakes, with powder from baobab leaves, or* tsigi*—couscous, the Arabou call it. And water only, not* dolo: *strong drink is shameful.*

It isn't so hard to live well.

Lila is beside me, driving the truck. We are heading out of camp on a run to the well when Ushi crosses our path a few yards ahead. Lila's grip on the gearshift tightens. Tendons stir beneath the skin of her hand. She cuts the wheel and noses the truck left to bring her window to Ushi. Lila looks down from the cab on her.

"I want a word with you."

"Of course," Ushi says.

"These television spots," Lila says. "The camp can use the attention, but I don't want to see anybody exploited."

"I don't understand."

"You are not going to turn Serata into your ecological poster child."

"I am not putting words in her mouth," Ushi says.

"Timbuktu Earthwealth is keeping her alive."

"I am not here to make trouble," Ushi says. "I want to help, if I can."

"I heard you in Vienna. You're out to stop Timbuktu."

"I know they feed you. I know you need them. I only want you to be safe."

"It's going to be a long time until everyone here is safe. For now, what's good for Timbuktu is good for this camp. I don't like it much either, but that's the way it is."

"I just want to help," Ushi says. "What can I do? Not Greenfleet, but me. I want to be a part of this." The refugees' need has gotten into her. It's reverberating under the surface, shaking her up like one of my seismic shots.

Lila sees that, and her whole body relents. She cuts the engine and climbs down from the truck. "We still need so much help."

I get out and walk around the truck. Lila takes my arm in a firm grip. She is leading me with a startling sibling possessiveness. It seems beneath Ushi's notice. Politely, Ushi absorbs Lila's monologue: "No matter how much money Timbuktu throws at us, supplies are undependable. This water purifier, I could run pee through it and get potable water. It's cranky, though. In the dust the generator keeps conking out. Air filters are tough to get, so instead of changing the filter on schedule, we wash it and reuse it a few times. We're taking a chance, but that's the only way."

Lila lowers her voice, confiding. "You know, we keep a canister of used sharps. We've never reused any syringes yet, but I keep thinking, you never know—"

Ushi asks her, "Are you a doctor?"

"Me?" Lila draws in her arms, closing subtly up. "No. I don't know what I am, I do everything."

"You have the objectivity of a physician." Lila's suspicion dissipates: Ushi is not challenging her credentials. "I don't know how you do it," Ushi says. "You're all so close, like family."

Lila coughs, or chokes, and careens away from the topic: "Yeah, I try, anyway, the lack of security is killing us. You came in a convoy, you didn't see it, but the road from the south is full of bandits, rebels, they call themselves . . ."

Ushi watches her silently, putting the rush of words away where puzzles are mulled. Whatever emotion we have seen, it revealed itself only in disappearing, like a mouse rustling in the granary. Ushi asks, "How much does it cost to supply you for a month?"

"Depends on the population, but money isn't the problem. Logistical screwups, that's the problem. You get hoes but no handles. Or you get diesel but no oil. Or drugs and no syringes. Timbuktu feeds us all on one Beltway death merchant's salary. We get what the hoods who drive the trucks don't want."

Fatimatou comes with wide grave eyes. A wordless flutter passes between them, something familiar and horrific. "Gotta go," Lila says, her voice pinched and stretched. She rushes off with little tight strides.

14

*I wander the camp with Ushi, letting her interest guide me like a bea-*con. Ushi's beacon is sweeping the camp for Lila. She wavers between offhand comments about camp life and fretful questions: *Is she all right? Does she need you?* There's no voyeurism there: Ushi is plainly distressed.

A tense vigil draws us to the mothers' tent. Three young men huddle outside, around the flysheet. One says, "Do you know the girl?"

Ushi says, "Who, Lila? Is she all right?"

"Lila is there too," he says.

"Can I see her?"

The man shrugs.

The dimness of the tent is like a church. Heads are averted or bowed. In the dimmest corner Lila kneels at a cot. She holds a prostrate girl's limp hand.

Whatever she murmurs is not for my ears. Lila chokes each word back like a wracking cough. With all but the consolation strained out, her voice is barely there. I can't be sure what I hear: *It's OK, raggy-bag . . . I know . . .*

Lila shudders and rocks over the girl's limp body. She touches the girl's face, holds her hand, takes the visible pulse on her skeletal wrist. The girl's only response is to breathe. Her lips close and part but her eyes are vacant, her fingers slack in Lila's hand.

The women with the dying girl are not from her clan. They must have taken her in. They are one misfortune away from a death like hers. Perhaps they are too weak to suffer the way Lila does; grief like hers must take a lifetime of stoking. I stoop and lay a hand on Lila's shoulder, and flinch from the vibrating anguish of her back.

The refugees watch, wet with composed tears that don't roil the face, as though Lila has depleted their grief. To a corner of my mind it seems unfair, as if she's taking what is theirs.

Watching Lila, I can see the girl has died. Someone must have run for a volunteer. He is a tall young Berber with a blasphemous look of reproach. He picks Lila up and carries her off. A woman closes the dead girl's eyes and stares after Lila.

I find Fatimatou in the Rubbhall. She knows why I have come.

"What happened?"

"Some deaths grieve Lila more," she says. "Don't ask her why. She will tell you if she wants to."

"So you understand it?"

Affirming it silently, she also refuses to speak.

"I won't mention it," I say.

Fatimatou sifts through sentences in her head, editing and discarding, then says, "Death happens for a reason here. That is a comfort, sometimes."

Lila is not in the mothers' tent. She would normally be asleep by now. The mothers tell me *Aye taara duna*. She has gone to the dunes. Can she find her way back?

"She never gets lost."

The dunes wipe the camp away before I've gone half a mile. They vary their aspect and all but change places in a stealthy shell game. They make me twist and turn so much I doubt the stars that mark my way back home.

I've given up finding her, when I see a dark shape where a steep dune kinks. I approach her in silence, uncertain now.

"Shh," she says. "The dunes—they're booming tonight. Hear it?"

Lila is tracing patterns in the sand. Her head rocks, rears, bows. She swallows with a painful crunch. Something is coming. I'm holding my breath.

"I had a sister, Trish," she says. "We were twins. Not identical twins, fraternal twins, but we were inseparable. Mom used to say we were Siamese twins sharing one great big mouth. We never fought. A lot of kids hung around us, but nobody could keep up with us. We had our own language that was a hundred times faster than English. It was like a secret code made of jokes.

"Trish got her first period a week after me. That year was the most fun I ever had. The dinner table was like a stage for us, a performance. I'd laugh something new out my nose every night. We made things out of food, played catch with it. The dog learned to wait under the table for stuff that came flying off. We'd get sent to our room a lot, but that just meant we'd spend more time together.

"But after a while, Trish didn't seem so playful. She would sulk at the table. My parents always seemed to be picking on her. She'd get mad and get up and go for long walks alone.

"Then they told me she had a problem, she didn't want to eat. That made me feel sick about the food games: I thought I must have been too disgusting when I blopped out food on my tongue or screamed maggots.

"I tried to make her eat, but my mother told me I shouldn't, it only made things worse. I didn't know what to do. I told myself that if I could say a whole Our Father in my head, Trish would get better, but I almost never could. I would hear shouts in my head, *Go to hell, Trish,* and I would have to start all over.

"Trish just got littler and littler, and she got lines in her face like a sad little old lady. They put her in the hospital. I went to see her every day after school. I wouldn't have gone at all, if my mother didn't make me. Trish scared me.

"One day Trish was all hooked up to machines, needles in her arms and tubes in her nose, and I tried to make her laugh but she just closed her eyes. My mother was talking to the nurse outside. I shouted to wake her up, and touched her arm. That was the first time I thought she might die. Only then."

Booom. Booomm. *Ala ka boom.* God is great. That's how they say it here. I always thought it must have come from the booming sound the dunes make: a sound of blessed release, as if a great burden has shifted and afforded some relief.

I awaken in the dark to a light hand on my shoulder and a hissing whisper, "Be still." The boys in the tent stir and giggle. Ushi's here.

"Please come with us?"

"Where?"

"To the waste dump."

"You can't go there," I say.

"If you'd rather stay in bed, I will tell you what I find. But it's better if you see for yourself, true?"

"I've been there. It's hazardous. It's guarded."

"All right. Go back to sleep."

"You're risking your life if you go there. Do you understand me?"

"Of course. Good-bye, my friend." I can see her smile in the pitch dark.

"Wait," I say. "I'm coming." I can tell Bud I went along to keep tabs on her. If I witness Ushi's capture, it might save her life. Unless they summarily shoot us both.

We walk out of the camp to a waiting Greenfleet Hummer. Ushi murmurs to a slight Songhai guide named Ali, and he eases into gear. She hands me a compact flashlight with a strap-on leg sheath.

Ali drives without lights. With no fear of obstacles, he creeps ahead by feel, probing for traction. As we approach I can make out a crane as a black rip in the Milky Way.

We stop a mile from the nearest pit, and Ali nestles more than parks behind a rock outcrop. He drapes a camouflage net over it and we continue on foot. When I look back the Hummer is part of the rock.

We slink toward the pit along a gully, stooping or creeping when the guide signals. Hearing the whine of a Saracen, we lie motionless for what seems like ten minutes.

We worm on our bellies past a black pile of muck among tires twice my height. Booms and blades hang overhead, blocking half the sky.

A tin shed sits under a squat tower of girders. We enter, and for the first time, Ali switches on his light. The concrete floor has a bottomless pit with a ladder hanging in it. The verticals of the ladder are built like two heavy bicycle chains. It looks like an elevator under construction. I say, "Where's the cage?"

"Somewhere below," he says. "This is the emergency shaft. It's got a few cages for casualties. Able-bodied men will use the rungs."

Makeshift, even for Africa. Bud's pinching pennies. Ali pushes a black button with his thumb, and it sinks in past the first joint. A motor starts to whine.

"Won't they hear that?"

"The guards won't pass this way for another hour," he says. "Even then, they will be in vehicles, looking, not listening."

Ushi has disappeared. "Where did she go?"

"Quick, follow her," Ali says. He points his light at the shaft. I see two ladders rattling in there now, one behind the other. One goes up, one goes down, moving a bit too fast. "Watch your step."

"What's underneath?"

"Don't worry about that."

I shuffle toward the ladder and stop dead two feet from the pit. I hear "Don't look down," but I do, and see black.

"There's a stationary rung above your head. Just look at that." He tenses, hissing at me as Ushi sinks into blackness. She might be fifty feet below by now, the way the ladder's moving. I grab a slick stanchion with my left hand, clamp onto the overhead rung with my right.

"Now grab one of the moving rungs."

Now I get it. Grab the overhead rung, grab the moving rung, let go of the overhead. Nothing to it. The fight-or-flight rush is intriguing to me. I almost forgot what adrenaline's like.

I touch a moving rung. I grasp the next rung as it sinks away from me. Both hands clamp tight and the moving rung wrenches loose. Sharp twinges in my shoulder shoot up to my hand.

"Relax, take hold, step on," he says. "When you get on, lock your knee behind a rung. It's a long ride down."

But I am frozen; not afraid but congealed.

"Come back out," he barks. "Just stay here." He grabs me by the collar, pulls me back onto the floor, and hops over the abyss onto the ladder.

Now I'm alone. I hold the stationary rung and hang there rehearsing in my head. I let a dozen rungs go by. I put a hand on the ladder, then a hand and a foot. *What if a cage comes down?*

I see a pinpoint lamp above me, coming down. The cage? I put my weight on the moving ladder but my other hand won't let go and I'm swinging by one hand, pumping my leg against the rungs that go by. I've lost my footing on the floor behind me.

I grab a rung and let it rip me off the overhead. Swinging one-handed, I bash my wrist bones clawing at the ladder as it bucks and thrashes in the black.

Far below, someone is clapping.

The ladder gradually stops gyrating as I sink through space. I lock my leg behind the rung, as directed. My hands feel waxy, pliable but uncooperative. Pressure builds in my ears, but I can't get a good pop out of them.

After several minutes I start to climb down the ladder. Ushi and Ali must be off it by now. I'm starting to wonder hard about where, and how, we get off.

Below me I think I see weak light reflecting off a dull surface. A faint voice carries up to me: "Ty. Push off the ladder when we tell you."

"Is this the bottom?"

"No." Something in his voice says the bottom is a long way down.

I hear Ali's voice getting closer: "When I say *Now,* push off hard. We will catch you. Not yet, not yet, not yet, *NOW!*" and I launch myself backward, springing full force with arms and legs, arcing up, and crack my head on rock.

I am on my hands and knees with tense hands on my shoulders

and arms. I don't recall touching the ground. Ushi turns my head with a warm hand on my cheek. Ali shines his light in my eyes.

"His pupils are the same, *Gott sei dank,*" Ushi says. "Ah, Ty."

Ushi's cheery calm embarrasses me. The pain in my head infuriates me. I snap at her: "So where are we?"

Ali says, "We're three hundred meters down the emergency shaft. This is the first adit, a tunnel that leads to the main shaft. There are two more adits below us before you get to the bottom."

I'm trying to get my night vision back. Now all I see is their lights. Ushi's beam is a slashing sword. Ali's is a broom, slanting stolidly down.

"Let's go," Ushi says.

"Go where?"

"We're going to scrape around," she says. "I can't say what I'm looking for, I only want to see."

She pulls a folding knife out of a leather pouch and picks at the rock. "We need to take a sample back," she says.

"That's a basalt mass," I say. "It will ruin your knife before you get a handful."

"We have to get some," Ushi says. The blade is scraping, not catching, with a thin irritating sound.

"Why do the walls sparkle like that?" Flicking her lamp, she sets off a million sparks.

I say, "Crystals of some metallic compound."

"Look at that big one," she says. "It looks like gold, is it gold?" She seems avid as a prospector.

"I doubt it," I say.

"But Mali has mined gold since ancient times. There are lost mines. Couldn't it be?"

I say, "Maybe—so what?"

"Ali, light the wall for him?" Ushi's question is a brusque order.

I stoop to find a good-sized crystal. "Give me the knife," I say. I scratch at it, play the light over it, scratch some more.

"Well?" Ushi presses me from behind, prompting a forlorn erection.

"Iron pyrite. Fool's gold. Sorry."

"Fool's gold?" Oddly, Ushi does not seem disappointed.

I look up. "The rock is shot through with it."

Something's dawning on her. A smile starts small on one side and spreads. She takes my face in warm dry palms and kisses me on the mouth.

I want to say *What?* but I'm goggling at her open-mouthed.

The sound behind me wakes me up like an ammonia ampoule. I turn toward the shaft, where the ladders are creaking to a halt.

The silence is absolute: not a breath, not a movement to rustle our clothes. Ali reaches over and grabs my hand, shutting off the lamp with a hollow drawn-out click. Ushi catches my arm and pulls me toward her: "Don't resist. They have guns."

Janissary's guns are the least of my worries. What if they turn Ushi over to Bud?

The ladder stays dead for long minutes. Ushi says, "Maybe they just shut it off and left. We'll have to climb."

"No," Ali says. "The cages block your way."

Even in a whisper, Ushi's voice has a battlefield rasp of reckless command. "What's that way?"

"The main shaft," Ali says.

She says, "Go."

"There's no lift!"

"What is there?"

"A concrete pit," he says.

"What's at the bottom?"

"Oily water, sixty meters deep."

"We will stick put there, and hide."

The tunnel is maybe a hundred feet long, but it stretches out in the short beam of the flashlight. Ushi strides through Ali's patch of light, dragging it along the floor. Ali sidles behind, hissing, "Slow down! There's no railing at the edge!" All his deference is gone now. This is survival.

I hear her stamp her foot and stop short.

Ali is leaning away from the hole, reaching for her. "For God's sake, be careful."

"What is this?" She is a teetering tripod, on her knees, back arched, with one hand on the ground. She cranes her neck over the pit, waving the lantern to the right. "What is this here?"

She scuffs in the gloom, grunts, and swings out of sight behind the wall. She's out over the hole, hanging or perching on who knows what. I can feel Ali stiffen from two feet away.

With a giddy squeal in her voice she says, "A ladder!"

Her light shines back toward us from the shaft. It makes a half circle where it drops off the edge. I creep on all fours toward the hole. The torch's flawed reflector makes bright spots like yellow worms on the tunnel floor. The concrete looks fluffy at the edge. Beyond it the light glints on water too far down. "Look here."

I lie on my side and stick my head out over the pit. The shaft is lined with concrete. Molded into the lining is a vertical column of twelve-inch-square holes. A lip at the bottom of each hole makes an ill-adapted handgrip. Ushi hangs there, all arms and legs, twisting in a way that makes me hug the ground. She calls past me to Ali, "Does it go all the way up?"

"A thousand rungs, Ushi," he says. "Have you ever climbed a thousand steps?"

"In the gym I'd climb ladder machines for hours, to stay slim. How many steps is that?"

"Ushi," Ali moans.

"Let's go," she says.

"You can't climb in the pitch dark." I'm snarling, my voice too urgent to mute.

"I count to one thousand, and then I'm at the top."

Ali says, "Then you're at the bottom of a sixty-foot ring of steel pilings. I don't know how you get out of that."

"Oh, there must be a way."

Ali keeps talking sense to her but she has stopped answering: She's on her way up.

I stretch out and grope for a handhold, ripples of panic flushing everything else away.

The edges that I'm holding make lousy rungs. They curve gradually back toward me. I can't wrap my fingers around them, and the fine-grained concrete doesn't grab my hands now that I'm sweating. I stop myself from counting. I don't want to know. I climb hard until I can hear Ushi's breath, short disciplined puffs.

"Is that you, Ty?"

"Yeah." Already it's hard to speak.

"From the beginning I knew you were strong, but it seemed you were hurt in some way. I think now you are healing. That makes me glad."

She's picking up the pace but I would follow her rung for rung up to the surface and on to where Holy Mary Mother of God sits in heaven tucking little pieces of herself into women who by rights should run the world. We never should have switched from goddesses to gods.

"Ali will come along soon," she says. "He will get very angry with me, and then he will come, muttering and cursing. He is a hooot."

I'm lying in a pile with Ushi and Ali on steel plate, numb hands just starting to feel the raised lozenge pattern, rubbery arms throbbing at my sides, dried-out breaths tearing through a pinhole inside me, nose still sticky from laughing or crying at where I am right now, here, instead of that frozen moment in the jungle when my life stopped dead four years ago.

It's dark and quiet. Maybe someone just turned off the hoist and left. Maybe they figured the roughnecks left it on. Why should they suspect intruders? It's a big hole. A kid might want to explore it, but the kids here are too hungry for adolescent stunts. I wish I were an adolescent again so I could more fully appreciate the Dungeons and Dragons glory of sneaking into the world's deepest hole with a reckless lingerie Amazon.

Ushi moved on last week, kissing babies, hugging mommies, waving herself like a flag. She was off to a reef somewhere, back on the ecological job.

I'm leaving, too. Some scrupulous wood-paneled court has freed us to choose among the proposals. I am going back to the remote abstractions of Vienna, where I'll peer through computerized mathematical goggles that shrink the world like the wrong end of a telescope.

I fly in some privileged airline class, in an empty compartment of wide leather seats. The flight lays over in some European capital, but I don't venture from the airport. The airline lounge has showers, massages, and dim New Age rooms, and I don't need to see another rich-world city; they're all alike.

Vienna is misty and cold and so dim I can see into the hotel lobby from outside. It's close and hot in my room. I push the balcony door aside and Faye pops out next door. "Ty."

The city hasn't dampened her spirits. She says, "How's your girlfriend?"

"Girlfriend?"

"The refugee girl. What's her name?"

"Lila? They're good. Ushi showed up."

"Did she wreak havoc?"

"Not like usual," I say.

"Her TV spots run ten times a day here. They're beautiful, but nobody quite knows what the point is."

Later on Faye tries to help me catch up. The panel is putting questions to the bidders, trying to rattle them with our worst nightmares: scalding radwaste seeping out natural breccia pipes. A shipful of penetrators lost at sea, sunk but not buried and rusting away. An "event" in a smelter of the kind we dare not name lest the terrorists catch on. Faye is lying on the floor of my hotel room, scanning a spread-out sheaf of charts. She props herself up on her elbows. A long-lost part of me is butting my zipper. This is different than my mopey platonic Lila ruminations. Ushi's subterranean derring-do seems to have opened some internal stopcock. The adrenaline rush must have zapped me like a shock treatment.

Faye has muted the TV. A newscast flashes on the screen. Even if I turn away the flickering screen drags my eyes back. At first I felt a need to know—the panel's work is not newsworthy, but news can turn us upside down at any time. By now it's a tic of the eyes or hits of a drug, continual quick glances at the screen for events in Mali or Russia, wrangles at the U.N., public protests, bidders' ploys.

I glance again, look back, then stare. This is one of the spots from the camp. In the background, Ushi's face glows in warm firelight. Seen from behind, Serata is in the foreground, facing Ushi across a cooking fire. The fire silhouettes Serata. The camera blurs her. Still, you can tell that something is wrong. In the flickering light your eyes hop nervously from Ushi to Serata's unsettling contours, seeking ears or hair or any feature to hold on to.

I turn up the volume. Ushi whispers in a voice-over: *As a young girl Serata fell into a cooking fire. They say a spirit went into her and made her do it. She lost her beauty and her sight, but the spirit took pity and gave her the powers of a* marabout, *a conjurer and prophet.*

Then Serata's words, Fatimatou's voice: *We used to live simply. You could spin your own cotton or weave bamboo. A girl had no need of clothes until she reached the age of marriage. Young men would share a set of clothes. Now people feel they must have factory clothes, more than they can wear! We raise houses like babies: Is the straw tight? Is the dung crumbling? We have more money, less to eat. To be rich we must spend our money on this thing, then that thing and the other. How did I come to need these things I do not want?*

Ushi's face is somber, chastened, mirroring her shame in the absurd excess of her life, and ours.

Everything is like fat on the dog's mouth, sucked up straightaway. Men drink till milk spills down their cheeks. They pay for maize from far away. Food in a tin, whatever it is—well, you are happy as a white man until it's gone. Even the sauce is too much now. Not just salt fish but herbs, onions, peppers, stock cubes. We trade away goats for cigarettes and soon we need smoke more than meat. In the market they commit aljaran, *hiking the price of the grain while shrinking the pot.*

Sometimes I fear we're running toward a cliff.

I hear Faye saying, "Ty," and her intonation says she has been fighting to get my attention. "Are you a Serata fan too?"

"She's a sweetheart," I say.

"You know Serata? You've met her?" Faye is wide-eyed, astonished.

"I used to see her every day."

Faye sits up, intent. "Is she really the way the film clips make her seem? You can dismiss Ushi as a poor little rich girl, but this woman, she's lived her whole life with literally nothing."

"You don't want to trade places with her, believe me." Some stray thought is gnawing at me, and I can't find it.

"But it's humbling, how little she needs, how little she demands."

"She's blind and disfigured and destitute, and she's used to it."

Fay backs off and lets the tension subside, curious but not offended. She's watching me closely. I say, "Sorry," and search for the nerve the clip has hit. Something in the brief spot jarred me: not the furtive camera work, not the firelight on Serata's ravaged head.

"Running toward a cliff," Faye says. "I got chills when she said that. I don't know why."

That's it.

The panel is assembled in the conference room. We stare at a video screen on a cart: spinning satellites and macho syncopation mean we're on hold for our one o'clock conference call. We're deferring to Sam; he knows how to act in this curious meeting. Sam is used to talking heads on screens; foreign dignitaries use video calls to interfere in Africa while staying away.

Now the screen blinks and a window opens on Niger. Niger, poorest country in the world, last anybody looked. Where did they get the money to rent a satellite transponder? The president of Niger sits before us, scowling almost life-size from the screen. He doesn't know he's on yet. Alerted, he starts to read to us, a sales pitch with an odd querulous tone: "It would seem that the government of Mali has a monopoly on waste disposal. They have no monopoly on desert land. Now, we don't know the terms of Mali's bargain with Timbuktu Earthwealth, but we can do better. Niger will take the waste for a nominal impact fee of twenty thousand dollars a ton."

Sam says, "You should propose this idea to Timbuktu Earthwealth."

"But you can make sure they don't shut us out." The president wants to know the fix is in. "They can dump in the Aïr just as well."

Sam says, "We can't tell them how to get the job done."

"Fair play, that's all we ask." The wide-angle lens spreads his jowls as he leans in on us.

Bud summons me to meet him. He has given me elaborate directions to a new safe house. (Take the U-Bahn to Spittelau. Take the escalator out and right back down, and watch for tails. A cola can in the gutter means it's not safe, abort.) The gutter turned out to be free of cans. Bud seems to have chosen well. These flats are filled with students, driven and preoccupied, with pocket computers and natty interview suits.

I end up in a flat that seems too opulent to be safe. I sit in a sinuous spine-shaped chair. My feet sweat in waterproofed shoes on the heated marble floor.

Bud yells and stomps until I wonder whether he bought the apartment below us, too. "You fucked up," he says. "Why didn't you tell me Niger was getting into the act? I could have seen this coming."

"Seen what coming?"

"The Niger government sent a commercial mission to our headquarters. They submitted a formal bid to take any waste we dump. For good measure they sent a team into Mali and abducted one of our survey crews. Now Mauritania wants a piece of the action too. North and South Sudan are fighting for a cut—two ministers had a physical altercation outside my office, two old men in a shoving match. I was mortified."

"Sorry," I say, "but I never expected this would happen."

"You are supposed to be keeping an eye on Theriault."

"Theriault? What does he have to do with—"

"Theriault is behind all this," Bud says. "Where do you think they got the idea to take our waste?"

"Theriault's dumping in the ocean, not the desert. What does he care who your partners are?"

"He's stirring up old rivalries to disrupt our plans. These countries are his pawns—the Frogs own those regimes. They keep their strongmen on a very short leash. The Frogs say jump, the Africans say how high."

"But Theriault works for a U.N. agency. He's not allowed to act on behalf of France."

Bud gives me a pitying look. "This issue is more fundamental than national interest. It's more fundamental than communism or democracy. The issue is, Who's going to run Africa, Anglophones or Francophones? Is Africa going to think like us or think like them? That's their choice, to use Africans as pawns, but we're going to beat them at their own game."

"By manipulating Africans?"

"This has to be fought at a careful remove," he says. "Africans fighting it out with Africans, that's one thing: the stakes are not too high. Direct conflict, U.S. versus France, that's dangerous. Even if we keep it covert, things might escalate."

He lowers his voice a notch and continues, "We've got an arrangement they call *non dit:* the Frogs are keeping some of our touchiest secrets—TWA Flight 800 is the least of it—and we've got dirt on them, too. If they expose us, we'd have no choice but to do the same. It would be political Armageddon, mutually assured destruction: a presidential administration disgraced, and maybe a whole party; the French government falls and France loses control of the European Union."

"So this is proxy war. Who's our proxy, Bud?"

"You have no need to know."

Back at the hotel my mind is ticking so fast I don't bother to wish for sleep. I'm drinking a yeasty sweet beer.

That's Faye's knock. It's two A.M., but she's bouncing with some news at my door. She's pulled something off the Web. I can feel her watching as I absorb the printout.

U.N. BUREAUCRAT ARRESTED FOR MALFEASANCE

KINGSTON (AP)—Jamaican authorities today arrested U.N. executive Alain Theriault on fraud and embezzlement charges. Theriault directed a little-known U.N. agency called The Authority. The Authority administers the Law of the Sea Treaty, a contentious international convention that Western countries have refused to sign.

In a postindictment press conference, Inspector T. E. Eginton of Interpol stated, "The pattern of criminal activity indicates utter contempt for the law. Perhaps this is what we should expect from the head of an organization that calls itself The Authority. Mr. Theriault appears to believe he is above the law and accountable to no one."

Theriault's legal counsel limited itself to a terse written statement: "The charges against Mr. Theriault are fabricated." In response Eginton said, "We have an airtight case. The defendant left an unmistakable trail."

The U.N. has frozen The Authority's accounts. The Authority has suspended Theriault and is scrambling to replace him. Theriault's most important project is a seabed nuclear-waste dumping plan of his own devising. A highly placed U.N. source said, "Theriault has made himself irreplaceable. He encrypts critical documents and personally controls access. He disperses information among staff and contractors, and he alone knows who has what. The project is dead without him."

Tonight the safe house is a festive place. Behind the drawn blinds Bud is crowing. "Theriault claims he's been framed. I'd like to see him prove that."

Bud seems awfully triumphant for an innocent bystander. Out of idle curiosity I tweak him to see if I can learn anything. "So Theriault overestimates us. We're not so good at dirty tricks after all."

"Think about what it would take to frame him," Bud says. "First, you would have to find one of Theriault's secret offshore nominee accounts. You would have to wire U.N. money into that account. To get the money out of the U.N.'s account you would have to penetrate their firewall. It's a bastion host firewall, the toughest kind."

Bud gets out of his chair and bends over me. "To implicate Theriault you would have to carry out some extremely sophisticated identity theft. You would have to fake his digital signature, and that's no easy task. Theriault hashes his signature with an MD-5 algorithm.

"Now, let's say you can do all this." He's pacing. "You've framed the guy for embezzlement, but so what? The authorities will never know. *Unless* he was unlucky enough to run afoul of Treasury OFAC. You know them? They chase dirty money. Let's say you route a wire transfer through one of the offshore banks on OFAC's watch list. OFAC catches it and Theriault is framed with airtight evidence.

"But who could do all that?" Bud's smiling an unnerving bright-eyed smile. "He says he was framed. Impossible."

Late at night in my room, Faye and I are talking shop. Rumors are spreading like plagues: the Russian Mafiya paid Minatom's bid bond. Timbuktu Earthwealth's nonperforming loans have been called in. The Japanese have built a fusion torch that turns waste to gold.

Smoke from Faye's fat spliff twists in front of the television. This animation festival is the room's only light. The phantasmagoric cartoons are no more surreal than these rumors.

I've had a few beers. I suspect Faye's pot is getting to me, too. I feel flashes of awe and a concupiscent warmth from the play of light and color on her form. When Faye shifts her position on the floor you can see her pleasure in the muscles she's stretching: back, thighs, or shoulders. But this hormonal geyser won't settle on a single object. When I was little my dad would put a plastic clown head on a hose and it would whip around and spray water, and me and the dogs would run and scream. My sexual stirrings are whipping around like that clown head, sprinkling Faye, Ushi, Lila, Faye, Ushi, Lila.

Why is my libido hosing Lila down at all? Of all people, Lila, that scrappy little beguine. She scorns feminine wiles. I guess she had sex once, with Bud, but she only did it to alleviate world hunger. What am I doing to myself?

The television screen slows its flicking and dims. The fluty New Age music signals one of Ushi's spots, and I'm back in the camp again. Serata's face, mercifully blurred, shakes on the screen in the dark.

The whole world is driven by visions and dreams. We imagine them, we give them life and they carry the world where they will. They are no longer our dreams. They are our world.

"Listen to that," I say. "A perfect statement of Ushi's philosophy, in Serata's words. Ushi's making an ascetic prophet out of her. She listened to Serata for weeks. She must have edited phrase by phrase until she had what she wanted."

"That's not what I'm hearing," Faye says. "To me, she's talking about models like the Crystal Ball that we invent and adopt and rely on until they run the world. There's no way Serata could have an inkling of the models we use. You'd have to educate her for years before you could even explain it to her. But somehow she knows what it's like to dream up a little toy world and watch it take over the real one."

"They say she's a *marabout,* a diviner. Maybe she was born to be a U.N. technocrat."

Serata pulls us back to the screen. She is stern, chastising us. We show contempt for the old ways. *Eating the plants that have human souls.* Faye says Wow. *Burying dead dwarfs rather than pitching them into the river, as you ought.* This is weirder than the cartoons.

In their visions the white men have found where the snake's head fell. They dig in Wangara again, they think.

Faye is sitting up. "Now, you can't tell me that's Ushi's propaganda. Who knows what that means? Wangara—where's that?"

"No such place, I don't think."

Within days, thousands of people descend on the Timbuktu Earthwealth pits. They are mostly unarmed, but their numbers overwhelm Janissary's garrison. They come from all directions, returning when ejected, braving barricades, armed patrols, razor ribbon, and desert. They die in the hundreds or gorge makeshift detention cells. Bud's supply chain cannot cope—it was meant for a skeleton crew of roughnecks and geologists.

The migrants are everywhere: riding convoys like hobos or stowing away, skulking in the pits by night, combing through mounds of earth. Suddenly no-man's-land is teeming. The warlords see it slipping out of balance, and they begin to posture for control.

Timbuktu Earthwealth is reeling. Bud roars at me in late-night phone calls: *What's going on?* I lived there; why can't I explain?

In Vienna, remote from the upheaval, we are staring slackly into the Crystal Ball. Its equations are useless to explain this swarm. We have been waiting for Sam. He has been delayed in Africa for days. Perhaps he will know, when he arrives.

Sam comes in now, looking his age, graying hair and papery graying skin. We show him no solicitude, yanking him with questions from all sides.

"I slept in the airport for two days," he says. "Twice I was nearly trampled in line."

"But what's going on?"

"Half the flights have been diverted for an emergency air bridge to Mali."

"Why?"

He says, "Gold rush."

Faye says, "That's not a gold rush, it's a mass migration."

"You have to understand," Sam says. "If word spreads of work, hundreds leave their homes and sleep rough for weeks. One hoax about a U.S. visa lottery caused a refugee crisis outside the consulate. Imagine the power of this rumor."

"What rumor?"

"The last time Serata appeared on TV, she seemed to be saying Timbuktu Earthwealth found the gold mines of Wangara."

"Wangara—we heard that, remember, Ty?" Faye turns to Sam. "Is that where they're digging?"

"Who knows?" Sam says. "Wangara is a lost city. Its location was always a secret. It's the place where Amadou the Taciturn cut off the snake god's head, if that helps. People thought it was on the

Niger River floodplain, but no one knows. If a *marabout* on television says it's in the desert, it's in the desert. That's why half of Mali is there now."

Faye asks me, "What are you smirking about?"

Now I see why Ushi was so happy to find fool's gold.

Bud reacted quickly. The next day, at noon, every TV in Mali fell silent for two minutes. Villages had time to assemble, drunks in the expat bars had time to listen up, and everyone had time to wait on tenterhooks for:

When the words disappear, Bud Van Sickle is on the screen. He is grave, sad, and profoundly disappointed at once.

"Many Africans are risking everything to cross the Sahara. They hope to change their lives by finding gold.

"Over two hundred people have died seeking gold in the Timbuktu Earthwealth demonstration site. Some have trespassed in hazardous areas, fallen to their deaths down deep pits, been crushed by giant machines. We have rescued some of the misguided prospectors. Many clutch rocks like this." Bud holds a nugget that shines in the TV lights.

“Is this gold?” Bud says. “No.”

“This is iron pyrite—fool’s gold. It shines yellow like gold, but it contains no gold at all. It is valueless rock. The rumor of gold in the Sahara is a cruel hoax spread by environmental agitators. They are playing with the hopes and lives of Africans.”

Ushi’s attack was a one-two punch. Bud ducked her jab and found a roundhouse zooming toward his head. Bud’s televised message repeats hourly for a week, quelling the gold rush with prudent words. But each time Bud’s broadcast fades to black, Ushi takes his place on the screen.

Squatting in the shade of an oasis, Ushi tousles a goat’s coat. Tuareg children stand in a ring behind her, fixing the camera with wounded looks. Water splashes in treble tones from a hand-pumped well.

Ushi’s face implores us in a close-up shot. “Timbuktu Earthwealth has publicly acknowledged the presence of iron pyrite at its desert dump site. When iron pyrite is exposed to the air, it oxidizes. Oxidation creates sulfuric acid. The acid will slowly dissolve the containment vessels until they crumble and release radioactive poison into Africa’s groundwater.”

A rock glitters in her tapering fingers as she shakes it accusingly. “This problem has occurred before, and the defense contractors of Timbuktu Earthwealth know it. It happened in Washington, D.C., their headquarters. They exposed pyrites to air when they dug the tunnels for the Washington Metro. Sulfuric acid began to attack the tunnel lining. Greenfleet’s analysis indicates that the iron-rich rock of the Sahara will release much larger quantities of acid.

“The project threatens an entire continent with disaster. We must stop it.” Ushi hugs the goat, inclines her head against its neck. It bleats softly. The camera closes in on her face.

“Please help.”

Bud got through it. Over a period of weeks, he ferried the prospectors home or to the camp, where they could be fed, just. Lila took it in stride, although she and Fatimatou looked thinner in the pictures she sent back.

Ushi's sulfuric acid scare hissed and smoked and settled down in time. While we sat on our hands in Vienna, Bud spent some more borrowed millions to study the sulfuric acid problem. His tame scientists proved that acid in the shaft is no big deal. The rocks stop seeping acid once they're sealed in again with concrete. Probability of a waste leak is point zero zero zero seven under conservative assumptions. Everyone but the Greens have calmed down.

Now excavation is proceeding again. Bud seems distracted, though. He seems to have another project going on the side. In the safe house he is always on the phone, invoking Mumm.

A frigid wind burns my face. Dawn whitens the sky above the Ural foothills. The taiga stretches endlessly off to the east. We are in the great swath of Russia that has been sacrificed to the atom. This is where Minatom wants us to dump the world's waste.

It is Minatom's turn to demonstrate their plan. I have taken a series of smaller planes, jinking like a gnat in the steppe winds. Ushi is here, flashing eyes and teeth from the chinks between her black sheepskin hat and electric-blue ski suit. I've just begun to notice the Russian bigwig in her shadow. He's a gaunt scientist from Minatom, Dr. Belov.

My wind-whipped ears transmit more pain than sound, but Belov's rumbling Slavic accent makes it through. "The Pol'arnyj Ural is ecologically dead. Perfect for you."

The only sign of life is a squat gray box on the slope of a nearby hill. It looks like a prison, ringed with concentric fences that stretch behind the hilltop.

I stamp my feet and the ground shocks my heels like rock. Frozen moss crackles underfoot. We tack through the gusts toward a hole in the ground. It's thirty feet across. A yard-thick concrete lining rims it.

"Now please descend," he says. He's pointing to two rectangular bars that protrude from the hole at shoulder width, waist high: the top of a ladder. Ushi gives me a shared-secret smile and waves me ahead.

This hole's just a shallow prototype, but it's a long way down. I think I'd rather climb it in the dark. The ladder twists and shivers with each shift of our weight. Ushi bends and looks down at me. She says, "Russian work seems rickety, but that's just their style. No frills."

Belov is following us down, shouting, "The ladder is strong—titanium. The site design benefits from Russian military experience with hardened ballistic-missile silos."

We're rattling around in a big empty can. Belov has joined us at the bottom. He passes out metal hard hats. "To demonstrate what we have learned, we will detonate an underground conventional explosion thirty meters from the site. The size of the blast will simulate the peak force generated by a magnitude-seven earthquake. Please note that an earthquake of that magnitude has not occurred here throughout recorded history. This area is seismically quite stable.

"You won't even know when the explosion occurs unless I tell you. Please bear in mind that if you stood outside the repository, the blast would knock you off your feet, even though it is sixty meters underground."

A whining motor overhead pulls a shadow up the wall. A crescent of gray sky is disappearing behind a concrete dome.

"For this demonstration we will seal the repository mechanically, with a temporary dome, not structurally. For that reason, our isolation from external forces will not be complete. Even so, the results will demonstrate the security of our storage sites."

When the dome squeals shut it causes an odd trick of acoustics. When you speak, you can get two or three words out before the echoes crowd in and shout down the rest of it. Belov counts down, "Thirty sec . . . twenty . . . ten . . ." The last ten seconds drown one another out. He is frozen in a wince as though he's bracing for a slap in the face.

"Nowowow." The floor gives a fleeting shiver. That's all. Belov points to the turning drum of a seismograph. It spiked viciously and subsided. "Magnitude eigh . . ." he says, pointing to the spike. Two technicians clown furtively and laugh. Belov watches the ceiling, which groans and squeaks.

We've shuffled around down here for a while. I get what he's trying to show us, and I am ready to see the sun, pale and weak though it is up there. I'm speaking one word at a time, in weighty individual pronouncements. "What. Now?"

"We. Wait," Belov says. "For the bull." Belov waits and tries again. "Bulldozers."

"What?" The echoes of my question take some time to die out.

"Crater," Belov says. "Digging out. Few hours."

The dome groans open and cold air drops on us in a gluey lump. At the top of the ladder the wind swipes, knife-edged and blinding. One gust staggers me back toward the hole. I plant one hand on the ground and scuttle away from it. Then I turn from the wind to catch my breath.

The wind has paused as if it's backing up to come on at a run. The glass-shard feeling on my face has begun to abate.

There's a plume of smoke slanting from the ring-fenced plant on the hill. Something's rumbling over there. Ushi's hair jumps forward on her head. She winces as it hits us both in the ears like a swat from a cupped palm: shock wave. And another, smaller one, a loud pop all around me. A flash sends red smoky comets up and out from where the building used to stand. The fire is more like a ball of light than a flame, white in the center and yellow around the edge. Scraps of debris spin out and away.

Belov is speaking on the fat handset of an old field radio. He is pale when he sticks it back in his belt. He takes Ushi aside, confers with her. "We will leave now," he says. "You will take this car."

I get in. The seat feels like dry ice but the driver keeps the heater fan off.

Belov pushes Ushi toward the car. He shouts at the driver in Russian, then runs to another car as our driver wheels around and floors it. The ruts are bigger at this speed, but the distant hills crawl by as slowly as when we came.

"What happened?" My voice is too loud for the car.

"An incident in the uranium processing plant," Ushi says. Underneath the plume of smoke it's still white-hot.

"The plant hasn't been in use for months—why should this happen now?" Ushi is sneaking shallow breaths, squeezing her words out through almost-empty lungs. Her forehead's white and sweating in the cold. "Belov says it's sabotage. Someone is trying to discredit Minatom."

It was a long trip back to Vienna: airsick, hungry, and maybe ionized by radiation. I'm back now, but I'm no more comfortable here. Bud has left me a series of messages at the hotel. When I reach him he says, "Are you all right?" His voice is hushed and anxious.

"You tell me. I was right there when it happened."

"You'd better get to a doctor. You may need some iodine—or blood chelation, maybe. That's no picnic."

"Is it that bad? There's nothing in the news here."

"Well, of course not," Bud says. "Everything I know I'm getting from my spook buddies. There's been a release. Fortunately, the plume is going northeast, toward sparsely populated areas."

"How big is the release?"

"Apparently that's classified for now."

"Is it dangerous?"

"It's dangerous, all right."

I say it softly, sweetly as I can: "Bud, did you blow them up?"

"My sources speculate that the underground explosion impaired the structural integrity of a sintering furnace, causing it to fail." Bud sounds like the words are going by on a TelePrompTer.

"That furnace has been mothballed for months."

"A likely story." I can hear him sneer at the other end. "Is Minatom accusing us of sabotage?"

"They're not accusing anyone. But they're telling me it's sabotage."

"They can't prove that. Anyway, nobody cares what they think. Minatom just blew it in a very public way."

“I guess no one is going to trust them with hot waste now,” I say.

Bud chortles down the line. “Guess not.”

Not after seeing the steppes glow green on the televised false-color satellite shots. Especially not once the plume changed course and closed on Finland like a giant claw.

My doctor in Vienna has dosed me with iodine. I will be all right, he says. My hair will be patchy for another month or so. I should keep a eye on my thyroid from now on.

When I can, I leave the panel to eat lunch outside. In this way I get time alone. It's not the desert, but for an hour I don't have to speak, listen, and look into eyes, or watch my demeanor and fight off my thoughts. I have taken possession of a bench in the Stadtpark, chosen for its discomfort and defended with my most forbidding face. A deranged woman with matted hair prowls these benches, scaring most visitors off. On the next bench she preens her plait and croaks contentedly. My ominous radioactive mange helps me guard my bench.

Despite that, a young girl is approaching. She sits beside me undaunted, a scruffy henna-headed waif with a trout fly hooked through her eyebrow. I am just about to abandon my bench when she passes me a note. "It's important, please consider it," she says. She gets up.

I turn to the envelope and work a finger under the flap. It holds one sheet of thick cotton stationery with the cursive monogram U.L. No date or address. It reads:

Please meet with me on the Greenfleet barge. We must liaise in private.

Ushi

I report the letter to Bud—no sense making my own decision about it—and soon I'm with him in the safe house again. He's pouring me scotch, beaming all around like a lighthouse. "Outstanding. She wants to meet secretly, that's good. She's desperate now. Maybe she wants to talk turkey. Maybe she wants to suborn you. Either way, we'll learn a lot from this."

The meeting will require some stealth. Ushi's barge is steaming down the Danube canals to an undisclosed location. All along her route the canals are thronged with badly dressed well-wishers, waste strikers doing their part to drag the world into waste-not-want-not poverty.

I hire a fumy sloshing motorboat east of Budapest. I keep pace with Ushi on the nearby river until the crowds thin out. At two A.M. on the second night, I board the barge, unkempt and slow-witted from lack of sleep.

The deck is gritty underfoot. A mate leads me like a blind man, which I am; they have turned out the lights on deck. Belowdecks I pass wall-mounted blubber knives and festoons of knotted drift nets, symbols of marine depredations past. Ushi's cabin is at the stern.

These days most of the old European barges are toys for the wealthy, all teak and brass. Ushi's boat has been renovated at evident expense to look dingy and industrial, as if to mortify her senses. The decks have been sanded and stained sooty black. Winches and pallets were blued and left in place. A big grimy crate serves as a vault for Greenfleet records.

Ushi receives me in her stateroom. Wilted tallow candles stand unlighted on an oil drum in the corner. Slaughterhouse machinery sits against the wall, grinders and blades compliantly ferocious like the jaws of mounted game. The room's light oozes gently from some ingenious hidden source. Ushi lies on her back on pillows and a mat, leafing through papers. One calf is balanced on the opposite knee. Her clothes are thick dark stuff in mournful Puritan colors: muted brown, faded black, charcoal gray. They are loose enough to spill off her body and settle in folds around her.

Ushi motions me to a corner of the mat, the only furniture in the little metal cell. She is sniffling, but not crying; she appears to have a cold. She mops her nose with a sleeve that comes down to her fingertips. "You must excuse me, I am too long sick. I have no strength to clean myself up."

"I hope I didn't disturb your sleep," I say. "I can wait until tomorrow if you'd rather talk then."

"I must prepare for Bulgaria." She pauses and lets her teeth peek between parted lips. "There is a nuclear plant there. The Bulgarians, they have learned some tricks from their neighbors in Ukraine. They fire up their reactor. Europe watches, heart in mouth, and the Bulgarians torment them: 'Damn old rust bucket . . . do I smell something burning?' Soon the Europeans are throwing money at them: a thousand tons of coal, more credits, anything, just turn that monster off.

"The leaders are happy to spend their money on Bulgaria. It piles up in the banks unused, unneeded. Up and down the Donau I spoke about simplicity. The strikers have deserted the shops in Vaci Utca in Budapest, the Graben in Vienna. A slump, they call it."

Her eyes widen and her voice drops so I can hardly hear. "A slump will not stop the death merchants, you know. They are too powerful for me.

"I can't stop them alone," she says, "but perhaps you and I can find a way." I recognize that expression; I have seen it before, hundreds of times. Captured on film, it sold a million barrels of corpse-collagen face cream. Ushi is not at her best on film. Photographs don't show the kind of stealthy facial-expression maneuvers she's using on me now. Video does not permit this stupefacient touching. She could make a martial art of it.

"Together, we can stop them. We can do that, can't we, together? It is easy to disrupt." She has me in an eyelock. "Timbuktu is a house of cards: natural enemies in an uneasy truce, each trying to cheat the others.

"A puff of breath"—she puffs me—"and the house of cards collapses. This is all I ask." She sits up and puffs again, lips pursing and uncoiling to an intimate smile.

I'm stammering. "You're right, it's easy to disrupt. But when you do, alliances fall apart, partners go their own way, tempers flare." I look for a metaphor that will strike a chord: "You've got a kind of habitat here, a delicate political one. We can't predict what will happen if we disrupt it."

Her fingertips stir on the back of my hand. She says, "The unpredictable doesn't frighten me. Timbuktu does."

Our meeting goes on until dawn. I do most of the talking. Ushi can take on the blank receptivity of a video camera. She never interrupts or reacts. She only echoes me, or prompts me. The intensity of her attention is hypnotic.

I'm ill at ease speaking so much and learning so little from her. Part of me needs to hear that she has made her own pact with the devil. I try a feeble challenge. "Strange bedfellows, Greenfleet and the Russians."

"The Russians have poisoned their half of the world, to be sure," she says. "It is lost to us. They have so much waste that it seems to them fitting they should keep it all, and grow rich."

"Won't the Russians expect you to condone their spills, their dumps, their mines?"

But Ushi has no interest in debate. Making some choice, she speaks in a peeping voice. I strain to hear. "Lila is so strong. I fear the littlest things. I have brown spots on my skin—what are they called?"

"Moles," I say.

"Yes, moles. These imperfections frightened me. I thought about them all the time. I imagined they itched, or burned. I rubbed my skin, checking them over and over, the need to touch them building like an itch. Wherever I was, I went to doctors and had them checked. I would leave the clinic and think of another mole that must be checked.

"My agent told me not to worry. She said they direct the eye around my body. She told me moles make a woman look real.

"One day it seemed I had scratched one; it started to bleed. It was beneath my ear, and they covered it with foundation for the day's shooting. I imagined the foundation seeping into it, into me, and mixing with the poison of the infection or the cancer in my face and I could not stand it. I left the picture session, ran to a doctor, angered everyone." She's getting hoarse with the kind of laryngitis that makes female voices sultry. "This doctor thought it best to remove it, but we didn't dare endanger my million-dollar face. My agent made me get other opinions: she got two yes and three no. It took days to find a plastic surgeon that would take proper care with my face. I was never so afraid. I looked ugly for lack of sleep. Finally, they took it off."

"And?"

"It was nothing. I think you can see where they took it off."

"Not from here."

"Perhaps not. The light is bad in here."

"Is that why you quit modeling?"

"I was too tired to live in fear of my body. I could not stand it. I wanted to forget myself, think about other things, bigger things."

"So you joined Greenfleet." *And turned your hypochondria on the whole world. Dumps instead of sores, spills instead of germs.*

My eyes are closing. "You are tired," she says. "Shall we sleep?"

It's bright out. The pillow next to mine has a head-hollow covered with tufts of Ushi's hair. She got a whopping dose in the Urals too. I wonder if she meant for me to sleep here. With both of us shedding it looks like a dog's bed in spring.

In their wardroom Ushi is wide awake, sweatered as always in muddy hues. She sits cross-legged on a bench against the wall. Four asexual beings in baggy black occupy an arc of chairs around her. She gnaws with her molars on a pencil stub. I pull up a metal stool outside the ring of chairs. They ignore me and conspire.

Ushi is withholding assent from a slight black-clad adviser with a wispy Lenin beard and eyeball-sized metal spectacles. He's thrusting with his face, reaching with his hands, saying, "You've never taken on an interest group like this. Your adversaries will stop at nothing. Your own tactics have to be eclectic."

"*Ach so.* Eclectic."

"You need a range of options." His eyebrows flap like wings above the tiny glasses. "You need waves of coordinated waste strikes, of course, but you need martyrs, too: detentions, video-taped beatings. A bit of self-immolation wouldn't hurt. We also need to organize hard-line groups for sabotage and terror. Nothing too awful; a little terror goes a long way."

Ushi studies him as you would a painting, or closes her face and looks down. She has buried her hands inside crossed legs.

"The students in Mali are the best," he says. "They've toppled a couple of regimes, and they're spoiling for another chance to flex their muscles. Militant as Korean students, but no dominant ideology—a blank slate for indoctrination. With two weeks of sleep deprivation and group work, they will be ready for anything."

He tents his fingers, reveling in what is to be done. "We've laid out a high-impact protest campaign. At the climax the protesters are going to seize the television station and get airtime on national TV. You must stay out of it, of course. We will time it to coincide with your public statements. The public will see polarization, escalation, environmental fears boiling over into civil unrest. Here are some suggestions of what you might say, and when."

He offers her a paper but her hands stay knotted in her legs. "The fourth statement is a plea for restraint. That's the protesters' cue to blow up a barge filled with pesticides."

"I do not want this," she says.

"Of course not—but you can't control Mali, nobody can. It's tipping over into anarchy."

I catch what she murmurs by watching her face. "I want some time to think."

Her activists file out. Ushi sits next to me and skewers me with a look. "Some Greens are impatient. That man is a sort of pirate. He tries to keep to the high seas so he can ignore inconvenient laws."

"He still needs to watch his step," I say. "He could get *Simpleton* torpedoed."

"I can meet him halfway, or I can lose him. With no one to rein him in, he will become another Carlos." She leans forward and inspects some microscopic feature of my right eye. "We must appease him."

Ushi made her first statement on Earth Day, cuing twelve hundred protesters to barricade the trunk road north of Gao. They set fire to a Timbuktu Earthwealth jeep and stoned other cars. The protesters beat a disciplined retreat when the tear gas came out.

The protests made a nice diversion for hostage taking: the interior minister, some ECOWAS diplomats, a U.N. envoy. Glassy-eyed revolutionaries took them in their offices and affixed them to shotguns for the cameras.

I wouldn't have thought that Mali was vulnerable to information warfare. I never knew its air traffic control system runs on six store-bought desktop computers. Mali bought them cheap from the defense contractors in the first lean years after the Cold War. A nifty strain of the Hellraiser virus scrambled their disks. It might have been two hours' work for a maladjusted adolescent. Mali was effectively lopped off the civilian air routes for five days.

The impromptu feel of the unrest forestalled outside intervention. To the experts it looked like a spontaneous upheaval, a green Tiananmen. To the world at large it looked like the same old African chaos.

Muru's men suppressed the hijinks with offhand brutality. In some cases the brutality was more than offhand. Some of the

Greenfleet organizers brought back rumors of amputations, blindings, clamps and tongs, presided over by a white man with short thick black brows and the sloping forehead of a caveman.

This time Bud has brought me to a different safe house: a cottage in the Vienna woods south of Grinzing. Until he draws the drapes I can see sparse washed-out stars and a valley full of lights. The dark wood walls seem immaterial in the room's dim light. Our chairs are works of art, but it's clear no one sat in them to test the design. My spine sags, my seat slides, sharp corners wedge themselves between my elbow bones.

Bud says, "There's one more thing to take care of before we get to work dumping."

"What's that?"

"We need to pay a call on one of the elders in Mali. Maybe you'd like to sit in. You can check on the local support, economic impact, infrastructure—all part of your due diligence, right?"

"Who is it you're going to see?"

"He's the leader of an ethnic Malinke movement. Mansa Muru."

"Muru? Jesus, Bud, he's not an elder, he's a self-proclaimed emperor. A fugitive with a private army. He's accused of war crimes."

"No one's ever proven any war crimes."

"His doctrine is genocidal. His people are genocidal. His actions have been uniformly genocidal."

"We work closely with him," Bud says. "Muru's a new man. He embraces the concept of foreign direct investment. His primary concern is stability and security."

"Bud, everybody knows this guy is trouble."

"Amnesty has the run of Mali, and they haven't been able to document a single human-rights violation."

"You mean they can't tell who got killed and who just starved."

Bud shows me his palms with a pontifical gesture, patient and calm and slow. "We all know Mali was unstable for a while. Muru was more or less in charge, and he got the blame—that's only natural. Mali has no tradition of public debate, so the rhetoric is naturally vituperative. We've heard it all: he's the African Pol Pot, he's the next Idi Amin. It just doesn't hold up under scrutiny."

"For Christ's sake, can't you find someone more—presentable?"

"He'll do fine. We keep him in line."

Bud and I can travel together. No one will question it: a trip to Mali is no compromising luxury junket. These days it's best to fly into Niger and enter Mali from the southeast. That way all the checkpoints are Muru's. All the shakedowns are coordinated. We stay south of the Niger River and pass through the peaceful part where the cliff dwellers live.

Muru's compound is built around a mud mosque in the town of Djenné. Muru is basically a prehistoric-style animist but he got saved somehow, too, and his personal savior has encouraged him to make a pleasure dome of the mosque. Muru chooses his attendants at the traditional parade of young virgins he has instituted. Upon menarche they are retired, tightly sutured for eternal fidelity.

We have come to pay our respects. Parked dusty technicals ring the mosque. As we walk toward a gap between two of them, Bud swaggers, but he's too stiff to carry it off. He's edgy too. The gunners on the trucks don't care.

"I'm here to see Mansa Muru," Bud says.

A sergeant calls down from the nearest truck. "Impossible, my friend. You give me no reason, no purpose for Mansa Muru to see you."

"Forget it, you're not getting paid. I have a message from Timbuktu Earthwealth."

"I will see," the sergeant says. He climbs down and goes inside. Thirty seconds later he comes out again. He stops to urinate against the wall.

"Well?"

The sergeant seems to have forgotten. Then, "No."

Bud walks off and takes out a phone.

Another man comes out from behind the technicals. Another sergeant. They're all sergeants, distinguished only by varying degrees of rapacity. This one is among the more wolfish, but he says, "Mansa Muru will see the representative from Timbuktu Earthwealth."

Bud turns to the first sergeant and says, "I will tell Mansa Muru you kept me from him to get a bribe." Both sergeants sneer.

The place is a temple of decay. It is the rainy season, and the rain is spitting down now. The mosque crumbles around Muru; the annual struggle to plaster it up has ceased. The supporting logs protrude like teeth from receding gums.

We walk through a dissolving doorway into an oozing mud swamp. Green slime floats in puddles on the floor. Maggots writhe furiously in the rib cage of a dead bird on the floor.

In a sanctum in the center of it all, Muru sits at a listing wood table stained with black mold. His buttocks slop over the chair. He fondles a grave child who pours him tea. Muru has a wide mouth, a small forehead, and a goiter. He looks at me with protruding eyes, pressing delicate hands on the table.

He toys with a handsome matchbook lying open on his desk. One match remains in it. If he used that last match he would have no pretense for keeping it. So he lets it lie unused on his desk, a mute testament to his importance.

Most people would not recognize the matchbook, which shows a gold bear rearing in a black cave mouth. Only the insiders know it as the Home Guard's emblem. He got it from Bear Mountain.

We taught Muru everything he knows. Muru is our proxy in Bud's war against the French.

"What do you want?" Muru's voice is a croak, slow and simple in English.

"We need your help relocating some people."

"What people?"

"The squatters in the Adrar des Iforas," Bud says.

Muru belches softly with his mouth closed, puffing up his cheeks. "That's in no-man's-land," he says. "That zone is empty."

I say, "There's a refugee camp there."

"A camp?"

"Ecumenical Alms used to run it," I say.

"Oh. That camp." Muru's face gives his bulging eyes a quick piqued pinch. "That camp is not going anywhere. It's there because the French put it there."

There are moments when you see things from a height. You make out patterns that obliterate your purposes in life. Sometimes it's a relief to shrink from view, to know your hopes and fears are equally trivial. But not this time. I follow the conversation not to higher ground but to a vantage from which human beings are interchangeable as ants, too small to cry or even crunch when crushed.

The colonial era is over. The free ports and hongs are gone. Foreign investment is as rulebound as a game: International competitive bidding. Domestic preference. Local content and participation. Timbuktu Earthwealth and the Authority have taken particular care to foster local content and participation.

For Timbuktu Earthwealth, Muru is a friendly face. He speaks English. He does not provoke his neighbors. He butchers blacks sparingly and does not enslave them. So Timbuktu Earthwealth has reached a quiet understanding with Mansa Muru.

For the Authority, as for the rest of the world, Inhad is repugnant. But he can still beguile. Frenchmen like Theriault cherish the nostalgic tug of the nomad myth. Inhad plays to that, rendering picturesque nomad idioms in fluent French. His mots suffuse the French intelligence community. Like Pol Pot and Stalin, he is *charmant.* What's more, Inhad can be useful. Those colorful nomad proverbs are not figures of speech for him; they comprise a precise technical nomenclature of feuds, raids, and reprisals.

Lila understands only dimly how she came to the Adrar. Back when I was in seclusion in the desert, Lila was working her wonders in Tabankort town. Miscegenation mixed Tabankort's races. Everyone plants and herds alike. Blacks marry Tuaregs, slaves grow rich. In a place like Tabankort it's difficult to cull salable slaves from mongrel Arabs. In such places Inhad finds it simpler to exterminate the lot. In the ordinary course of events, Lila and her refugees would likely have been slaughtered, not moved, but the realities of power saved them, invisibly, as the petty contention of pagan gods once briefly protected Troy.

Even then, Bud was vying for nuclear waste. At that time he seemed sure to prevail with his crass Anglophone "hardball" and his Hollywood publicity. Theriault reacted with characteristic subtlety. His thoughts turned to Inhad. If Inhad could be persuaded to nudge some innocents into the path of Bud's bulldozers, progress would stop.

Inhad did as he was bid, sparing Tabankort. He drove Lila and her refugees north to Bud's dump site, buying valuable time for the Authority. Timbuktu Earthwealth put a brave face on the setback, making a mascot of Lila, but they were stymied. As Bud Van Sickle was driving for the goal line, playing football, Theriault played an altogether more elegant and cerebral game: tic-tac-toe.

Lila is an *X* blocking a row of *O*'s.

Tic-tac-toe, skillfully played, always results in a draw. A draw is not acceptable to the men who rule the world. So the contest must continue. The matter will be decided in another way.

With a lover's rapt attention Bud is trying things and feeling the response. Now he has adopted the intonations appropriate for an audience with Emperor Muru. "This project can't continue without your help."

Muru tells him, "Truck them out yourself."

"We haven't got the resources. Since the gold-rush hoax we can barely feed the camp, much less move it."

"Just be patient," Muru says. "Without that white girl to scrounge food for them, the camp will disband."

"She's not going anywhere," I say.

Muru blinks carefully and draws his closed mouth into a smile. "Patience. The camp has become an Algerian rebel base. Soon enough some fanatic will cut her throat."

When we get back to Bud's Hummer I punch in Lila's number on the satellite phone.

"Who are you calling?" Bud wants to know, but I'm already

talking to one of the volunteers. The woman says, "Lila?" I detect an ominous awkwardness in the silence. *They're going to tell me she's dead. They're going to tell me she went home.* My is mind caroming off the possibilities, a strobe-light succession of light and dark, hope and fear, desert brown and jungle green.

Lila's voice. I breathe again. It simply took time to find her. She hasn't yet learned to wear her satellite phone. She says "Ty?" warily, as if she hears a rustle in the dark.

"How is it there?"

"Incredible. No one's died in weeks. A child was *born.* You know what it's like to see more life here, not less?"

Lila's world is so small.

"Is it safe?" Bud clamps my arm. I'll only be allowed to say so much.

Laughing, she says, "Safe? You mean, are people running and starving and dying? No. They're not. Here, they're not. You look at the new faces, there's no shock in their eyes. There's greed in their eyes, or outrage, or a search for familiar faces. All different kinds of hope."

"Do you need anything?"

"Are you kidding? I'm the mayor! I get whatever I want."

"Have you been taking in many Algerian refugees?"

"I don't ask," she says. "If you're an Algerian and you have any sense, you burn your papers so they can't send you back."

I tell her, "Please be careful." Bud pushes a button and cuts me off.

At times the city of Timbuktu seems to mock Bud's venture. His technocrats hope for a 2 percent return. The *marabouts* outside double your money by sorcery. Our minutely chronicled "forecast horizon" is 120 months. Here in Timbuktu, centuries sink without a trace. Now at the Timbuktu office we have pressed the computer into service as a television, modern and prosaic at once. But the image on the screen is a totem from another time.

This is not like Ushi's other spots. Serata is speaking alone, up close, in rotten-fruit colors and shapes. Her scars hump and twist with a puppet's unnatural animation. The hand in the puppet is palsied or shaking with rage.

Serata's own voice is audible this time, a lump-tongued yowl. Fatimatou's voice shouts English over it, breathless and stammering, dragged along behind, appalled, possessed. Serata's face cuts through my reasoning mind and dredges up fears that antedate thought. Her voice sinks in deep, filling primitive lobes with mute dread. This is true prophecy: fear compels obedience.

This sowing of hot salts in the earth, this will end life.

There will be plagues—the big spots and the small spots, and leprosy most hateful. The sores that make us send the sick away. The men will kill with clubs, not guns: there are not enough bullets in the world. Slow death unending: first you, then you, then you.

We will know a new kind of wandering, stripped of our animals and driven without rest. No salt lands, no green, but piles of stones, scraps on sticks, buried death everywhere, taking our legs as we go. The shoots will not push through the grease from all the unwashed corpses in the ground . . .

Towns throughout Mali erupted then, not in riots but in panic, the kind of wildfire hysteria that grips people by their superstitious bones and makes old stories manifestly true.

The smiths in Gao sell magic charms that look a lot like knives. Mobs in Ménaka find sorcerers to suffocate in pits. Here in Timbuktu, fitful gunfire crackles. Shouts come too close, then recede. Bud sits up with a pair of MAC-10s, cleaning one, keeping the other in reach. The magazines are longer than the guns.

In the camp, all is quiet. Lila and the refugees watch, appalled but not afraid. Serata's spark did not catch there. In the camp she's just the same, a timid cheery saint. Serata does not recall saying the sharp words we heard.

That's because the spirit had her, others say.

Mass hysteria boils up frequently in Africa. It always seemed natural to me, a hair-trigger response to a dangerous environment. Your protective reflexes outrun your critical faculties. Your body snatches up a fear and presses it into service to spur flight. Any fear will do, rational or not.

Some people chalk it up to inadequate education: children here don't outgrow bogeymen. It's just one more sad consequence of ignorance. Ignorance makes Africans fall prey to terror, corruption, and disease; ignorance makes Africans fall prey to irrational fears.

That said, I've never experienced it, or even witnessed it. I can't dismiss the people who think it's more than that: Serata, for example.

I recall kneeling around a fire one chilly evening. Serata's stiff mouth and cooked tongue change her words, but she speaks slowly and we understand. *The European does not take fright. He is too wise for that. He understands fear, he thinks. No mystery in it: a herd of antelopes bolt at nothing. A herd of Africans take fright from fancies of ghosts.*

Ah, but to feel it, to be part of it—in that moment you believe in something with your whole soul, you are sure of it as you can never be sure of your name or your mama or the earth underfoot. It is a kind of understanding that comes all at once, too fast. That is what makes it terrible. Fear such as this is a glimpse of what God sees.

Timbuktu is quiet now. Muru's Creepers have imposed order, using enough mundane here-and-now terror to outweigh the most fearful superstitions.

Bud is back to business, instructing me in my duties. "Lila trusts you. Talk to her, tell her it's time to pull up stakes."

"How are you going to get them out?"

"We gave them trucks; they can leave any time."

"Half a dozen trucks won't get twelve hundred people through a desert full of mines. Lila tried that once, and hundreds of people died on her watch. She's not going to budge."

"She has no option," Bud says, "and neither do we."

"You're paying Janissary—put them to work. Let them handle the evacuation."

"Under the current circumstances, that would be a provocation. We've got a delicate balance between the two warlords. We're leaning toward Muru, and Inhad knows it. If we inserted a force in no-man's-land, Inhad would go apeshit."

"Bud, you told me Janissary could pacify the place in a day."

"I don't have the budget to contain a civil war, and civil war is what we'd have if I sent a force in there now."

"So let it slide awhile," I say.

"We can't. Algerian refugees are percolating across the border, and the camp is taking them in. They look like noncombatants, but you know a lot of them are Islamic resistance fighters. We can't contain Algeria while that's going on."

"If you want Lila out of there, you're going to have to move her."

"Lila needs to understand that the situation has changed. The camp has changed. One night one of her grateful refugees will come into her tent and carve her up. Is that what you want?"

Bud's generosity has tricked out the camp's computer with

two-way video. Fatimatou helps me set up a call. She chases Lila down and puts her on. It's no better breaking the news from here. I shrink from her glare at a distance of four hundred miles.

"Are you out of your mind? A forced march through the desert? Forget it. When the raids have stopped and the mines are cleared, we can go home. Not before."

"But it's not safe where you are."

"Then make it safe. Bud's got all his soldiers of fortune sitting on their thumbs. Put them to work."

"Lila, look, I can't explain everything to you, but please believe me. The camp sits on a valuable piece of real estate."

"And you're evicting us." Mother Teresa's compassion, Medea's temper.

"It has nothing to do with you. It's like a steamroller coming down the street. You just know to get out of the way."

The screen crackles as she blinks off.

Timbuktu Earthwealth headquarters feels like a tire about to blow on a desert road: too much pressure and too much heat, spinning remorselessly, way too fast. At the big marble table we exhale in squeezed-out gusts. In the intervening silence of our stopped-up lungs Bud drums callus-and-bone fingers on the table. It sounds like marching jackboots.

Bud has summoned some fixers from his staff. One has a hatchet face and a thin-lipped leer. The other has skin like a pricey briefcase and electric-blue eyes. Their appearance suggests no particular country. They seem to come from a stratum of the earth that underlies countries, where living creatures are compressed diamond-hard. Like Bud, they work for everyone and no one. Bureaucratic jargon muddies their role: they have "Timbuktu Earthwealth billets with a dotted-line report to Janissary Systems," but they are freelancers, on contract, detailed from somewhere else. Who the boss is, I don't know. They could be waiting for instructions from Satan.

"Muru can't cut it," Bud says. "He hasn't challenged Inhad in the buffer zone for years. With all the envoys and technocrats kissing his ass, he thinks he's a statesman. He's lost his nerve."

“Just gig the little toad, then. We own all his cronies—give one of them a turn.”

“You guys made a basic mistake,” Bud says. “You recruited people you like, and now we’re paying for it. All our assets are pussies.” Bud is raising his voice a notch every few words, prying his eyes wider with each sentence. “We need somebody hard-nosed. Each new asset, I kept prodding you: Does he fit the profile? Firstborn, violent upbringing? Rising star in a snake pit: the slave cartels, the Ninjas? No. They’re pantywaists.”

One underling murmuring, one grunting, they eye Bud. “Maybe Mumm can suggest something.”

Bud’s eyes widen and droop at the sides, almost imperceptibly. Anxiety. I’ve never seen it there before. Instantly it’s gone, and Bud is snarling, asserting dominance. “*I* will decide when we go to Mumm.”

Bud’s guys back down and grovel for him, but Bud has acquiesced. This Mumm must be invoked.

Mumm is on his way. He’s clearly an important man, with powerful connections and better ideas. Maybe he can arrange an airlift. Bud has kept us up most of the night, banging file drawers, muttering at his computer, asking questions when he knows the answer. He mostly leafs through files in silence now, but when my eyelids droop he speaks: *Keep your mouth shut unless someone asks you a question. Nobody will be asking for opinions, only facts. Keep it short.*

You ought to mark up this map with some notes. You need to be up on your topography. If you can’t contribute, I’ll be the one who looks bad.

I look around for a little mousy noise. It’s coming from the papers Bud is holding. His hands are shaking. He presses them angrily down on the table when I look.

Mumm works at Janissary, and Janissary works for Bud. Yet some secret renown dictates a little vocal genuflection in every reference to Mumm. No one takes his name in vain.

Mumm is here now. He has a sallow face and a taut crease of a mouth. Blank eyes, motionless hands. Short thick black brows under the sloping forehead of a caveman.

His silence is a raised club. Even Bud will not lock eyes with him. Bud's guys are playing dead. Authority is irrelevant here, and power pointless. Mumm is not the boss; he is the kind of primate that decides who will eat, who will mate, and who will die.

"You need to get Muru an adviser." Mumm's words, in pin-drop silence.

The others check Mumm's face with quick glances. Mumm will acknowledge some of the glances with a brief tensing of his jaw. The others compete for this sign of favor. Mumm clamps his lips on a fuming cheroot, but his eyes send the message that an utterance is coming. He savors the expectant silence. "What you need is a refugee wrangler."

I say, "Is that some kind of aid specialist?"

Mumm says to Bud, "What is he doing here?" Bud cringes. Mumm laughs in abrupt derisive spits. *T*'s.

Mumm turns to tutor me. "Refugee wranglers displace populations. A fundamental skill. Make some refugees. The aid agencies fly in to take care of them. Now you got yourself a camp. Your men can come and go, get fed for free, get billeted in nice tents. Great pickings for your press-gangs.

"Muru lacks the know-how." Mumm's declaiming lumps of words. "We need somebody who can do it for him. Shell the camp right and you can drive the refugees like a car."

I don't know what's in my eyes but Mumm says to me, "You got a problem with that?"

"No, he does not," Bud says. "We can do it with minimal casualties."

"That's true," Mumm says, speaking slowly, frowning in puzzlement at this irrelevance. "Properly done, this is an operation of surgical precision. Munitions are not what they were when you were in Iraq, Bud. You can kill twelve, or ten, or just a single preselected asshole. The virtuosos can just scare them away."

One of the underlings says, "This adviser—how about somebody from the Ghanda Koye movement?"

"They're air force. All Muru's cronies are ex-Ninjas. Read the fucking briefing book." Bud is climbing over him, fighting to be beta male. "For three K a day I expect—"

He stops as Mumm opens his mouth. "Rebels from pastoral tribes do it best: they're herders, you know? They're bred for it. Their livestock is dead, they miss the cattle drives. This is the next best thing."

Lila, and Fatimatou, and Serata and the children who snuggle in her lap. The next best thing to cattle.

Mumm says, "It so happens we have the best refugee wrangler on the continent right here in town. They call him Fatso. He stepped over a line in Uganda: the natives get touchy about ritual cannibalism. The neighbors went multilateral on him. Now he's holed up here. He's here with what's left of his resistance army: his kids, Sonny and Junior."

"Fatso is here?" Bud's seen-it-all-before face gives out. Fatso is a celebrated person of a very special sort.

"Apparently Mali's extradition treaty lapsed when the government fell. Fatso's happy here though, the medical care is better. Imagine that." Mumm twists his face and laughs. *T*'s.

"Bud, I'm going to see Fatso." Mumm glances at me and says to Bud, "He knows the terrain around the camp? Where wheeled vehicles are OK, and where you need tracks?"

"Yes," Bud says.

"You're coming too," he says to me.

I don't like Bud. I don't trust him. But parting from him to go off with Mumm, I find myself locking eyes with Bud, hanging on. I'm going beyond Bud's pale. That's bad.

Fatso was the Sudan's weapon against Uganda: an obscure psychopath in the tradition of Idi Amin. With Sudanese money and arms he became a rebel leader. He has not been abandoned in defeat; defeated African rebels take refuge in another shard of Africa. They are not lonely in exile: prudent rich-world spies know their time may come again.

A Hummer is waiting outside with a thick-limbed silent driver at the wheel. Mumm and I get in back. Mumm pulls out a map teeming with tiny features. He puts it in my hand. "You will give Fatso the lay of the land.

"Look at that detail. European Space Agency commercial resolution." He points to the map. He's smiling now—we're buddies, having fun. "The natives used to lock up foreign engineers if they caught them with topo maps. State secrets, they called them. I would go down to the security ministry and say, 'Here is a map, my gift to you. Suitably digitized, it can guide a cruise missile to the bedroom window of the presidential palace. Anyone in the world can buy one of these for fifty dollars.' Half the time they're so embarrassed they let the poor bastards go without a bribe."

We pull up at a Soviet-gray concrete high-rise. An iron fence surrounds it. Head-high and sturdy, it's topped with decorative work like a rich man's fence: rods that curve back and forth, flame-like, tapering to a sharp point. Mumm leaves the driver with the Hummer and we walk to the gate.

Garbage is hurled out of broken windows here—we pass through a trampled-down gap in a stinking midden that rings the building. We climb six flights over more garbage and what's left of the windows.

When we reach the top floor Mumm heads for one of the steel doors like he's coming home at night. He pounds on the door, puts his back into it. Here in Mali it's a foreign sound, this storm-trooper knock, and it reverberates like shouted obscenities. "Hey, Fatso, open up."

The door hasn't stopped rattling when a metallic crackle carries through from inside: racking and cocking of guns in sure hands. Mumm sneers. "You hear that? They're down to shotguns. They're packing Baikal shotguns like a bunch of Haratine sand niggers. When they were on top, they had Hecklers, Uzis, anything they wanted."

Mumm bellows again, "Smile, Fatso, you're the luckiest guy in Africa."

The door squeals open on two leveled shotguns and other things I do not notice. His voice low and loud, Mumm says, "Nobody calls him Fatso to his face, especially these days."

In a stained cushioned chair sits living death. He wears a damp diaper and nothing else. His thighs swell into rock-hard knees. The skin traces the skeleton in sharp relief, dropping precipitously off each bone's edge into deep recesses. The button where his ribs meet is etched in fine detail. Skin clings to every chink and suture in his skull. The eyes are huge and dry and they pulse with hate. You would think he was too wasted to hate like that, with the cunning and imagination in those eyes. Now I see why Fatso is the best. Hate makes him clever, courageous, persistent, and patient. His kind of hate comprehends all virtues.

"Pat them down," the skeleton says. There is no caution in his tone; he is not gauging a threat but making one, affirming helplessness.

One of the men puts down his shotgun. He spins me into the wall, kicks my feet apart, and squeezes me in his hands. "What's this," he says, digging his fingers into my scrotum, tighter and tighter until I'm on the ground thrashing, breath squeezed out of me but still yowling.

The squeezing stops. The pain changes, throbbing with a shrill warning that shoots deep into my belly like something torn loose and whiplashing inside me. My stomach makes a fist and shoots heat into my throat and I am choking it back.

I twist my head to look for Mumm. He is watching me impassively. They watch him, waiting for fear to take hold.

Mumm says, "Shouldn't have done that, Sonny." He steps over to the skeleton, cradles the skull-face in his hands.

Two shotgun muzzles touch Mumm's head.

Mumm speaks inches from Fatso's face. They are breathing one another's breath. "If you shot me, do you know what would happen? The president of the United States would send LRRPs after you. Big ones, white supremacists, fucked-up inbred redneck psychos who have practiced killing you for years. They will fight for the privilege of coming after you, and when they find you they will peel you in strips until you're pink like me."

Mumm cocks his head, pushes it in a little closer. "Everybody in the world wants you dead. Everyone but me."

In a cottony voice the skeleton says, "Put the guns down," and, to Mumm, "If I spit in your eye you'll be dead next spring."

Mumm says, "I bring the gift of life."

Turning to the man who hurt me, Mumm produces two vials.

"This is for your dad. A month of this and he'll be on his feet. The disease will disappear. But if he stops taking it, if he can't get it any more, he dies.

"This stops the new resistant strains. Africans can't afford these drugs. Dutch junkies can't afford them. Even rich American fags can't afford these drugs. But I have given *you* the gift of life."

I climb up a table to my feet, freezing and twisting to wait out the pain, but there's a bruisy pressure building as the yanked-out works creep back in place. I glance furtively back over my shoulder, where the sons nurse their father, holding a cup to the flaccid lips, tenderly murmuring, eyes shining with love.

"Now I'll tell you what you owe me."

Fatso has lain down to rest. Sonny and Junior huddle in the corner with Mumm, awestruck and submissive, dovetailing smoothly into a new hierarchy with Mumm at the top and me palpably at the bottom. Mumm is brisk and bureaucratic now as he briefs them on the mission, as he calls it.

Mumm unrolls the map. "Here's the Adrar." He shows us the Janissary Systems encampments, blue triangles on the tan map. With a finger he peens the red triangle that marks the camp and says, "I want them out of there. You do what it takes to move them."

"Move them where?" one son says.

"I don't care, but I want an orderly march. No casualty footage, no screaming bare-assed little girls running in flames."

"We can move them west."

The yell breaks out of me, "That's all impassable dunes with no wells. The trucks will bog down and they'll die."

Mumm says, "Bust his balls again, he's out of order."

Junior hits me backhand on the nose. I sit and take it. Mumm tells me, "Shut up until I tell you what to say."

Sonny gestures at the Janissary outposts and says, "What about these security forces?"

"Just stay out of their way. They will stand down."

Junior scowls, then rises and looks out the window. His back expands and hunches as he calls, "Your driver's shot!"

"They can't take the Hummer, I've got the key," Mumm says.

"They're sniffing around the stairwell," Junior says.

Mumm spits air in disgust. "Give me that shotgun. Sonny, come with me. Fuckin' delinquents."

On the way out Mumm stops and says, "When I come back I want a route for the squatters marked on that map. Work with him, Junior."

There's no way out for the refugees. But maybe I can get Mumm stuck, out of range of the camp. I'm lying frantically: "You can't set up a battery there. You'll be buried in sand within the hour."

"Wait," Junior says. "Mumm told us the dump-site supply route goes that way." He sees me hesitate and twitch and says, "What are you trying to do?"

He stands up, taking his time, but it's clear my chance to explain will come after the beating.

His eyes jump behind me. It makes me look. A shotgun is leaning in the corner. I'm closer to it. I push the chair in his path and dive for the gun, ramming my shoulder into the floor. I squirm up the wall and swing the gun around. He freezes like a pointer dog, every muscle taut.

He sees something in my eyes. Maybe he's seen it in child conscripts. It tells him I don't want to kill and now he's coming, head down, brows down, hands clawed and I blow a leg off Fatso's firstborn son.

Fatso is risen, shaking like the living dead and glaring with the rancor of the damned. I poke him in the face with the gun butt and his head snaps sideways and down. He lands like thrown clothes, light and limp, and I think I've killed him too but his eyes open and the hate in them panics me and I'm tearing out the door.

I'm downstairs before I start to think. I have the shotgun, but no shells. Tossed, it clatters in the stairwell.

Mumm's voice comes around the corner. I skid to a stop and

wheel around. *Hide.* I squeeze into the garbage under the bottom flight of stairs. The gun is in the corner in a different pile of trash, right on top.

Mumm's voice is above me now, dripping down: "Good soldier. Tended to freeze up, though. That's why he's dead."

When they see what happened they'll come back down for me. I have to run. I climb out, shake off slimy greens and rags and take off, out through the gap in the midden, toward the gate. Which window is Fatso's? Are they looking out right now?

I pass the Hummer we came in. It's unattended except for an African kid climbing the fence alongside it. No, this boy's not climbing. His feet scrabble against the fence. His arms dangle broken at his sides. He hangs by his lower jaw, which is hooked through one of the metal spikes on the fence. The spike sticks out his open mouth.

Mumm has made an example of him.

21

I dodge through the narrower alleys, brushing by alert locals. I'm faking a destination and some self-control but my toes bounce me up and my hips fight my legs—I want to run. If I make a wrong turn I'll acquire a mob of beggar kids. They all moonlight as informants for the Creepers. I come to a street broad enough to carry vehicular traffic. Every truck is a taxi here, especially for a foreigner with real money. I flag down a truck heading south. It screeches and pulls left and stops well beyond me, bumpers bouncing. Paint gone, shocks shot, no brakes—this vehicle will not stand out. The bed is one-tenth loaded with a dozen bags of rice. The driver is a jolly tactile man with stumpy dreads.

"I bi taa min?" He wants to know where I'm going.

"Korioumé." The port.

For five dollars he takes me. He rolls up the windows to protect us from the hot wind, and we bake in stagnant air. He's ecstatic, but it will be a quiet ride. My Bambara vocabulary won't take us far.

By the time I smell the rank river it's dark. A steamer is taking on passengers. I squeeze into the queue and press a dollar into the ticket man's hand.

I should be hunched in deepest shadow, but I can't stand still. If the boat's not moving, I have to. The passengers have boarded and

I'm staring at the black bank. The engine revs and the mooring lines thump on the deck. The boat is under way.

I have no sense of going anywhere. I can't see the landmarks we're leaving behind, and the sounds don't last long enough to fade as we go by. A truck's brakes, metal on metal. A cry, male or female. In between, nothing: the sound of a curfew. No one has imposed one. People know to stay inside at night.

The river sloshes against the boat's hull. The deck moves under me, not with a swell or a chop but with an ague. This is an afflicted river. The mosquitoes will be fighting for a place on my socks, down where I can't hear them.

Muru owns the river from here to the border with Niger. If the river were navigable, which it's not, in Niger I could—do what? Watch it happen from a safe distance? No. They will go into the desert invisibly, in silence, like water going into air. At some indeterminate point they will be gone.

But now there's a sound, continuous and steadily louder, and I'm clutched up inside, hugging the wall: this sound means a launch, coming up behind. A searchlight sweeps the deck. Everything slows. It's Mumm here to spike me on the fence with that boy.

To find me, they only had to ask after me. I forgot what a prodigy a white face is in a torn-up African town.

The crew seems not to have reacted. I must be running but I don't feel my feet on the deck. I see a hatch. *Get down to third class.* I skid to a stop in the black: *Where's the top stair?* My feet can't find anything so I squat and grope. It's a ladder. I ease myself frantically down.

Am I trapped down here? I should have gone over the railing.

It's dark down here except for one tiny light. The mantle of a naphtha lamp glows pure white. It shows faces staring at me and shadows that move and stop and melt away. It gives little enough light that a single broken porthole glows blue-black in the next room. I see a semicircle of it through a half-open hatch. It opens to port. The launch is bumping the hull on the other side. This may be my way out.

That must be a toilet behind the hatch. I feel wisps of river air from the porthole, an intermittent fluttering draft. But a stench turns into a taste as I grope toward the circle of sky.

The passengers do not speak to me. They watch me feel my way toward the hatch. I step on fingers and shy at the yelp, duck from a shadow that looks like a wall at my face.

I squeeze through the hatch. Inside is a toilet swathed in some kind of fibrous mold. It's slimy underfoot as I feel my way behind the toilet to the porthole. The fittings are rusted shut but the glass is in shards and the shouting voices are down here, their beams raking faces.

I knock out the shards with the heel of my hand. One cuts so deep my whole body gives. I'm climbing out. Hanging on with the cut palm I stretch the gash open to a big red mouth. I let my legs through the porthole and I'm squirming, humping, ripping in the ring of broken glass. No pain now. I throw my arms up overhead. My shoulders won't go through, they're straining stuck, but I squeeze back in, tilt one shoulder down, thread it through, the voices are louder now, their lamps shine in here but the beams haven't found me, not yet. I'm afraid to look with my shiny white face. Now my collarbone's hung up on a glass notch and I'm shoving off, scrabbling at the hull. The glass snaps, and I drop.

I tried not to splash, but the slap of the water on my face and arms must have made a noise. I'm underwater and I hear the air coming off me. I want to look and see if they're lighting up the water, but I can't tell which way is up yet. The river tastes like rancid eggs and kidneys and oil.

I'm rising now, and I'm looking where the surface ought to be. Only the dimmest glow, no lights. But I don't dare come up right under the porthole. They may be looking out. I bump against the hull and think of the screw going by. I push off, thrash away, but I can feel it pulling me in. I've drawn up my legs, I don't dare kick but I'm clawing at the water, arcing toward the screw sucking me in, I'm flailing and I hear it pounding and it spins me around and goes past me.

As my head breaks the surface I gulp up and duck back down. I dribble the water and scum from my mouth and dive. I'm churning underwater, swimming straight, I hope. The water has an awful and unnatural variety of textures: oozing and slippery with clingy tufts and yielding lumps.

I have to breathe now. I drift up and gasp, leaving an ear and an eye out. The steamer is moving off. The launch is still with it. Someone must have seen me belowdecks. They'll start searching the water when they don't find me on board. I have to get away.

I can see lights in the distance. Is the riverbank that far?

I've puked several times. The first time was easy and painless. But now dry heaves are knotting me up and holding me underwater. A few vigorous strokes can set off a new spasm. I'm creeping through the water on my back; the current's got me and it's taking me somewhere faster than I can swim: maybe back out into the channel. I can't tell. The lights are gone and I don't know where the riverbank is. I give up flopping in place and dog-paddle so I can pant better. My feet keep sinking. Again and again I get locked in my head, senses shut off, thoughts blinking out until I snort water and choke.

I know I'm not dying; when I fade there's no radiance and no comfort, only Fatso's eyes and Serata's two dents and Muru's wide froggy mouth telling me what's going to happen.

Strong hands pull me up into a boat that lists and ships water. The fisherman is gaping. A tiny lamp dilutes the blackness. The man kneeling over me speaks no French or English. He looks stricken. To cook a fish from the river is one thing, but to dunk in it . . .

I spit meagerly over the side, expelling some of the microbes rioting in my mouth, leaving the rest to regroup each time: leptospirosis from rat piss. Yellow fever. Polio from shit, wandering loose in my body, snipping nerves. AIDS.

I strip and take a blanket from him. I have to scrub—you can rub the worms off before they tunnel into you, mash them as they squirm unseen on your skin. Each one that survives will dig until it finds a vein, ride my bloodstream to my lungs, crawl out to my throat, slide down to my guts, settle in and suck my blood.

As he sets me on the shore my stomach is still bubbling. Nausea nags like prudent advice: *Puke once more, get it over with.* I do, and lose more time. A boy turns me over, punches me halfheartedly, and frisks me, but I don't have anything he wants.

I feel cleaner now, after my river bath. I'm not with Mumm and Fatso anymore.

I open my eyes and see another African squatting over me. His eyes are different—not avid but kind. Long face, firm nose. A sleeveless Malian shirt, not foreign castoffs like the gangs wear.

He asks me, "Are you sick?"

"I fell into the water," I say.

"That's not good."

"I have to get away from here."

"Rest a minute," he says. "Where are you going?"

I have no idea. "Toward Kidal." And the camp.

"Into the Sahara?"

"Yes."

"There is a bus. I will take you to the depot. You may have to wait."

Not the depot. Mumm will stake that out. "I don't want to be seen."

"Who is looking for you? Foreigners?"

I don't answer.

"I only ask because you should go in a truck if you want to avoid foreigners. I can arrange one." He lugs me to a doorway, where I sit like a drunk in the dark. I can't see where he's pointing when he says, "That jug is for travelers—drink if you want. It's thirsty on the truck."

It's easy to feel safe. A danger recedes, the mind rests. Traveling in a locked truck, released twice a day to void, or not (the women, supernaturally, do not, ever), I feel invisible, lost to the world. What Westerner would tolerate this?

This conveyance is no special deal for me. It's a routine part of life. I'm locked in the truck with a dozen others. We are not locked in to confine us; the truck is made for cargo and the door latches only from outside.

The truck bed is the size of a standard container with no top. The passengers have pulled the tarp off. The square of sky penned in by the sides has more stars than all the cities in the world. The Milky Way is thick and deep. Saturn is sallow and Jupiter, piercing white. The Pleiades are blurry lumps of light. With no moon we are black and gray when we stir, and nonexistent when we are still. People are heaped at the front of the bed. Cargo is stacked in back.

A bare patch of empty gray truck bed invites me to sleep. I move there and quickly learn that this is where the truck bucks most violently. Before I can scrabble back, I bounce and crack elbows and knees on the corrugated steel. I squeeze back into the crush. They don't like the way I smell either, but they are tolerant. My foolishness doesn't amuse them. Their hushed voices and halting French echo the boatman's concern. They call me *kōro,* brother, as if we shared one mother's milk.

All the cruelty here seems to breed kindness, more of it than anywhere on earth. My nameless helper refused payment when he put me on this truck. "You've given up your home and you've got nothing now," he said. Even visitors evoke compassion here.

The truck slumps to a stop. The driver needs a stretch. They open the cargo doors and the men fan out quickly. They will have no more time than the driver needs. The women do not come out. Manners prescribe dehydration, which shields them from the indignity of urinating in the open air.

I need to drink. I will dehydrate quickly if I don't. Even in the cold night air I'm gulping with each breath.

"Is there a well here?" The driver shakes his head.

A woman says, "Yes, yes there is, down the slope."

"No time," he says. "If you go we'll be gone before you get back."

Is it too much to ask? Can I live without a drink? These people don't complain. But I've seen too many men drop dead from thirst. At Ramadan, when they can't have a drop all day, they work in the sun, honor God with their thirst, and die.

The pounding in my head relents and I am lying on my face in the sand. The men pick me up and take me back to the truck. My nose fits comfortably between two ridges on the corrugated metal.

I can hear the women. They are demanding water, not for themselves but for me. They rush outside, and the truck does not move for long minutes. One returns with my bottle. She keeps it from me until the silt settles. *"Ji kadi."* It's good water. It's from a little rill, she says.

Surface water. In that case I should seal the bottle and let it sit two days until the worms die. A corner of my mind drones on like that, refusing to accept the African imperatives that govern my new life. I suck at the bottle until the muddy lees are dry.

The passengers have crowded back in, and the door shuts. I need more water.

A woman hands me a bottle of cold green tea. Her man peers

over her shoulder in the gloom. *"I ni se."* Thank you. I drain it, unable to let go, and the man starts. Not because I am jeopardizing his life, but because of my need. People here have trained themselves to ignore thirst. They see thirst as a kind of dipsomania: a weakness that leads to dependence, as if water were a vice. Urine is brown here from this unnatural temperance.

I wake in perfect peace, floating unresisting until I come to feel my head bouncing off the truck bed. The women hover over me. They have taken charge of the work of nursing me.

The rusty steel is shaking less and less, but it's pulling at me. It is slowing. "Another oasis?" I ask.

A woman shakes her head. "No, there's nothing here."

A murmur approaches from the door, *"Sûreté."* The police. Another word, quicker and quieter: "No." A hissing whisper: *"Ninjas."*

The Ninjas have some official name that doesn't fit as well. They're not a secret police. It's no secret, what they do: the dissidents who issue from the jails crippled and silent, they are the Ninjas' work. Bozo dragged them into the light of day and punished a few of the worst. Bozo is gone now, and the emperor Muru has restored them.

Frantic hands drag me to the back. They stuff me under bags of meal until I'm pressed with weights, barely able to breathe, sucking in air with contortions of shoulders and sides. Will they see the bags move as I breathe? No matter: I have to breathe.

The door bangs open. "Everyone out." A voice from outside, the driver's, I think, but pitched high now.

The Ninjas rattle and bang in the truck bed. They speak to one another, not to me. They bang the walls and floor; I start, but the bags hold me tight. I can hear them shifting bags near my head. Rice rustles and bags plop, closer and closer. One bag, moved, shifts more weight onto my ribs and stops me breathing. I try new muscles that might draw in air, in my back, my shoulders, my waist. I'm a pig in the coils of a patient python now. The air in me is all I'll get.

There is silence. I hear the beat of my heart and in my left ear, the rustle of mealworms in a bag. I can feel the truck rock as they jump from the bed and scrape in the dirt outside until it's time to breathe again, and I can't. My nerves want to windmill my arms, but they're pinned. My whole body is writhing humping twisting in place, muscles tearing, lungs empty now no matter what I do.

A mouth is on mine, sticky and sour, and I'm filling with the smell. Someone is breathing for me. They feel the suck of my breath and break off. A light hand touches my chest. *What's wrong with me?* Perhaps I am ill.

They speak irrelevant words to me. The same thing several times, it seems. Finally the words coalesce in my mind.

"Don't thank us." I must have been thanking him. "They warned us of you, a white man on the run. If the Ninjas found you here, they would break our bones. It was too late to turn you in."

Now I remember. They buried me to hide me. They suffocated me, then revived me.

A man's shape shows against the sky. "Are you Russian?"

"American," I say.

"Ah-hah." Proud of his idiom, forming the sounds like they're words. In English he says, "I knew it. Those teeth aren't Russian teeth. Too good.

"What is your name?" He's not curious but attentive, listening for something.

I tell him.

"Do you know where you are?"

Yes, I do.

"No damage to your brain. You'll be all right," he says. "I'm a doctor. I studied in Paris, then stayed there as long as I could. I saved many lives there, so they did me the honor of deporting me on a commercial airliner. No chains, no guards, with dignity, just like a Polak."

The truck's closest approach to the camp was four miles south of it. The nearest stop, five miles west of it. It is three A.M. and in the cool of the early morning I can walk that far. But I don't know how long I can wallow through this deep slippery sand. The mountains look different from here. I can't tell where our well is.

My thirst is starting to build again. I slog faster; it's too cool to make me sweat, but the dry air wrings moisture from every breath. The horizon is brightening. It won't stay cool for long.

The light begins to show me subtle shapes that don't fit here: smooth flat arcs; surfaces without enough relief. All at once it comes together as a concrete road. It must go to Bud's dump, but for now it takes me toward the camp.

I step up onto it and continue, using walking muscles now instead of slogging muscles. This way I know I can make it to camp. A broad steel sign is backlit by the brightening sky, and tiny at this distance. It pulls me toward it until I'm trotting flat-footed.

The biggest lettering is at the top center, three short lines. As I near the sign, black smudges resolve themselves into long and short blots, then textures that promise individual characters. The sense of the words takes over and flashes RADWASTE HAZARD KEEP OUT in three languages.

The words slow me to a walk. That can't be true. They can't ship waste here yet. That's just put there to scare off Ushi's gold bugs.

The sky silhouettes the stair-stepped steel piles, a new pit, and a drilling derrick. I can see towers of metal struts with dim shapes underneath. They come to life one by one, rattling, roaring, or clanking. I leave the road—now is not the time to meet a Saracen full of Janissary men.

In the distance, fenced off by great tangled coils of razor ribbon, a dark textured rash mottles the sand. In the twilight it could be muck from the shaft, or refuse from the work. Only a wisp of smoke marks it as the camp.

23

Razor ribbon hems the camp in on three sides like jaws closing. The fence added a couple of miles to my walk but I'm in the camp now. No one sees me yet. My head keeps wobbling back into a staticky buzz. Now I'm on all fours. Getting up makes the world ratchet back and forth so I settle back down. Fatimatou is kneeling over me, dripping water down my gullet. She was nowhere in sight before.

I'm in and out for a while—less than a day, I think. I spend the time in a tent. I wake to drink from the bottle on the ground and roll back over to sleep. Someone's keeping it full, but I'm never awake to see them.

Now I'm awake facing Lila and Fatimatou, who perch on the next cot. Fatimatou leans forward in intent solicitude. "Did you break down?"

"A truck dropped me off."

"A trader?"

"Yes."

Lila asks, "Did you hear anything about Muru coming here? That's what the traders are saying."

"It's true. He's got something to tell you. You have to be ready to hear it."

Lila puts her facial dukes up. "It better not be more of that 'on your way' crap. Bud won't put up with that."

Lila ducks outside and I try to mute the pounding in my head. I get up to follow her. Fatimatou starts forward. "You've been ill," she says. "We'll try some pills on you."

Ten minutes later, Lila hasn't gone far. She's turning and twisting, answering questions, conferring with volunteers three at a time. The volunteers are tense: rumors are multiplying. Lila is quiet now, not boisterous. She projects a sickbed gentleness that reassures no one.

Lila seems to have a new familiar now: a barrel-chested Arab. He comes up close when he speaks with her, but that's the Arab way. He speaks in barrages of questions and thrusts his head forward to smile. He seems manipulative, probing like a con man, demanding assent, leading her somewhere a step at a time.

I join the crowd competing for her ear. "Lila, we need to talk about Muru's visit."

"Don't start anything now," she says.

The new guy doesn't like me, and his nostrils flare. He glowers at me when I speak to her, horns in by blocking me with his body. He seems to speak only bad French. I call over his head in English, "Lila, who's your man Friday?"

Lila grins. "That's Abikel. He's all right, I guess," she says. "Sort of a hustler. He bird-dogged me soon as he got here. He's . . . inquisitive." Abikel listens with blank suspicion.

"What does he want?"

"Maybe he's trying to get lucky. Some of these guys think Western women are love machines. Especially the Algerians. The Islamists have got them so repressed, they could explode."

"He's Algerian?"

She shrugs. "He's got no papers, but he hangs around with the Algerians."

We have waited days for Muru's visit. The tension in the camp has slackened with fatigue. I can almost believe he might not come.

I'm regaining my strength, but uncertainty saps me now. I drift around the tents, noting things that need fixing. Everything I might do is contingent on the continued existence of the camp.

Lila is scanning the horizon from the roof of a truck nearby. Her knees quiver slightly as she shifts her weight. She must be watching for Muru.

She cowers for a second, then stands up tall. I follow her eyes to an approaching jeep. I search her face for denial or hysteria, but all I see is sad resolve. That means she doesn't understand.

The technical trundles into camp, all primer spots and dust and maybe black paint. A rear wheel wobbles like a rolling penny. A machine gun yaws unattended.

A sneering adolescent sergeant climbs down. He has active eyes and a shaved bullet head. He wears shorts, flip-flops, and a cigarette ad of a shirt. He holds an automatic rifle by the breech. His hands are relaxed, but I see a bit too much white in his eyes. They get first pick of the relief agencies' pharmaceuticals.

He speaks to me: "Mansa Muru wishes to meet the relief staff. He is taking the time to personally convey an important directive."

Lila squares off, nudging me with a shoulder. "Under what authority is he issuing directives?"

He ignores her and speaks to me. "You will receive him at ten o'clock."

"Talk to her," I say. "She's in charge." I hope I said that out of respect for her, and not to shirk responsibility for what happens next.

He looks her up and down with the rapist's habit of exploratory intimidation. He turns to go and calls back over his shoulder, "Ten o'clock."

They did not come at ten, or at ten-thirty. At eleven we go back inside the mothers' tent to wait. We will know when Muru comes: word has spread through the camp, and hundreds of eyes are fixed on the southern horizon.

Alone in the tent, Lila and I drink tea and lick sweat from cracked lips. She speaks doggedly of camp life, shortages and expedients, silencing me with a new rush of words when I take a breath to speak.

I recline and lay my head on a crooked arm. Lila's life-and-death small talk winds down. With my eyes closed it feels almost like our old comfortable silences.

I say, "You know what Muru's going to tell us, don't you?"

"Why don't you stop acting like his spokesman?" She says it with the kind of anger that bleeds off fear.

"Don't kill the messenger, Lila."

"What makes you think you know, anyway?"

"I learned a lot while I was back in the world. Things I never knew about this place. About our guardian angel Bud."

"What do you mean, guardian angel? Is that sarcasm?"

"His relationship to us is . . . complicated."

"Bud is keeping all of us alive," she says. "Maybe you don't like the way I threw myself at him. It might make you feel better to know he didn't want me. I saw his nose wrinkle up when I got close, because I stink."

She sees what she expected in my face. "All this time you thought I slept with him. I told you, it was you he wanted. He needed a spy on the expert panel."

"Bud got that a long time ago. Now Bud wants us to move on. Muru will be saying the words, but the message comes straight from Bud: Time to go."

"No." She gets to her feet. "Not this time."

"It doesn't have to be like last time. Maybe the U.N. can get us out."

"A hundred people have dysentery. You put them in trucks, you might as well bury them. And what about the mines?"

"Lila—we are about to be moved. Mines or no mines. Dysentery or no dysentery. We're in the way. That's why we have to move."

"You think I don't know how it is? They kick us around, and now they're kicking us out. Even a wasteland is too good for us. But I'm not going along this time. I will not lead a death march into the desert."

"You don't know what this Muru is like," I say.

"Yes, we do," Lila says. "We've seen the video too."

"What video?"

"Muru's coming-out party," she says. "Ushi sent it over the Internet. Fatimatou has it saved somewhere. Let me see if I can find it."

It's on their laptop, in the volunteers' tent. She turns the laptop upside down and shakes it. Fine dust falls from the keyboard. I hunch over the screen with my face close to hers to see.

The video shimmies on the screen: a blond-paneled auditorium. The camera pans across an audience of suits and finds Bud up front, sitting at a dais with Muru. Muru's tie chafes his neck. He wants it off, you can tell. He's shrugging and tugging at the tailored suit. Bud's finding a way to praise his new partner.

Now Muru starts reading in a monotone. At intervals he stops and looks up as if he smells something, stares at someone in the audience, and settles back down. Maybe he's trying to engage his audience, but it comes across like paranoia.

Muru has invited questions. The camera swings to a redheaded Aussie woman with big shoulder pads. "I have a question for Mr. Muru."

"Yes," Bud says.

"Mr. Muru, doesn't the plan violate the Pelindaba Treaty?"

Bud cuts in: "You mean the treaty's dumping ban? The dumping ban does not apply to us. Our plan is not dumping but emplacement: the careful siting of safely shielded material. Our material is not raw waste. We process it for safety by vitrifying it. This makes it insoluble in water and prevents any future use by terrorists. At any rate, the National Assembly of Mali has chosen to reject the Pelindaba Treaty. A broad coalition supports nonacceptance. We expect a vote when the assembly goes into session next month."

The woman pulls out papers. She crimps them with her fingers so they stand up stiff and heavy like a cleaver in her hand. "I have a document here: Draft Declaration of Nonacceptance of the Pelindaba Treaty. Word for word, it's identical to the assembly resolution. Except it's on Timbuktu Earthwealth letterhead."

Bud puffs up like an adder. "That is Timbuktu proprietary material."

"Mr. Van Sickle, it looks like you've put together a complete treaty-abrogation kit: declarations, public relations material, a digest of precedents in the International Court of Justice. Can you comment on that?"

"We have earned the trust of the government of Mali. We offer advice candidly and openly. In some cases it is accepted. Next question." But no one is vying to be recognized now. This woman has Bud on the hook, and her rivals listen in silence.

"We've spoken to a number of assemblymen," she says. "None of them seem to know much about this resolution, except that they're all for it."

"The party leaders know what they're doing," Bud says.

"Some party leaders say Mansa Muru will resume raids if the resolution fails to pass." Shouts from people jumping up: *Mansa Muru . . . attack Bamako again? Disband the assembly?*

Muru rumbles. The reporters erupt, yelling, "What did he say?"

"Nothing," Bud says.

"Why don't you let him speak for himself?"

Muru is not listening. He stares open-mouthed. The camera swings to a tall Tuareg woman who rises with difficulty. Two men help her up.

She says, "Mansa Muru, I bear your mark." She lifts her flowered blouse. Intersecting ruts gouge her stomach.

I had always dismissed the reports claiming that Muru raises man-eating rats for punishment. People say rats have no taste for flesh: even starved and trapped against the skin in pots, they eat their way out only reluctantly. It sounded like a myth to me, too archetypal to be true.

The woman says, "Emperor Muru, it is for you that the Creepers kill and torture the people of Mali. How will you answer for your crimes against humanity?"

Muru is on his feet, sputtering. He has reverted to Malinke, which spurts out in full-throated snarls. Bud is tugging on Muru's microphone and shouting over him: something about not reopening old wounds, working together for the good of Mali. Bud makes some kind of cutthroat sign with stiff fingers, and the screen goes black.

When she first saw the tape Fatimatou scoured the camp to find someone who spoke Malinke. He watched the video three times with an ear cocked close. He tried to render Muru's words into English. The sound quality was good, but the strange idioms and the shouting and the contested microphone made it difficult to be sure that he really heard Muru say things like *the new black Songhai empire or the purification of Mali or filthy nomad roaches.*

A double clap outside the tent. Lila bursts out between the flaps and I hear Fatimatou say, "A convoy."

I follow Lila outside in a flare of sunlight. Flat-footed in the heat, we jog up a rise to the broad watchful side of a growing crowd. Three trucks skim over a mirage, dust wafting behind in the wriggling distance. They keep tricking my eyes as they move through the haze, growing and shrinking, changing from buses to trucks to tanks. Now, having changed to four-by-fours, they stay that way. The lead truck rolls slowly into camp and coasts to a stop with a gentle crunch of stones. I can't see into the windows. The vehicles behind it separate and stand back.

The nearest truck has been stopped there for minutes, it seems. The refugees wait transfixed: they want to hide, but they have to know. I don't hear a murmur or a breath.

The crowd shies back as the door opens. The driver gets out and probes the camp's faces with a penetrating stare. He opens the rear door and Muru rises ponderously. He's built like a biker, powerful under the fat. He wears mirrored sunglasses and a peak-capped khaki uniform. A knot on the left side cheers, three clipped syllables. So much for Lila's little bubble of peace. Muru billets his fighters here too.

The passenger door is open now. A black skull rises above a jittering stick figure, long-toothed mandibles jutting forward over a walking stick, red eyes skittering in sockets wreathed with slack skin, then locking on me, impossibly alive and bright.

Fatso: skeletal still but back from the dead, corpse-face unshrouded and obscene, naked of flesh. A hoodless grim reaper, pointing at me.

24

Muru stands tall, feigning a tribal chief's silent authority, but his hands hang restlessly, crawling from belt to bandolier to knife. He is a figurehead, tossed aside.

Fatso shows his teeth, stretching skin across pointed bones until I wait for the tearing sound. "Mumm said I would find you here."

Lila wheels and looks at me. "You know him?"

"Through Bud," I say. "We all work for Bud."

She fights the idea in silence: she has her role to play, and these ghouls have theirs.

Fatso says, "It is no longer safe for you here."

Lila's eyes open wide to let a memory flood through, and she grabs my arm. Inhad used those very words to drive her out of Tabankort. Deadly exile having become routine, the continent has developed polite formulas for it. Lila is hearing those words again, and it's not a nightmare, she is living it. She is hooked into me, nails digging into my skin, thumb twisting a tendon, sending the charge of panic and helplessness through me.

"It's going to be different this time," I lie, meaning no one will be butchered, knowing no one will be spared.

It is up to me to plead. "There are too many sick, and not enough trucks."

"Do what you can."

"All we can do is stay here."

"No."

"Then we will move," I say. "You are bringing trucks to move us?"

"No."

"Who will be moving us, then?"

"Anyone you choose. Today."

"No one can do it but the Creepers of Niani. No one else has the power."

"No."

Desperate to break through the wall of refusal, I challenge Fatso: "You don't have enough trucks? Mumm can get them for you. Don't be afraid to ask him."

Fatso shrinks his eyes to slits, refuses to take the bait. He will not prove himself to me. I turn to Emperor Muru, giving him a chance to assert his imperial authority. "What is your decision? You are the *mansa*."

Muru gulps air to bellow with an eye on Fatso, waiting for a sign. Fatso ignores him and he deflates.

I turn back to Fatso, who is calculating what I will pay for my affront: Challenging his primacy. Trying to use his subjection to Mumm.

And he has not forgotten that I crippled his son. He turns away. I see rage coursing through him as the virus once did. He is fighting it back with some unpracticed emotional reserve. He would replace my mind with pain in some traditional way, except that he's in thrall to Mumm. The frustration of Mumm's directive, *no atrocities,* it galls him. I gall him. It will be all the worse for us in the end.

"The relief agencies will send trucks. They just need time. They will come here if you let them." I'm pleading now, groveling, wallowing in the reversal of our fortunes. Sheltering under Mumm's wing I was white U.S. might and the power of life and death. Now I am all those things, neutered and helpless and waiting to pay.

Muru and Fatso have left. It's clear to them we will not, cannot leave. Fatso took one long last look at me, not to communicate but to fix my face in his mind. He will have to imagine what is happening to me, downrange.

I have never known such stillness here. The solemnity of twelve hundred condemned is more like silence than my solitary thoughts.

Fatso is a drover of victims by trade. Workmanlike pride ensures the shelling will be deft. But he will not be judged by weighing life and death; all that really matters is our panic and our flight. Unnecessary death would be a minor lapse of form. I can't know how much death is enough.

No one else feels this uncertainty. They assume what comes next will kill them—bombardments are for destruction, any fool knows that. By staying or by leaving, the refugees are simply choosing their death: instant obliteration, or foot bones stripped bare by a mine. One night without entrails or a march, a breakdown, then thirst, then radiator water, then convulsions and death.

I heard Mumm tell Fatso to go easy on the killing. My knowledge could be fatal to the camp. Fatso might imagine me bracing the refugees, telling them, *It's a bluff, he just wants to frighten us.* To prove he's not bluffing he might choose to spatter some flesh.

I don't like guessing Fatso's thoughts. It feels like mortal sin.

Fatso keeps us waiting until the sun and the moon have both set. Even when it's dark as it will get, he waits, letting our minds work.

The first jet of flame is gone almost before we turn toward it. It comes not from the south, as we had expected, but from the hills near our well. Above us there must be a slow ascent and an instant of poise. It lasts too long—the shell could not have gone that high.

The whine is just audible now. Undeniable now. Louder and louder, it's a shrill whistle, and a rough hand yanks my arm with a ferocity that topples me, and as I fall a concussion rolls me. I twist in the air and see Fatimatou, teeth bared, snapping at me, *Down,* like I'm a dog. I land lightly on my shoulders, my legs on top of Fatimatou, and a white flash swipes at my eyes, a crack slaps at my ears, inserting pain, and soil showers me. Something pings off the truck and I am beginning to understand.

And that was only one shell. My fantastic idea of the proper rhythm of a barrage came from fireworks displays: a stately series of pretty bursts culminating in a climax. The rhythm of this is internal, soundless and sightless: the wave of pain from tormented eardrums cresting, then fading, the violent start from the next shot and the long clenched wait for the impact of the shell, then more pain, more pounding, sometimes from two blasts, or three, because this spasm of burrowing panic will not let you count the flashes, and whipcrack stripes from fragments set you grinding face, pelvis, chest, thighs into the sand with more than sexual urgency.

In a split second lull that settles like a drugged stupor, Fatimatou drags me ripping and jerking to the latrine. I slide headfirst into the muck. The chlorine is sharp but too wet to choke me. A truck's cab soars impossibly overhead, and fire showers down.

White light casts black flashbulb shadows of the truck's smoke. Red light comes from everywhere.

I have felt nothing for some time. Now I feel Fatimatou stir. She is a slight girl again, not a fury but trembling and weak, mewling out mouthfuls of breath.

Her eyes are white all around the dark. "This is our chance to go. Now!" She understands the rhythm of these things, the pause to let the panic take control, the cue for induced blind instinctual flight.

We come out of the pit and see Lila scaling the ground like it's a mountain. Fatimatou creeps over the plowed earth. I am there with them in time to feel more than hear *No.* Lila's voice, a muffled buzz, *No.*

And I see Fatimatou grappling, screeching, pleading convulsed, and Lila's laying on of gentle hands.

Four have died in the eastern margin of the camp, where Fatso chose to nudge us. Two had taken shelter in a truck, trusting its white flag to protect them and ignoring its pyrotechnic potential. An old man of forty lay on his son to shield him. A shell commingled them. Hissi is shot through with the fine wire that wraps each charge. Some of it bristles from her skin like silver stubble. She is alive for now, but we cannot touch her.

Muru be bin na. Muru is coming. His convoy is approaching from the hills. It labors through the sand, slowing as it nears. It will spare us from bombardment while it's here.

When they arrive Muru's guards set up two camp chairs. The chair legs dig deep as Muru sits. Fatso folds into his seat with soft snaps of crepitus.

Muru's epaulets shine red and green in the sun. His mirrored glasses shrink the gathered refugees to anonymous mites. Lila and Fatimatou are mirrored slightly larger than the rest where they stand before him. Fatimatou is petitioning the emperor. Lila is preparing to cast out demons.

Muru pats and caresses a spotless gun. Plain though it is, all steel struts and black works, his gun is an emblem of state and only incidentally a weapon. Like the bombardment, it substantiates his authority. More powerful and real than any of his regalia is Fatso propped in his chair, unmoldering bright-eyed at Muru's right hand.

"You need only move on," Muru says.

"We can, with your help." Fatimatou clasps her hands at her waist.

Lila squares off. "Every one that dies, *you* killed them like you shot them in the face." Each word jolts her.

Muru points the rifle, bellows, *"You are defying the state,"* and more, but he's reverted to Malinke and we don't understand. His voice buffets us, the whites of his eyes redden, a vein pumps in his head.

Muru falls silent, stopping time. I can't read his face. Has he concluded that fear won't work?

Sudden ululating cries, another death. Lila turns toward it, traces it back with her eyes toward the girl who has been the next to die for days, the wasted adolescent girl. Her face crumples.

Fatso's eyes glint scalpel-sharp as they dissect her. Now he understands; he has found the single sinew that ensures collapse if cut. He knows souls have Achilles tendons too.

Fatso puts a hand on Muru's featureless mound of a shoulder. He rises and takes his leave. Muru lumbers after him.

Fatso's guns spared the volunteers' tent, leaving the TV intact. We are huddled around it, begging *What now?* but it's meaningless news, world news. We are not part of that world, with its conferences and statecraft.

Serata appears on the screen again, and I don't want foresight anymore.

The camera cuts and wiggles in a sick-making way, glancing at Serata, glancing away. The coy camera work is hard to watch, but the part of your mind that reads faces is riveted. You look for eyes in the shadowy concave depths. You try to make a nose out of two flat slots. You search for lips to make a mouth of that writhing hole.

One hole for three seeds, that was the old way. Men wouldn't even use carts, for fear of ruts. This plowing madness has nothing to do with food. You have gone mad, wanting more and more, looking up, not down as you would with a hoe, averting your eyes from the earth. The plows crack the fields, the rains burst the cracks, and the earth shatters like a pot. Your animals run away from you. Dry dung poisons the soil. You trade your child for food and your house fills with graves.

How is the harvest this year? Ask the rats and the crickets and worms. Be ready—wild grapes and shea-tree fruit will keep you alive, or leaves from trees, or birds' eggs. When you are forced to eat your seed corn, you can steal more seeds from the termite's mounds to plant. Catch locusts to eat as they take the last of your grain—dig a pit and cover it when they swarm into the cool earth. You may wish to dig up rats from the bush. Then there is a kind of clay you can eat.

Survival foods. That's what you call them if you don't eat them, if you don't know that survival is a matter of degree. Serata knows them well. As she ticked them off for the camera she was clutching Fatimatou's hand. Afterward Fatimatou asked why. Serata only shook her head and groaned.

We wait for the next bombardment, unable to sleep, not needing to eat. In time, with a timid, flinching awareness, we come to know the guns have stopped for good. The encircling calm is complete.

Lila takes me into the Rubbhall. The blower roars. Her voice cracks, shouting over it, "This is it. This is all we've got."

"What do you mean?"

"The shipments have stopped," she says. "Convoys are starting to get ambushed again, and the drivers refuse to go out anymore."

Of course. Timbuktu Earthwealth ordered their mercenaries to stand down. Bud is still keeping up appearances, buying supplies, secure in the knowledge they will not reach us. The rehydration salts are gone. The food will not last long.

I see in Lila's eyes that she has assumed God's responsibility for each new day's deaths, one of which passes by in the sharp-edged light outside the doorway: a form borne on a litter, empty arms crooked as if to cradle a baby and shaking stiffly with the shock of each step.

The whole camp saw Muru's visit, and the whole camp understood its import, even played out in a foreign tongue.

Ten or twenty families have decided to leave. Lila and Fatimatou give them five days' rations. Two days' travel will take them to a caravan route. There they can wait for a slaver's truck.

Your self: it's one last thing that you can trade for food.

They will leave tonight when it begins to get cold. A knot of refugees has assembled to see them go. Lila said her good-byes before, family by family, then withdrew to her tent. She is there now. I don't dare go in.

But Abikel is going there. He will leave tonight too. He looks around as he stoops at her flysheet, but he doesn't see me. He does not clap to announce himself. I don't like his stealth.

He lifts the flap and goes in, and fear drives me over there. I'm slipping in the sand, clawing with stiff arms, thinking of the slashed Algerian family in the baking car. Muru's toad face is croaking out the words for me, *They will cut her throat.* This Abikel's the one.

I break in the flysheet and see Lila slumping on her cot. Her eyes are shocked wide, but at me, not at him. From where he's sitting beside her, Abikel turns to me, annoyed. Just annoyed, not preparing to kill.

He seems to be consoling her. Lila yells, "What?" She thinks something has happened outside.

I'm panting it out: "Everything OK?"

Lila screws up her face and shakes her head to clear it. "What is this?"

"I thought . . ."

"What?"

"People have made threats," I say. "I'm told the Algerians have it in for you."

"Who said that?"

"Muru. Bud."

"What do they know?"

Abikel rises, glowering. I've done something to his honor. It will take a big altercation to fix it. But he doesn't feel a murderer's adrenaline surge, that's clear. Lila jumps up and puts a hand on him, murmuring in bad French to distract us both. "Abikel came to say, Hang on. It will be all right. Yes?"

I keep my intonations low, rolling, contrite. "I'm sorry. I was stupid. It was not personal."

"He's trying to buck us up, Ty. I think that's nice." In English she says, "Unconvincing, but nice."

He says, "I *know.*" He looks at her once more, then walks out, pulled into himself. Lila's twisting her lips, fighting something off. She has said many difficult good-byes today. But she was not prepared for encouragement. It takes more strength to hold still for that.

The Rubbhall is three-quarters full. It holds food for a month. Despite that, mute fear is building like the tingle before a lightning strike.

It is *daraka,* breakfast time. Fatimatou and I ladle porridge from fifty-liter pots. We're sharing out generous portions today; no one wants to compound anxiety with hunger. But the queue lacks its usual lassitude. Bellies press backs, sway and buckle to either side.

I see a face for a second time, a snarling boy's face, and I call for the Mind Your Manners Men to escort this boy to the back of the line but it collapses around him, milling toward the pot with clinging hands and drowning eyes. Women plunge their bowls into the pot, shriek, and suck burned fingers, men tug it, slopping scalding muck. Someone knocks me down, and feet bend my ribs as I curl up in the dust.

Fatimatou screeches and I see her falling into scuffling legs. A sandaled foot hits my nose. It's not a blow, it's someone tripping over me, falling on me, and this is being trampled, I think, and clutching clothes I pull myself to my feet, roaring, *Fatimatou,* but she is gone.

The Rubbhall door is open and bodies are milling in it, pressing in, flailing arms. A hand closes over a face, shoves it viciously back. Bared teeth close on a wrist, an elbow thuds on a breastbone. Now a violent backwash pushes a flying wedge of gouging men out the door. Screams flit around the men like lightning in clouds. Behind the wedge, two men with a carton of meal surge out grimacing, shoved from behind and it's looting now in ones and twos and I can cling but I cannot stand.

An open hand thuds on my face, stiff fingers crook around my nose. I recoil, butt a face with my crown and fall, and the legs disperse like a flock of birds with birdlike cries.

My arms make a cage for my head. My whole tongue tastes my blood, the sweet and sour and salt parts together, and the sand clumps red by my eyes. Through the crook of my arm I see the Mind Your Manners Men threshing thin bodies with thick sticks, the same drowning panic in their eyes, and I'm scrabbling on my belly, darting a glance left, no stomping feet there, just Fatimatou.

She slumps on her knees, her eyes slitted and streaming, muddying her face. She is mourning a permanent loss, a shared death. She does not struggle as Lila does. Her lips repose. Fatimatou has kept this agonal vigil before. As before she's helpless, watching a community in throes.

Food riots happen all the time at other camps, but never here.

Lila and Fatimatou are trying to stitch some work crews together. By this means they hope to inhibit disturbances and pilfering, and keep comfort in reach of the strongest, who might lash out.

A couple of the Mind Your Manners Men have taken a jeep to the well. They formed a work crew of frisking boys. To go is a special privilege for the best boys. Cool water straight from the well is a rare treat. I can see them crawling down the road, hardly raising dust. The driver is tentative, not unskilled, but gentle with the jeep—when you're too thin your hipbones grate on the bouncing seat. They are about to move out of sight behind the hill when the jeep hops over a flash. We hear the blast just as the jeep lands and rolls, spewing a fan of orange fire.

The mine had been placed on the trail within sight of the camp. Its meaning is clear: we are not to have water anymore. A chorus of shrieks rises and falls raggedly, then tapers to an uncanny silence. All but the weakest are on their feet, eyes converging on the same point and peeled down to the soul with the same slow shock.

I look to Lila. She crumples, her face first, then her spine, dropping to her hands and knees. As she picks her face up she is modulating pure tone with an instinctive precision that words cannot approach, howling.

☢

We have water enough for nine days. No more porridge now; the compact food we chew dry. Couscous we suck and swallow in little pinches. Water we take by itself in cups, ladled carefully out like the precious gift it is.

Thirst has gotten ahead of us, and drinking enough would painfully distend the gut. Our carefully measured cupfuls are mercifully insufficient. They puddle comfortably in shriveled stomachs and do nothing for the thirst.

Furtively, over several days, Lila locked everything wet in the truck: gasoline, diesel, coolant, bleach, motor oil. There is a thirst that these will slake. Thirst can shout down anything in you: reason, fear, pain. And thirst is strident now in all of us.

In Lila, certainly: I reach for her hand, pinch the skin behind her knuckle and make a little tab that stays up for long seconds. She stares at it. “I’m all right,” she says, her tongue loudly struggling free of ropy spit.

“You didn’t have to warn us,” she says. “You came back even though you knew,” and with a scant throatful of breath, “Why?”

“You act like it all depends on you. It tears me up when things go well. I couldn’t imagine you on your own now.”

She grips three of my fingers with awkward strength. No tears, of course, just a slurping giggle.

I could walk to the well; I’ll just watch out for mines. Rest a minute and then go. It’s hot now but I’m not going to just lie here.

26

I must have nodded off. I'll go to the well now. I hear the sound that woke me. It makes the air shake. Guns? No: little thuds, fast, but not as fast as automatic-weapons fire. More like a machine, like an earthmover at the dump site. No. It's not coming from there, and it's coming too fast.

Lila's eyes open and stare. I roll to the tent flap, bat at it, pull it aside. Floodlights and sheets of dust. A helicopter—big, twin rotors. Another. Maybe they will take me to the well.

I crawl out of the tent. Hatches open, voices come in Morse-code bursts, lamps swing. I know that voice; can't be. The white lights bob toward us, spread out, and shine back in: camera crews fighting for an angle.

Movie lights blazing, live on news around the world, it's Ushi.

Each pilot cuts his engines, and we can hear as well as see cartons and cans carried at a trot, the prostrate crowd, Ushi's feet in big boots.

"Water and syringes first. I want Helo Three out of here. Food and bottles in four caches." Ushi stoops over a prone boy and puts a canteen to his lips. She stands, hair flat, face smudged, shakes herself and yells, "Careful with the water filter."

The lights and cameras have gone somewhere else. Ushi squats in front of me. "Thank goodness you're all right. Drink up."

I am sucking at Ushi's water, closing over the canteen, Adam's apple tripping over itself to swallow faster and faster. *More* is all I can think. My stomach hurts. Someone sets a gallon jug down. "Keep drinking," Ushi says. "There's enough for everyone, for now.

"These supplies will last two weeks," she says. "That should be enough time, if we're careful with the water."

Someone at my side sticks my arm and eases something wonderful into it. My body is not screaming for liquid now. "How come Muru didn't shoot you down?"

"He never saw us," she says. "We came from the north."

"From *Algeria*?"

"Yes. Why are you looking at me like that?"

"It would have been safer to buzz Muru."

"No," she says. "The Algerians were wonderful. The government, the patriots, the Islamists all helped."

"But the revolution . . ."

She shrugs. "They conduct it in such a way that life goes on."

She has trotted back to one of the helicopters. The crews are rushing to get some liquid into everyone before daylight. For many of us, one more day of sweating would be all. They tag the tents and shelters as they treat the occupants. The orange patches are multiplying as the strongest refugees pitch in.

Ushi comes back. "You're looking better. As soon as you're up to it, you're leaving."

Lila hasn't spoken since the helicopters came. She's sitting cross-legged with our shared gallon jug in her lap. She doesn't drink unless I help her pick it up.

"You need me here," I say. "These people need rehydration, therapeutic feeding."

Ushi says, "You have other fish to fry."

The sky lights up in the south. Floating flares burn hot white, casting black shadows. Tracers tangle overhead.

"We're not moving," a male voice says. "If we fly now they'll blow us out of the sky."

The flare light feints all around. Ushi is kneeling alongside me, talking over her shoulder to the fliers who crouch behind her.

"We should dig in," a pilot says. The shadows play on their faces, waxing and waning and splitting until a flare holds the sky steady and I can see they all have the same hooded, flinching eyes and taut lips.

Another voice says, "Any one of these rounds could be an HE shell." High explosive, ending it all. I'm not too dry to fear it now.

Ushi says, "They won't shell the camp. The world is watching us."

One day has gone by; it's night again. I'm still weak and woozy but not beyond return. The flares and tracers outside the tent flit and crack like a desiccated thunderstorm. Ushi is on the satellite phone with the Greens, probing for a way out.

Ushi brought some familiar TV faces: the crazy Canadian who raided with the Sudanese rebels; the tiny Tamil woman who broadcast the battle of Irian Jaya from a shell hole; a couple of quavering anchors. We are watching our camp on the news, beamed around the world and back to us from Ushi's camera crew. The camp looks wrong on TV, too sharp, with the tunnel vision of long lenses.

The camp fades to black and Muru fills the screen, his wide toad's mouth fixed in a toothless grin. He explains why the camp must move, why he is not responsible for the lives in it. Why a march through mined desert is the only way.

"They're letting him talk," Lila says. "They must have sent him to charm school."

Muru's mouth snaps closed and the camera cuts away. To Bud.

Bud sits facing a woman reporter. His big sincere face is all concern. The reporter says, "Do you have anything to say to the people in the camp?"

"You are all in my prayers. Ushi, you have my heartfelt thanks."

The reporter asks, "Why don't you step in and stop it?"

"What?"

She says, "U.N. action would take months. ECOMOG is

paralyzed, and no Western government is prepared to intervene. Timbuktu Earthwealth is the camp's only hope. You retain Janissary Systems. Why can't they get the refugees out?"

One hand squeezing the knuckles of the other, Bud explains patiently: "The scope of Janissary's services is limited to security for our work crews. With no ongoing work, no contract to dump the waste, Janissary has no role."

"But Janissary Systems is on the spot."

Bud says, "Janissary is a security service, not an army. They don't have the right; they don't have the means."

"They don't have the means? When Janissary first came to Mali it took them two weeks to mow down every bandit east of Bamba."

"I have no authority. I'm a private citizen."

No, Bud. Looking out that cockpit you're a god. We are your creation.

It's cave-quiet in the hills where Muru waits. Our rescue seems all the more boisterous for that. I feel like we should keep it down. I'm doing light duties now, feebly, like a convalescent in therapy—inventory, today, in the Rubbhall. Ushi comes into the Rubbhall alone, feeling her way among piles of stores. I sense a few hairline cracks in her wonted poise. "The doctor says it's safe for you to go now, Ty."

"Go where?"

She says, "To meet a friend of ours."

"And then what?"

"Our friends have sensitive information that will save the camp. But they have no influence. They need our help to get a hearing. We have to put them in touch with the right person. Someone who will see what must be done. Some sort of spook will do. I do not know any spooks." She nods to start me nodding with her. "You must set up a meeting so they can warn your government."

She's counting on the government. We're through.

Ushi's face has changed. I have never, in any of her photos, seen this face: pleading eyes and a tremor in her lower lip and, incredibly, no histrionics. She has stopped playacting.

I don't like this. It's a breach of protocol. Deities shouldn't ask mortals for help. It scares them half to death.

We are considering what to do. I sit with Ushi, Lila, and Fatimatou in a circle in the sand, stubbornly choosing a futile course. The coming dawn casts enough light to show eyes as gray shadows on faces vague as fog.

I ask Ushi, "Who is this friend of yours?"

"He—or maybe she—sent us an E-mail message. He disguised his identity with remailers, proxies, things I don't understand. He is a Green, but a quiet one."

"So he says."

"I trust him," Ushi says.

It could be Timbuktu Earthwealth laying a trap. "He could be anybody," I say. "You'd better make him show some bona fides."

"He has proven himself. He gave us information about a secret chemical-weapons dump in Switzerland. Astonishing, but he gave us proof. He is a true Green."

"Ushi, how did they get this secret information?" That sounds like something that Bud might know.

"They learned of it by tricking a satellite somehow, and listening in. Anyway, Mr. V is our only chance."

"Mr. V?"

"We don't know what to call him," she says. "His computer I.D. is nonsense, scrambled."

Lila says, "Ushi, just go to the press with Mr. V's big scoop. You brought reporters from three continents. They can get the word out."

"In the first place, I don't know this secret. Only Mr. V does. Whatever it is he knows, it can't be made public. That would make matters worse."

"Why?"

Ushi says, "I don't know why—that is what Mr. V says."

I say, "So he needs our contacts to get his message across."

"Yes," Ushi says. "Greenfleet will send him wherever he needs to go. And someone from the camp, too, to help him and to vouch for him."

Lila says, "Maybe we should hook him up with the guy who runs the Authority."

"Theriault? Theriault is ruined. Discredited," I say. "He's in jail."

Lila says, "Ushi, how about your partners at Minatom? What if he breaks the news to them?"

"Minatom is kept in the dark," Ushi says. "They can't possibly help."

Fatimatou says, "Bozo."

I can't help the shrill edge in my voice: "Bozo? He's in exile." *In the jungle, in the place that took my wife.*

"Bozo is a good man. I have felt it in his handshake, seen it in his eyes. He will understand. He will do what's right."

"Fatimatou, he's your hero, I know. But he's been driven away." Lila coos to her, shutting us out, speaking in private with a friend.

Fatimatou says, "Bozo always had American advisers around him. He called them his spooks. They are Americans like you, Ty, careful and serious. They will not desert him now."

I feel as if I have to tell a child an ugly fact: *Dead people don't come back . . . Some friendly adults are bad . . .* "It won't do any good to tell my government." I say it gently as I can.

"Why not?" Ushi says.

"Bud works for the government. Or he did. It's all the same."

"No way," Lila says.

I tell them everything, the aerial view from the cockpit: the Algerian revolution, the real reason for Timbuktu Earthwealth. How Bud uses Lila and me. How Bud crushed his competitors, exiled Bozo, did what he needed to do.

Fatimatou says, "But Bozo's advisers are not like Bud."

I say, "Fatimatou—"

Lila lays a hand on me and asks her friend, "You're sure?"

Fatimatou says, "Yes."

"If Bozo gets this message, he can act on it?"

"He can."

Lila breathes in her friend's certitude. She says, "OK. Ty? Please take our new friend to see Bozo."

It has taken two nights of sleepless thrashing, but now I am ready to go back into the jungle. I fled from it as the place where my wife died. Now I am drawn to it as the place where she lived. Even at the worst, we could always feel a fluttering undercurrent of normalcy and peace. If I can slip in there and let it carry me along, indifference will shield me.

Even with no rule of law, it's a gentle shred of land. Despite what the warlords and bandits do, people seldom starve. When they burn your town you hide in the forest, where mangoes grow wild everywhere. When the soldiers leave you slink back to dig up your roots. Sometimes the fires have cooked them, just as you would. It's a lovely place, like Eden after the fall when God's not looking and you sneak back in.

Fatimatou is pecking at the laptop, arranging my meeting. She's conspiring in some remote dark alley of the Internet, cloaked by diverse black arts of concealment. She can hide behind faraway computers. She can carom messages from continent to continent, hiding her tracks, and scramble them so a simple yes or no fills half a screen.

Fatimatou beams her nonsense messages up at the satellite and off to Mr. V's hideaway. Where is it going? She looks at me quizzically. "To him," she says. "That's all we know."

"What's his name? What's his address?"

She smiles and shows me:

V~i8h21^eyTY)ffgj5YeoWir_4jdRp3kjgn)o16dp@nowhere.nu

"Mr. V knows how to whisper," she says.

For security we never mention Bozo. Kaga Bandoro, Central African Republic, that's all we will say. Mr. V will meet me there. It's easy to find, in the very center of the center of Africa. If Africa's a vortex, going down the drain, Kaga Bandoro is its whipping underwater tail. Just follow the sucking sound until it sucks you in.

The reply, when it comes, is a skittish appointment with lots of ways to bolt. Standoffish meetings will be called and canceled with random signals. Our paths will cross and cross again before we meet—where, we don't know. When, we don't know. It all depends. Whether the camp can be saved, or how, we don't know. It all depends.

27

It's time to fly out: the darkest hour of the darkest night this month. I've been awake all night, but ducking into the aircraft's hatch is like waking from consciousness to something sharper and more real.

Aloft in the helicopter, the earphones are no help against the engines' roar. The craft lurches and swings as though it's swatted by a giant hand. Tracers blaze all around. I'm clutching a handgrip, drawing an endless breath.

The pilot has explained how we will fly, and why: this recklessness protects us from hostile fire. When our recklessness is dangerous as Muru's guns, we are as safe as can be. This has been proven by men in computer-filled rooms.

We stopped to refuel in Niamey. In Kano there was food, too, but we couldn't refuel until after prayers. We stopped in Ngaoundéré, where they are of Fula stock, like Fatimatou. We slept in a hangar with poised quiet Fatimatous all around.

Now we are sinking into the Central African Republic. The helicopter sets me gently down on a neglected airstrip. At the strip's ragged end a crusty Korean four-by-four waits under encroaching trees. A Ubangi dressed in khaki and blue sits at the wheel. He turns the jeep over to me and walks away.

My way will be passable—these are the little rains, not the big rains. I have an old map, but there's only one road. All I need do is go straight.

The repellent is disorienting me. It's too familiar. When we lived here DEET smelled like children's modeling clay. Now, driving in the jungle where we lived, DEET smells like my wife. The smell lets my memories loose, and inside my head it's like Ngaragba prison when the rebels come to town. When a mutiny turns the tables, inmates rampage like these thoughts of Michelle.

I cling to the least awful thoughts. A tsetse bounces off the windshield. When we lived here tsetse flies seemed like insect cops, with the bulk and swaggering authority of unmarked yellow jackets. This one brings Michelle, in a rush: her gentle way with the flyswatter, her abiding distaste for bug goosh that was more mercy than squeamishness. I'm holding on, fighting off the next thought; my ferocious concentration distracts me, and I brake hard when I see the deadfall in my path.

A tree has fallen across the road. A bend hides it until you're almost on top of it. I bump it with the jeep to see if it will crumble. It's a stout trunk, solid at the core. I have a chain saw in the back, and an axe. I climb out and choose the chain saw, louder but faster. I don't like making noise, but I can't afford to stay put too long.

It's hot work that brings the mosquitoes to spiral confused and DEET-struck above my skin. When I've torn out a breach I drag it to the edge of the road. I glimpse something that freezes the sweat on my back, and I move numbly toward it.

Nobody says *jungle* anymore, they say *rain forest,* but this is not rain forest, it's jungle: the canopy doesn't inhibit the other vegetation, so it's an opaque, impassable tangle at ground level. Might as well be a wall hemming me in.

Hidden in the jungle it was hard to see, but now I'm right on top of it: the spot where the tree gave way. It's not a splintered break. It's neatly cut. A trap.

It's hard to turn around, because I know what I'll see. I try to pull the fear back in. When I can I turn back to the jeep and trip on flat ground in front of the little man sitting on the hood.

At first I take him for a Pygmy, but he can't be, he's too slight. Then I take him for a panicky flashback. But he's not. He's real.

It's just as it was four years ago: plants jostling in slow motion for bright spots in the green shade; whirring insects and wet heat; a lethal little boy. The memory hoods me, and my wife is with me again, red coming from her chest and spattering my sunglasses but I can see. The sniper rifle's half-inch shell passes through her and thumps on the ground beneath me. Flies settle instantly on the frothy pink scraps of her lungs and her empty chest. I see the sniper's face. He is a boy of less than ten. Big gun and small boy, lashed to the branch of a tree. He must have been painstakingly brutalized, as they all are, beaten if they spook at screams, fed pieces of prisoners. Still, it is clear this was his first kill. His laugh soars up.

I hear, "I kill you." There was no warning for Michelle then. This is happening now.

A lethal little boy just like the one that killed my wife, as if that very one has ripened and dropped off the branch. The same camo bush hat creased in half to keep it from covering his little beanhead like a bucket. The same stubby cigarette. The same thickly cuffed sleeves and little fingers reaching around his gun. He bares one outsized incisor along with a row of little rice teeth. He must be all of nine years old.

This time the malevolence is casual, with no admixture of fear. He isn't new to this. He bellows, *On the ground,* just like the big kids do. Then, if he wants, he will shoot me in the head.

Having spent endless hours contemplating the moment of her death, now I can follow her: and I am ashamed to find, having lived it and died it in my mind a thousand times, and having imagined the extinguishment of each of my senses in turn, my last fuddled thoughts, that I am unready. I don't want to be where Michelle is, or is not. I have turned my back on her. Fear gives way to the dejection of a compound failure. My torpor frustrates him, and nothing in his short life has instilled patience. I don't have long to wait.

I'm still waiting. Something in his bearing flicks a switch in me: a hint of artifice, but not mimicry of older killers. He remembers only dimly, but before he was conscripted he might have postured like this: he's clowning. His eyes push and pull in a way that says he doesn't want to kill. Not yet.

I set down the chain saw and say, "Oh, yeah?" high and adenoidal, stretching my mouth wide. He laughs. My shoulders bob, bowing of their own accord. There's something ping-ponging back and forth too fast for speech, almost too fast for thought, and it's sweeping us both up in an old ineradicable instinct: play. He has life-and-death power, canned food, and Camel cigarettes, everything a boy needs except unarmed playmates. I'm a Frankenstein, lumbering toward him, a crab scuttling past, feinting toward him, dodging away. He's staying out of reach and so am I, predator and prey changing places, changing back, second by second. Our dogs used to play with each other like this, even one-eared Ralph with his million scars who could scare off bears sometimes until I shot him. I sprawl dead on my back. I wake and attack, crawling, wracked with zombie tremors. He shoots over my head but you cannot kill the undead, *Aaargh.* He falls, covers up and squeals but there's nothing he can do, in a second he's down on the ground, curled up and I'm tickling his guts out.

I've found the part of him that's still a child.

These days the city of Kaga Bandoro is rubble and torn prefab steel in the care of a twitchy African peacekeeping force. They shake me gently down and send me on a scavenger hunt: seek out a particular shopkeeper; follow his map to a derelict wall; feel for a cavity in the wall; find directions to a rendezvous with Mr. V.

It's a sheet-steel box in the prefect's compound. Tiny jungles have erupted in neglected corners of the packed-dirt yard, and the trailer sits in one of them. I shuffle weakly up to it, inhaling the steam and sweating it out. I'm unused to the insects and they're deafening me. I'm glancing nervously around to see what I won't hear.

The sun is blinding on the flimsy white door. Everywhere else, creepers clothe the walls in trembling green. Braided vines snake groping through the air as if the house has put out feelers. One taps my arm.

I can't be sure I'm as close as it feels. The near-death rush of my meeting with the boy makes me avid to be inside. A klaxon in my brain stem's shrieking *Run*. The sheet metal door makes too much noise as I knock.

Nothing has prepared me for the face behind the door. She stares with a wariness I've never seen in her. She's strung tight as I am; no pothead relaxation in that rosewood face.

It takes a while before I get it out: "Faye?"

She is staring at me, dazed. "Ty?"

"What are you doing here?" Both of us say that.

"I'm looking for a guy we call Mr. V. He had an encrypted computer I.D., V-x-y-z or something like that. He was going to meet me here."

"I sent those messages to Ushi," she says. "Not to you—you disappeared."

"You saw Ushi on TV, saving the refugee camp? Well, I was there. I drew the short straw, so I came to meet Mr. V."

Faye says, "Ushi thinks Timbuktu Earthwealth is trying to starve out the refugees. She's trying to make them lift the blockade, and she appealed for help on the Internet. I can help."

"How can you possibly help, Faye?"

She turns to a wobbly wood table. A blue backpack sags on top of it. She picks through the pack and pulls out a stapled sheaf of papers. Holding it finger-and-thumb by one corner, she says, "This will stop Timbuktu dead."

"What is it?"

"This is the paper nobody would show me."

"That paper about the Crystal Ball?"

"Right," she says. "Take a look."

It looks forlorn, not sensitive, a specky copy of a scientific paper written for a tiny community of one-track minds. It reads like the technical papers I crammed at Bear Mountain. Reading those, I could puzzle out the general idea. Reading this, I'm lost:

ABSTRACT

The Foundation Model is an international trade model developed by the Demos Foundation, a multilateral research institute. The model takes many forms, but all are based on the relationships shown below:

$$\frac{d\rho_i}{dt} = \frac{\dfrac{\partial \Psi_i}{\partial t} - \dfrac{\partial \Phi_i}{\partial t} \cdot \dfrac{dY_i}{dt} - \xi\left(\dfrac{d\rho_\varepsilon}{dt}\right)}{\dfrac{\partial \Phi_i}{\partial \rho_i} - \dfrac{\partial \Psi_i}{\partial \rho_i} + \eta(\Phi_\varepsilon)}$$

Ψ: output, Φ: consumption, Y: income, ρ: price index
η, ξ as defined in Hardison (2)
$i \cup \varepsilon \subseteq \{\text{Countries}\},\ i \notin \varepsilon$

The Foundation Model is widely used in financial and currency markets to make split-second investment decisions known as "macro bets."

Macro bets may destabilize markets if they rely on overly complex predictive models. Complexity can jeopardize stability; as early as 1970 Gardner and Ashby demonstrated an inverse nonlinear relationship under certain general conditions. This paper extends the Gardner and Ashby results to gauge macroeconomic stability if a demand shock accelerates African growth. Statisically robust computer simulations indicate extreme

---

Halfway through, the words leave me behind. I hack through thickets of equations and proofs, looking for something to add or subtract. I'm lost.

I am paging slackly back and forth when Fay says, "Your lips have stopped moving. Is that a good sign, or a bad sign?"

"The warlords don't care, Faye. They're sitting in the hills outside camp with their big guns."

"The warlords will never know what hit them," she says. "If we show this to the right guy, ten governments will jump in and abort Timbuktu's plan on the spot. And Timbuktu Earthwealth is behind all this, right?"

"So just publish it."

"We don't dare," Faye says. "The controversy would be paralyzing. The implications are very clear, and very awful. We need someone who can get things done in secret. You know someone like that—don't you?"

"I hope so, Faye."

"Who are we going to show this to?"

I say, "Ex-president Bozo of Mali."

"Bozo? He's an exile. What's he going to do about it?"

"People swear he's under U.S. government protection. I don't believe it. Timbuktu Earthwealth kicked Bozo out, and Timbuktu Earthwealth *is* the U.S. government."

And Timbuktu Earthwealth is acutely disappointed in me. If Bud's government associates are here with Bozo, then I'm dead.

Bozo's friends have contacted us. They gave themselves plenty of time to check us out, and stake us out. A jeep is taking us to meet him, somewhere out of town.

The meeting place is a thatch-roofed trading post of laterite block. A stand of thick trees spreads to shade it. It's shut tight, but I hear movement inside when I knock. I try to time the long, long wait, but time keeps getting away.

The door opens on the smiling moon face of Aras Bozo.

"Mr. Bozo, I'm—"

"Mr. Ty Campbell. You come with Fatimatou's recommendation. That is enough for me."

There is more to Fatimatou than she lets on. She's coming into focus as a hard fighter in the thick of Bamako's street politics, on the run now but ready to jump back in someday.

The light inside is green-tinged forest gloom uncut by lamps. A flowery smell comes and goes on weak breezes. A desk holds a fat red passport and some kind of electronic memo gadget. “Let’s get down to business,” Bozo says. “You have a message for me.”

“She does,” I say.

Holding tight to her papers, Faye collects her thoughts. She’s trying to come down from her mystical plane. She says, “We have to stop Timbuktu’s dumping scheme. This paper proves it.”

Bozo takes the paper and scowls through it. Faye boils it down as he reads: “Serata said it best. When she was on television she said, ‘We’re running toward a cliff.’ That’s exactly what we’re doing. Look at this.” Faye points to a chart as he stares at it.

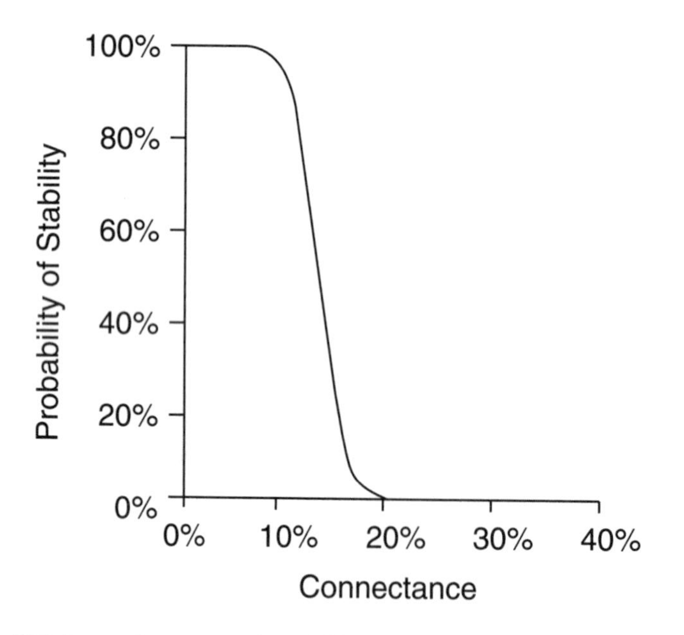

“We’re going over the cliff: from stability to chaos.” She confides to Bozo in some secret scientific shorthand. Bozo came from a tribe of fishermen, but he spent years at an American university. The pace picks up: interruptions, interjections, flat angry denials. Bozo slows and thinks, fights inside, and thinks some more.

“And Timbuktu’s project does that?” Bozo shakes his head, aghast. “It’s just a big construction job. That can’t be right.”

“Doesn’t matter if it’s right,” Faye says. “You ask any banker, any finance minister, any investor. They’re using this model; they’ll get this result. And they'll act on it. It's a self-fulfilling prophecy. Speed up the world with Bud's dumping plan, and she'll jump the rails and crash."

A man appears in an inside door: unreadable, but American. Bozo's handler and, I suppose, Bud's esteemed colleague.

He's tall and thin, with narrow shoulders and big hands. He records every inch of me in quick black eyes. No doubt he combines Bud's ruthless ambition and Mumm's sadism.

He turns to Faye and says, "This report—it needs to be compelling, if it means what you say."

"The reasoning is rock solid," Faye says. "Ask any of your analysts about *Nature,* volume 228, Gardner and Ashby."

"And this computer simulation: the Foundation Model?"

"Universally used by governments and private investors. This is how the world works now," Faye says.

"And you think you know what happens when the economy goes over the cliff?"

"I'll show you," Faye says.

She takes a little flat computer from her pack. She summons up a tiny world on the screen: a map centered on Africa, bound up in crossing arrows. "At the U.N. agencies they call this model the Crystal Ball. The Foundation Model is the guts of it. There's a whole world in there: countries trading with one another, getting richer, getting poorer. It's just a toy: first-order differential equations. But it acts like we do."

She pats the keys, nudging us to an invisible edge, and over. "You see?"

The spook grips his mouth and watches the map shimmer. The shimmer changes into a flicker. The change is not perceptible—but look away for a moment, watch the writhing rainbow ghosts in the room's dark corners. When you look back you can see the pace of change pick up. The faint tremor grows to a psychedelic purple-brown stroboscopic assault on the eyes. It vibrates like panic.

He says, "We'll take this under advisement."

They're interrogating Faye and her computer. They put her on the phone with men who hammer her. They twist and stretch assumptions to the breaking point, dreaming up a crazy man's litany of catastrophes. She's sure, but she's dripping with sweat.

The inquisitors rack her through the night. When they sign off, Faye goes limp. The spook twists his mouth. "Bud's bosses won't be happy about this."

I guess now is the time for him to deal with me.

Faye asks him, "You work with Bud?"

He rocks his head back. "What?"

"We know he works for some U.S. agency too."

The spook says, "Timbuktu Earthwealth is a private company. A very private company—it's a subsidiary of Janissary Systems."

I say, "No, Bud hired Janissary."

"That's the way Janissary works," he says. "They muddy the waters with shell companies and consulting contracts. That way no one can find out who the shareholders are."

"But Bud showed me—"

"Forget what he showed you. Bud is not working for the government. At one time he worked black contracts, but he's burned a lot of bridges since then. His entree to the black world is wearing thin."

"He's not—"

"Bud wants to sell his dump site as a military base. To do that he's trying to scare us with Algerian bogeymen. But Bud takes a very narrow view. From where we sit, Algeria's lost in the noise."

28

We are back in the jeep, driving away from the meet. The wall of green is pressing in and down. I ask, "Faye—what happened back there?"

Faye says, "The shimmering maps in the Crystal Ball, they mean chaos: chaos triggered by Timbuktu and the money they will spend. Booms and busts, back and forth from one to the other, spreading out in waves. Liquidity crises. Bubbles. Financial contagion."

"Bozo and his spook, are they convinced?"

"Ty, there is a law of nature. We've known about it since 1970. But it's only been proven inside computers: no one would dare experiment on the real world. Complexity affects stability. That's the law. When things get too interconnected, they go out of control."

Faye's getting mystical again, but she's not high and she's not confronting subatomic paradoxes. "How connected is too connected? In certain cases we know, exactly. There's a magic number: thirteen percent. When complexity gets past thirteen percent, the situation plunges into instability."

"Where does the, ah, *world* come in, Faye?"

"Here's what it means. The world right now, we don't all trade, not as much as we could. We've got tight-knit trade blocs, embargoed rogue states, and we've got Africa, a continent full of economic cripples: no capital flows to speak of, not much trade. So trade connectance is low, nine percent or so. Now factor in

Timbuktu's dumping plan. Suddenly Africa has money to spend, and the whole world is exporting, importing, investing. Great, right? Not according to this model.

"Look what you did to the connectance of the world economy. With all these new African trading partners, it jumps to fourteen percent. Look at that graph. You go over the cliff into instability."

"It's this beautiful model," I say. "It's wrong."

"Doesn't matter," she says. "Everybody uses this model: governments, businesses, parastatals. Everybody acts on its predictions."

"Publicize that report, and people will throw out their crystal balls."

"No one would dare publicize that report. The conclusions are too sensitive: it condemns Africa to another generation of poverty. That's why Bozo was fighting me. Governments will bury the report. But they have to read it, and act on it. They have to shut Timbuktu down. Without explanation."

So with a word, Bud is checkmated. But Bud won't take that lying down, and he still has mercenaries and warlords and arms suppliers in his corner. The people who run the world will handle it from here; Faye is confident of that. How, exactly, she's not sure.

Just ride it out. That's her way of telling me there's nothing we can do.

I have made it safely back to camp, but retracing the route shook my nerve. No ambush on the way out, just a string of cold-sweat random obstacles. Faye and I split up in Niamey to board separate Greenfleet helicopters. My flight back to camp was way too quiet. The helicopter lurched through the desert air as before, but we drew no fire—not so much as a tracer or a flare.

Now the camp's supplies dwindle in an eerie calm. Muru will give no word or sign, but no one will test his blockade. Lila's nerves have drawn the color from her face.

At the northern edge of camp, Fatimatou stands staring at the hills. I come up behind her. She is looking at a dusty pall that blots a patch of sky, all her muscles set in bunches under thin brown skin.

She puts out a hand and stops me: "Hush." Now that I'm still, I can hear it, or feel it: engines, wheels, and treads, too many to tease apart, from all around, not just from the hills.

"They're coming," she says.

I've seen foreboding in her stance, but never this fear. This distant stirring deviates from the awful routine she knows. The time for a massacre is past. Why now? Shells, yes, or starvation—but more intimate forms of terror are customarily used first, to shock and stampede. A descent on the camp at this point means a loss of control: frustration eroding discipline. Some new crisis, dictating an end to the siege. Or revenge for a crippled son, too long deferred.

Has the sound grown louder? I can't tell. I can hardly hear it for the thumping of my pulse. I've been holding my breath, for minutes it seems, but the sound eludes me.

I want to feel the shotgun in my hand. Suicide, reasoned and sure, my only degree of freedom. The prospect gives me all the comfort I need. I can reject Fatso's choice of death. It is only a mirage—I can't leave survivors to pay in my place. But to lay down the gun will be my choice, the last one I will make.

Fatimatou is trembling now. I put an arm around her and she clings to me but her eyes are wrong. The fear is gone. Maybe she is ready to face what comes next.

"No," she says, with a blurry-fast shake of her head.

"Fatimatou . . ."

Her hands on me a celebration, musty breath in my face, a hint of a squeal in the words: "They're not coming. They're going away. Listen."

The sound has subsided. The dust has crept along the horizon to the west.

"I do not understand," she says. "Why would they retreat?" She says it softly, as though they might hear and think again. She bolts from my side, and I follow. She is heading to the volunteers' tent with little bursts of sand spreading out behind her feet. She slips in past the flysheet. When I get inside she is setting up the computer. "Maybe there is news," she says.

I stand over her shoulder and watch her searching. She finds some glowing red runes, and her shoulders float higher. "Cu-cu-cu!" I can't see what prompted her exclamation. She dives down and down, too fast for me to follow.

She gives another incredulous hoot and rakes the stubble on her nape. "They are not coming. They are not retreating. They are racing."

On her screen is a bulletin.

News-stream Breaking News

Nuclear Waste
Disposal Project Aborted

Citing unspecified "technical factors impacting feasibility," Timbuktu Earthwealth today aborted its nuclear waste disposal project. In a terse announcement, Program Manager B. D. "Bud" Van Sickle stated that Timbuktu Earthwealth had already constructed extensive support facilities, and that it would donate them to the Government of Mali.

Critics point out that the dump site is not in government-controlled territory, and that the facilities most likely would be looted by rival warlords in the north. Van Sickle responded, "Timbuktu Earthwealth has dealt with all factions in the course of its work, and we trust all parties to show restraint."

Since the announcement, two local militia groups have laid claim to the facility and surrounding territory.

Faye's magic spell worked. Her hocus-pocus made Bud pull out. Somewhere in the rock guts of Bear Mountain, scientific prophecies are spreading fear and awe. Men of power understand no more of it than I do, but the meaning is clear: *It is forbidden*. These are the same old gods, trading comets, eclipses, and the burning bush for new portents.

Lila has come in. She watches silently, reads the bulletin with an interrogatory hand on Fatimatou's shoulder.

There is no breathy rush of relief in Lila's voice. Her throat is taut. "To pull out suddenly like that, Timbuktu must have left loot worth millions: abandoned equipment and supplies, weapons and ammunition. That will draw warlords and junior warlords and wanna-be warlords. When the dump site is picked clean, you know where they'll come next."

Yes. Here.

So this is only a respite. The Creepers will return with replenished supplies. Even if they haven't lost patience with us, their rivals will force their hand. They must loot the camp or watch it be looted, rape or lose their chance in the slaughter that follows.

One more quiet night has passed. Fatimatou has been standing, listening, since dawn. The sun is slashing down into the thin sky overhead, but she seeps sweat and stays put. I go to draw water for her. There's not much left now, but it may be more than enough.

She looks frail from a distance. Up close, with her little bones, she's a miner's canary about to drop in the act of alerting us. "Any sign they're coming?"

"Not yet," she says, "but they could come at any time. They only have to send a few. Muru will come to preside."

Fatso, too.

I wish I had fossilized water for her. I would make a sacrament of this drink. This moment feels like the peace of an empty Pre-cambrian world.

I give her the canteen. Her eyes close as she drinks, leaving me alone and mute as the pillar springs up, gray roiling with sunset red, bright and burgeoning at the top, world-sized, not at all like an earthbound palm-sized mushroom, this mushroom cloud.

Fatimatou gasps. She sees it through closed eyes.

An invisible broom sweeps toward us rocket-fast, pushing a wall of airborne earth stretching out of sight left and right. It reaches us, punches like squat Seychelles surf. I didn't feel it drop me, but I'm on the ground. My shirt is gone. A buzzing burn on my face makes me hold it without touching, open hands frozen an inch from the skin. I'm straining to see past the flashbulb blobs oozing in front of my eyes.

The tents are down and shapes are moving under them, crawling out. The Rubbhall is going flat. Fatimatou fell too. She's ignoring a split lip, scanning the camp with a slack jaw and giant eyes. I can tell she hasn't started to think what it means: Did they ship in a critical mass of waste?

The shock wave spared us. But what about the particles, the rays? When will the fallout start drifting down? I won't feel it burning me, but I will know what is happening. At Bear Mountain, I learned all about ionizing radiation. The night I learned, exhausted as I was, I couldn't sleep.

29

I see Ushi stumbling past, pink and panicked from a flash burn. I follow her to one of the trucks. She's fighting to get in. "How long before we die?"

Based on what they taught me at Bear Mountain, my guess is eighteen months. But we could live for years. Ushi is fumbling with a satellite phone.

"What are you doing?"

"I have to call Greenfleet." She yanks the door open and falls into the cab.

"Don't waste your time. If that was a nuclear blast, the electromagnetic pulse fried the circuits in the phone."

Hysteria in her voice: "I can't hear it." I can't hear much of anything. The phone is shaking in her hand. She has to brace against the seat to hold it still.

"No," she says. "It's working. But I can't get through."

"The phone is working? That can't be."

She gives it to me. I think I can just hear quick little beeps over the ringing in my ears.

"How about the computer? Is the computer destroyed?"

It's wrapped in a tent, but it works. The satellite dish is lying down flat, but apparently undamaged. We just have to find where to point it.

It takes six hours of fits and starts and setbacks, of staring and willing the news to appear. But we find a bulletin, lose it, claw it back, and wait without breathing as it creeps word by word down the screen.

Mushroom Cloud Observed in Sahara
News-stream Breaking News

Satellite imagery and local observers reported a mushroom cloud and a damaging shock wave in the Sahara desert. A blast broke windows twenty miles away and showered ash over the surrounding area. Satellite sensors indicated a multikiloton blast, but a U.S. official stated, "This was not a nuclear device. It was equivalent to several thousand tons of TNT: maybe an arms depot or a warehouse full of high explosives."

A specialist at Greenfleet contested the U.S. interpretation: "You don't fill up a warehouse with high explosives, for obvious reasons. You spread it around. That way, in case of accident you get a series of explosions. This was one big blast."

A Western diplomatic source stated, "It's clearly a big booby trap. To dig in the Adrar, Timbuktu Earthwealth would have to make sensitive deals with Mansa Muru. They lured Muru to the dump site and blew him up. That way the shady deals won't come to light."

Mansa Muru leads the Creepers of Niani, a paramilitary faction that controls much of Mali. Human-rights groups have charged that the Creepers benefit from U.S. weapons and training.

The Creepers confirmed that Mansa Muru was missing and presumed dead in the blast. A sequence of conflicting announcements reported the accession of "Mansa Musa II," "Mansa Fulani," and "Mansa Bobo" to succeed the deceased strongman.

Ushi keeps in contact with the Greens. They feed her news and rumor and off-the-record whispers from their friends. She imparts it to us each day, scoop by scoop.

With his rival gone, Inhad jumped into the power vacuum. He moved on Timbuktu and took the city for the Holy Garrison. They surrounded Timbuktu Earthwealth headquarters and captured Bud. Inhad sent Bud to the salt mines, where he can "work off his debt to the nomads of the desert he defiled."

NATO sent a force to secure Timbuktu's dump site and investigate the blast. They found that the shaft had collapsed; but they detected faint seismic signals like gunshots from below. Someone was alive a thousand feet down. It took two weeks to dig him out. He gave the name Mumm.

Mumm was in charge of the booby trap. His team had just tied the last knot in the detcord when they heard the Creepers coming. They left the warehouse and hid in the shaft.

Some of the Creepers went down the shaft to loot it. Mumm and his men retreated to one of the adits and fortified a position. They ambushed the Creepers there.

When the booby-trapped warehouse went up, the tunnel walls gave way. The rock shattered in spots and flowed like mud. Some of Mumm's men were buried to the waist. The pressure squeezed all the blood up from their legs. They turned raspberry red and died. Mumm was unhurt. He fought on until he had killed or captured all the Creepers.

Mumm ate them. It kept him alive. He saw skin merchants do it in the Congo but he never thought he'd find himself chewing belly fat and liver to keep his eyes from melting, eating muscles to fight wasting and despair. It was a matter of survival.

They say he took a doggie bag home.

The blast at the dump site injured more Creepers than it killed. The bulk of Muru's forces were a couple miles away when it blew. The NATO medics treat the casualties here at camp.

Fatimatou has been working with them, but now she's standing over me, straining stiff-necked against a shudder that throbs in her belly and seeps from her eyes. She says, "Did you see who's here?"

"Who?"

"The sick man who came with Muru. The one with the awful case of SIDA."

Not Fatso. Anyone but Fatso. It's not his revenge that frightens me. Fatso finds the hate in you, shapes and focuses it like a burning glass focuses the sun. He will find the men he needs, or make more.

We're playing with fire, bringing him here. Fatso is a spark from the conflagration sweeping Africa: the flickering firefights in the Great Lakes and the Congo Basin, the incendiary bomb bursts lighting up the Horn and all the splinters of Sudan. The fire passed by here once. It charred Mali then. If Mali ignites again now it will go up like smithies do, inundating towns in flame and turning sand to glass. It won't go out.

Fatimatou won't come with me to see him. He's outside the tent where the safe and the dying are culled from the ones on the edge. He lies on a litter, clothes cut off to expose a bright spatter of fragmentation wounds.

Fatso caught AIDS as a kind of food poisoning by eating prisoners' flesh while they watched. That's how he got fat. That's why he's a skeleton now. He's at the very top of the food chain, where poisons build up. Fatso's full of death and terror like a swordfish is full of mercury.

Fatso picks his skull up and stares. The blast took the skin off it, and there isn't much else on the bone. He's not staring at me, thank God. Where, though? The ray of his gaze twists me around. I stop where he focuses and find a little boy whispering to Serata.

Fatso looks at Serata. And eyeless Serata looks back at him. Not with eyes. Maybe not even with her eye sockets—I can't see where they used to be. Her mind's at one end of an unseen wire. Fatso's at the other end, and the wire's so taut it's singing up high where you can't hear it, like it's going to snap. But it doesn't snap. Serata rises to a crouch with tentative poise. She sways to her feet and starts to walk. She holds out her hands and takes tiny steps, canting her weight back, clearly blind, but she's following a geometric straight line to Fatso. The injured move out of her way. The dying get out of her way. No one wants to be between those poles in the force, whatever it is, arcing back and forth. Everyone in sight has stopped dead: refugees, medics, volunteers. We watch from all angles, fighting to draw in the sight like there's not enough broad daylight to go around.

She kneels by the figure of death. Fattened on diseased flesh, wasted from incautious rape, oozing imbibed blood from a thousand cuts, Death is weak. The incandescent hatred in his eyes has begun to flicker. I think maybe it's flickering at the dangerous frequency that triggers fits, because Serata is on the brink of one now. I know it like a dog knows when it waits stock-still by its epileptic master. Millions of neural shorts and shocks shoot down each erect hair on my skin, holding me like killer amps from a thick cable, and all of a sudden I know what's at stake.

Long ago Serata had a seizure and fell into a fire. If she falls into that smoldering pile of bones the spark will catch and sweep Mali with hate that starts as fear and ends in open trenches full of liquefying meat. Everything depends on Serata: I'd doubt my name or my mama or the earth underfoot before I'd doubt this visceral awe.

I hear a sound of percolation, then a rasp. Fatso's last gasp. I don't want to see Serata fall thrashing and frothing in Death's arms. Everyone saw something go up from them, I didn't but I'm running blind with the others, trampling the ones that fall and churning harder when someone pulls past me because I *can't* be left alone back there.

I'm alone on the empty sand before the panic lets go, heaving up bile past a smoldering knot in my side. Serata told us about this shared fear. She said it comes from seeing what God sees—that's what she told us, that night by the fire. God must be stronger than we imagine, to face sights like that.

I will never speak of this: not to a skeptic; not to the simplest and most superstitious desert pawn. Humiliation is the most fearful aspect of madness. We think we're too smart for mass hysteria; we could never fall for witch-hunts, cults, or posse murder. We have outgrown the primitive fear of an epileptic's afflictions. Most of us never feel reason drawn out of a crowd like air dispersing in a void. We can't imagine a state in which restraint is a mercy and beatings can soothe. Not until we're part of it.

Clinging to reason like a dying man clings to faith, I work up exasperation to squeeze the moths out from under my ribs. It's hard to walk back. A gritty wild wind is pushing me away. It's not rushing air. It's inside me.

No one watches now where Serata sits, head jiggling, in some vigil over Fatso's clutching corpse. In halting Bambara I ask her, *Mama,* what happened? and the honorific sails up in pitch to become a child's cry.

Ka de, abana, it's over, my child, *Ala ka boom.*

30

Several days have passed since our panic attack. I remember the stampede, but the terrors that triggered it are pale and dim; the world returned and dissipated them.

Ushi made the camp a cause, focusing the world on it. With the siege lifted, the world's sentiment is released and the camp is flooding with aid: Flocks of two-rotor cargo helicopters. Flotillas of hovercraft. Tanks with flails, popping the mines like caps, and, following them, convoys of trucks. Prefab warehouses for the mountains of food, inflatable hospitals for the tons of medical supplies, tent cities for the mobs of volunteer relief workers.

They call it "Ushi's camp" now, but Fatimatou is in charge by acclamation. Ushi stands mute in the background as Fatimatou lays down the law on global TV: *No more food. We have enough. We need hoes and seed and wells. If you can't bring those, stay home.* The world watched, appalled, as she ejected the Cherished Baby Trust for "getting in the way." Ushi is tickled to have found a new way to put the world in an uproar. Africans speaking for themselves—how subversive.

Lila is content to watch. She sits and smiles with the women in the sand. I have never seen this calm in her. I squat with them and greet them, *"Ani woola."* In the lisping accent of Ségou they run through rapid-fire Malian pleasantries, how's your mother, how's your father, how's your sister, how's your brother, how's your family?

"Maybe it's time to go home," Lila says.

I take her shoulders and shake her. "Good riddance. You're a big monkey wrench rattling around in the world's works."

She laughs. "Holding up progress and development."

Holding up the world, like a skinny little second-string Atlas staggering and bobbling and barely hanging on.

Smiling skyward, she says, "Not straight home. I would go the long way home. I want to see Zanzibar, Malabar, the South Seas. I want to go swimming, in the sea. At the earliest opportunity I will find a place with a bathtub, and soak."

She says, "Want to come? It's better traveling with someone."

Having picked up on the shy hitch in Lila's voice, the women are giggling. It's official: we're a town. We've got gossips. They say to me, "Lila *kagni.*" Silly nosy matchmakers pointing out how cute she is.

I say, *"Awou."* She is. I wonder what she's like when she's not holding up the world.

Acknowledgments

Thanks to Clyde Taylor of Curtis Brown and Tom Bissell of Henry Holt. The very best of this book is a product of their high standards and contagious enthusiasm. The rest of it is better for their judgment and expertise.

About the Author

As a consultant specializing in foreign direct investment, the author has worked with clients that include foreign joint ventures, international financial institutions, and the federal government. Readers' thoughts are much appreciated at littlefair@gmx.ch.